**Raves for Pamela Ribon's**
**"witty, wonderful, and wise" (*Maryland Gazette*) novels**

### *YOU TAKE IT FROM HERE*

"Hilarity and heartbreak compete, but ultimately hope wins in this thoroughly delightful story about what it means to be a woman, a mother, a best friend. I can't wait to pass this book along to every woman who ever mattered to me. Pamela Ribon has a huge, fresh voice, and this is her best book yet."

—Joshilyn Jackson, *New York Times* bestselling author of *Gods in Alabama* and *A Grown-Up Kind of Pretty*

"One of those rare books where the characters feel like your best friends from the first page. You'll laugh and cry as Pamela Ribon takes you on a colorful, rich, and unforgettable journey of friendship."

—Kristin Harmel, author of *The Sweetness of Forgetting*

### *GOING IN CIRCLES*

"Pamela Ribon's hilarious and touching writing makes you think, feel, and wish you still knew how to roller skate. Her best work yet."

—Caprice Crane, international bestselling author of *Family Affair*

"If Pam broke my heart with *Why Girls Are Weird*, she completely pulverized it with *Going in Circles*. . . . I'm not usually one to force people to read books, but seriously people, if you don't pick up *Going in Circles* thi͟ books enough."

—Ste

"Few writers are as funny as Pamela Ribon, who infuses her novels with satirical humor alongside honest glimpses into our most intimate relationships. . . . One of summer's most absorbing reads."

*—largehearted boy*

"It's refreshing to see a chick lit heroine who isn't just a designer label whore. Charlotte has depth. Sometimes she's wise, and sometimes she needs a guide to see the obvious—just like a real person. Ribon has taken us back to chick lit basics, and the floundering genre is all the better for it."

*—All About Romance*

"A more intense read than you'll get from something with a pink cover. Which is as it should be."

*—Lainey Gossip*

"Totally enjoyable reading. . . . I read it in a day and I learned about roller derby and I laughed out loud once and cried a little, and what more do you really want in a book?"

*—The Unimaginary Book Club*

"This book surprised and delighted me. . . . A highly enjoyable novel by a talented writer whose time has come."

*—Fierce & Nerdy*

"This is a fantastic book. I'm really going to attempt to rein in my enthusiasm. Really! This is me attempting to sound like I'm not pushing a book at you."

*—Book-Addicts.com*

## WHY MOMS ARE WEIRD

"A rollicking page-turner. . . . Fantastic and satisfying."

—*Albuquerque Journal*

"Compassionate. . . . Fans will identify with this kind, imperfect heroine."

—*Publishers Weekly*

"This joyous, single-sitting read is as bright and witty as it is wise and bittersweet. . . . Ribon is a sparkling talent."

—*South Florida Sun-Sentinel*

"Hilarious and heartfelt. *Why Moms Are Weird* tackles the absurd morass of family with joyful wit and brutal honesty. I barreled through this book."

—Jill Soloway, Emmy-nominated writer for *Six Feet Under*, *The United States of Tara*, and author of *Tiny Ladies in Shiny Pants*

## WHY GIRLS ARE WEIRD

"Chick lit at its most trenchant and truthful."

—Jennifer Weiner, *New York Times* bestselling author of *Then Came You*

"Light and entertaining."

—*Booklist*

"A whole lot of good reading."

—*Miami Herald*

"Irresistible. . . . [L]ike hanging out with your best friend just when you need to most."

—Melissa Senate, author of *The Love Goddess' Cooking School*

# you take it from here

## A NOVEL

# PAMELA RIBON

GALLERY BOOKS

NEW YORK  LONDON  TORONTO  SYDNEY  NEW DELHI

Gallery Books
A Division of Simon & Schuster, Inc.
1230 Avenue of the Americas
New York, NY 10020

This Gallery Books trade paperback edition July 2012

GALLERY BOOKS and colophon are registered trademarks of Simon & Schuster, Inc.

For information about special discounts for bulk purchases, please contact Simon & Schuster Special Sales at 1-866-506-1949 or business@simonandschuster.com.

The Simon & Schuster Speakers Bureau can bring authors to your live event. For more information or to book an event contact the Simon & Schuster Speakers Bureau at 1-866-248-3049 or visit our website at www.simonspeakers.com.

Designed by Jaime Putorti

Manufactured in the United States of America

10  9  8  7  6  5  4  3  2  1

Library of Congress Cataloging-in-Publication Data

Ribon, Pamela.
    You take it from here / Pamela Ribon.
        p. cm.
    1. Female friendship—Fiction. 2. Cancer—Patients—Family relationships—Fiction. 3. Domestic fiction. I. Title.
    PS3618.I24Y68  2012
    813'.6—dc23
                                                    2012008623

ISBN 978-1-4516-4623-8
ISBN 978-1-4516-4624-5 (ebook)

For Madeleine Chao

Sweet girl.
May you take over the world.

(*Meow*.)

you take it

from here

Jenny,

I've got this hunch that if you're reading this, your other hand is currently holding a lit match. But I think you should try to hold off destroying this letter long enough to read what it says.

I can only imagine you've been yearning to know the truth for a long time now. You never did like it when people kept things from you. That pride you got from your mother makes it so you'd rather pretend I dropped off the face of the earth. I'm sure she's proud of how much you've stuck to your guns.

But listen. I know what's happening to you tomorrow. That's no small thing, Miss Ma'am. This probably goes without saying, but as soon as I heard your news, I wanted to be there. I know, we don't always get what we want.

It's hard not to talk to you like you're still a young girl, awkward and defiant. I keep reminding myself that you are no longer that person, that there's a chance you're nothing like the Jenny I knew, the one I spent so much of my life *worrying about. How did you get to be so old? I can't even begin to imagine how much I've missed.*

*What you're about to read won't be easy for either of us. It doesn't always paint me in the best light, and I worry it'll be too hard for you in some parts. I'll try to warn you when the rough stuff is coming, but I think it's time you learned it all. Lord knows you're finally old enough. Most important, I think it's officially been enough time that your mother can't find a way to murder me for telling you everything.*

*I think she'd want you to know now. She'd want you to hear her entire story, all her reasons, and how they became mine.*

*So let's get started. We'll have to take it back quite some time. Back in ye olde 2010. You were thirteen. I think about that a lot, actually. You were only thirteen.*

*You've never left my thoughts. Not for one moment.*

*So please blow out that match. This is for your own good.*

# ONE

While it took over two decades to build the infrastructure that could lead to what happened, it all really started the year your mother and I were thirty-five, smack-dab in the lava-hot center of July.

Before I reached that age I couldn't imagine anything older, but now it seems like I was just a baby. I was balancing an overstuffed purse on my hip, my reading glasses forgotten on top of my head while cheap sunglasses slid down the bridge of my nose. My cell phone was in one hand while the other pulled my limp blond hair into a makeshift knot. All sense of pride in one's appearance quickly melts away in that sticky, miserable, Louisiana heat.

I was standing in that aggressively carpeted baggage claim area of the Ogden airport, desperately trying to absorb the remaining seconds of air-conditioning. I'd soon be diving into stifling humidity. The weather is half the reason I left Ogden in the first place. Living in that oppressive atmosphere always made me feel like some kind of exotic cockroach, scuttling around, seeking the cool of night.

I already missed the predictable weather back home in Los Angeles, where normally at that moment I'd be in a coffee shop on my computer. If I wasn't busy drawing up plans for a client, I would be updating my website with an entry boasting of a recent success, or procrastinating my workload via a healthy dose of Web surfing. I knew I'd be fine once I saw Smidge, and I'd be even better once we were off on our trip, but at the time I remember being frantic because my hair was already starting to frizz.

It was important to get in front of your mother's eyes before my hair went into massive failure, lest I again endure her favorite opening monologue, titled "All This on Your Head Is Wrong."

Smidge asked me to fly to her that year to kick off our annual trip. I use the word *ask,* but that does not describe what she did. There is no *asking* in Smidge's world. There is requesting, declaring, demanding, and ordering. And when those don't work: threats.

I'd been on the ground only ten minutes when I got recognized. In typical Ogden fashion, I probably knew half of the people standing around in that lobby. "Oh, I'd heard you were coming," some of them had already said to me while I was waiting, as if the local newspaper printed the airport's daily manifests. I couldn't figure out how else people always seemed to know when I was visiting. Your dad later told me it's because your mother would brag to everybody, like a celebrity was touching down in Ogden. It's still hard for me to imagine that, what with how unfamous I would feel beside her.

"Hey, California!" said the oversize man-boy smirking at me, his voice loud enough that everyone else turned to stare. "Looking good."

Tucker Collier started calling me "California" long before I moved away. He found out that I lived there for a time when I was three. "That explains it," he said, back when we were still in college. "Why you're so different." About me moving to Los Angeles, he still quips, "She went back to her home planet."

No matter how many years of my life I invested in Ogden—active, youthful years—no matter how many times I came back to visit, the fact remained that once I arrived I didn't stay. I didn't settle in for the long haul. From then on, whenever I was in Ogden, I was a visitor. An other. As much a mystery to those people as California.

Smidge was supposed to pick me up, but she was nowhere to be seen and apparently pretending to have misplaced her phone, seeing as how she wasn't answering calls or returning texts. Luckily for me, small Southern towns are filled with boys at the ready to swoop in and save the day. Mine had come in the form of a man standing next to me wearing his trademark wicked grin, the one that looks like he's thinking about a joke he can't share in public.

"Tucker Collier!" I shouted, because that's what old friends do down here when we haven't seen each other in forever. We shout first and last names like we're taking attendance.

"Danielle Meyers!"

Tucker lifted me an impressive distance from the ground as he squished me to his chest. Since he's six feet, three inches, two hundred and thirty pounds, there wasn't much else to do but take the brunt of the impact and label it "affection." He was still warm from outside, and there was a sweet stickiness from his damp skin underneath his clothes.

"My spleen!" I managed to whimper as I squirmed against him.

Tucker laughed as he gently returned me to the earth. I'd always been a sucker for his big green eyes and those sandy-blond curls he refused to do anything with other than smash underneath his beat-up blue ball cap. If he were even slightly vain he could have been a model. He had that deliciously careless, homegrown look about him, a dangerous combination of helpful and hell-bent. He'd be the first one to show up at your grandmother's funeral, and the last to leave the bar on a Sunday night.

I'm sure you know that's a compliment.

We might have gone to high school together in a town where it seemed everybody was legally bound to date everybody else at some point, but Tucker and I had never gotten around to getting together. I could make the excuse that he's slightly older than I am, but I think more likely it was because I was in the chess club. That's not me calling Tucker snobby. That's me not saying enough about how I was in the chess club.

Like how I was the president. For two years.

And made us wear T-shirts.

T-shirts that boasted *We've Got the Rook*.

"Sorry." Tucker jammed one giant hand into the back pocket of his jeans as he reached out with the other. He gave an awkward pat to my arm, stroking my limb like Lenny with a rabbit. "Didn't mean to smush ya."

He'd get talky after a few beers, but in public, with the "common people," as he'd like to say, Tucker preferred an air of solemn stoicism. It was as if he was intentionally bad at hiding his superhero alter ego, just to make sure we all *knew* he was a superhero. That way we could all pretend we *didn't* know so he could go around with that "thoughtful" expression, looking slightly over our heads like trouble was on the horizon, and he was just about to save the day.

But I knew the truth. That his stone-strong look was actually the result of being destroyed by someone he loved. We all knew each other's secrets and mistakes, but only talked about them when the person with the problem wasn't around. Some might call that gossip, but we did it out of respect.

"I like the hair," he said, meaning mine, and I immediately raked my hand through my scalp to unleash the messy bun, before twirling the ends at my shoulder like a fifth-grader. It must be the size of Tucker that always turned me embarrassingly, uncharacteristically girly. Or our history. If I hadn't known him so long, maybe it wouldn't have mattered so much that he found something nice to say.

"Oh, thanks," I stammered, mentally ordering myself to stand still.

"Yep," Tucker said, clearly enjoying making me turn red. "You're looking real good, California. Enough that I just had to say that again. Must be all those salads and movie stars rubbing off on you."

I resisted the urge to tell him all the ways he was wrong

about how I'm "looking." I could have easily pointed out my various patches of dry skin that were one doctor's visit away from being labeled eczema, or show him the location of the mini-constellation of brown spots I had recently found near my right temple—some kind of unfortunate birthday present my body gave itself after I turned thirty-five. Honestly, all I really had to do was gesture toward the coffee stain I got on the plane. It looked like I'd painted a nipple onto my tank top. Luckily I'd strategically placed my purse over it, grateful the oversize nature of my carry-on protected me from possible ridicule.

I had an immediate wish for Smidge to materialize right there in front of us, just so she could hear Tucker's kind words about my appearance. She was the reason I'd even bothered to compose myself before a seven-hour red-eye that included a harrowing layover in Houston that was more of a full-throttle sprint to reach the gate on time. If I'd been flying anywhere else, I would've just hidden under a hat and zonked out on the strongest pills I could find. After all, it's a red-eye, not the red carpet. But Smidge had a way of making my life take a few extra steps.

The usual criticism she would give upon first seeing me would range anywhere from "Hey, Puffy! Did you leave any sodium back on that plane?" to "Are those ankle socks you're wearing with those heels? Are you in the fifties? Do you need me to put some Buddy Holly on the jukebox, Mary Jane?"

Nicknames and body slams. Smidge is half stand-up comic, half disappointed football coach ordering a few extra laps.

Tucker and I hadn't seen each other in at least two years, and even then I seem to remember it was only briefly, as he was heading out with the boys to go golfing. That would've made it the night of the fireworks, the last time James came to Ogden with me before we separated. They got him drunk and chased him around with Roman candles, because he was dumb enough to tell them that he'd never played with fireworks before.

Do you remember James? You must. You had such a crush on him when you were little. One night you made him sleep in your princess bed, and as you tucked him in, shoving those pink Tinkerbell sheets under his shoulders one at a time, you solemnly told him that when he woke up he'd have magically turned into a prince, and you'd be married forever.

I couldn't blame you for falling in love with him. He called you Prettygirl. All one word like that. If you were in the same room with him, you demanded to sit in his lap. The first time you saw him holding my hand, you were mad at me for days. You simply refused to share, even when I tried to pull rank with "Finders keepers."

"He loves *me* more," you insisted. Eight years old and ready to settle down for the rest of your life. I was more than three times your age at that moment and nowhere near as sure as you were about him.

You were our flower girl. The only flower girl in history to weep hysterically down the aisle. You hurled clumps of petals at the ceremony like you were lobbing grenades.

You were eleven or so when you found out James and I had separated. I remember you had this smile on your face that made me momentarily wonder if you'd caused it to happen through some sort of spell or potion preteen girls are prone to conjure. I could easily imagine you writing the perfect anti-love chant combined with just enough wishes to finally get your prayers answered.

I hated you a little bit right then, Jenny. Because James never loved me the way he loved you. He never loved me just as I was.

It dawned on me that the reason Tucker was acting so friendly, so overly full of praise, patting me on the shoulder like I was a good horse, was because he'd heard my divorce was final. He never was a huge fan of James. It was kind of an instant aggression. "Any guy who'd wear a newsie cap is an asshole," he once told me. We left it at that.

The rubber belt for the baggage claim lurched to life, giving Tucker and me somewhere else to turn our focus. The other nine people from my flight took a few steps forward, claiming space.

We settled into a spot near the bend as it occurred to me why he might be there. "Did Smidge send you?" I asked.

"No, ma'am," Tucker said. "I was dropping my mom's friend off. She's on her way to visit her sister in Chicago." He pointed toward the tarmac, which you could easily see through the window. It was only a hundred yards or so from where we were standing. "I saw you coming down the steps of your plane and figured I'd like to say hi. Welcome you home. You still call this home, right?"

"Of course I do."

"Liar."

I went to grab my suitcase, but Tucker jumped in front of me, his gentleman button activated. I thanked him.

"I'm jealous of my mom's friend," he said. "Getting to go north of here, anywhere that's cooler, escaping this stank heat.

Why would you leave La-La Land for this place in the summer? I thought you were supposed to be the smart one."

I spotted my second suitcase. Again, Tucker grabbed it before I even had a chance to lean forward. "I can't believe it's been a year already since the last time y'all were gone," he said. "Where was that again? Italy?"

"No, last year was China. I'm not sure where we're going this time. She says it's a surprise."

"Well, I hope it's far. And I hope you get to pet a monkey."

Smidge would never pet a monkey.

"I'm guessing we are either going to end up in Mexico or she's planning on trapping me on a damn cruise ship like she's been wanting."

I glanced down at the cell phone in my hand, as if I'd somehow missed her message. I thought about renting a car, but it seemed like a waste of money.

Picking up on a cue I didn't mean to give, Tucker said, "I can take you to Smidge's."

"If it's not too much trouble."

Tucker reached up to fiddle with the frayed brim of his cap. "Lucky for you, it's Help a Pretty Girl Day," he said, superhero-proud of himself.

"Well, *shucks, Tucker!*" I drawled, mocking his accent. "That's mighty neighborly of you."

"Or you could just walk," he said. "It looks like real nice walking weather out there, don't it?"

"I'm sorry. Thank you for the ride."

Exiting the Ogden airport always felt like a punch line. All the cars are lined up at the curb just outside the exit door. That's the extent of the parking lot at this place: the *curb*.

Some people find the small size of Ogden comforting, but it made me feel like I was choking in a turtleneck sweater. I need space. Variety. The feeling of lots of things going on all around me. At any time in Ogden, you really only have about six choices. Smidge thrived in that world, maybe because she always found a way to make all six of those choices revolve solely around her.

Tucker tossed my suitcases into the back of his rusty brown Jeep with an easy carelessness, as if my luggage was filled with pillows. "Sorry about the state of this thing," he said, giving the side door a whack. "It hasn't had a good hosing since the last time my dog was in it."

I rolled a few patchy tennis balls from the passenger seat onto the floorboard. They bounced softly before nestling between two empty Gatorade containers. In order to make space for my feet, I kicked up a pile of empty Chick-fil-A bags and crumpled receipts.

The Jeep pitched with Tucker's weight as he dropped into his seat. As he turned the key, he rotated his ball cap with his free hand, resting the brim against the top of his sunglasses. He didn't bother to buckle up until long after he was in gear. I could hear music playing, too softly to recognize much more than a steady beat.

The backs of my legs were already sticking to the vinyl, sweat beading on my shins. I pulled my hair back with one hand, pressing it to the crown of my head.

"Hot," was all I could manage to say.

"Let me get some speed so we can cool down," Tucker said before taking off at an intersection. I closed my eyes and tried to ignore this outdoor sauna of a city as I prayed wherever

Smidge was taking us would be frigid compared to this. Let's go to Moscow, Norway, Alaska—someplace where the summer wouldn't matter, where we could wear lots of clothes and drink way too much.

If she even for one second tried to get me on a cruise ship, I would kill her. I would wrestle her to the ground and choke her with my two sweaty hands.

# TWO

——————

You were already trotting down to meet us—your focus firmly downward on your cell phone, midtext—as we pulled into your driveway. That sparkly, pink-and-purple machine never left your grip. During meals, when you were brushing your teeth, even in your sleep you held on. It was as if you'd accidentally installed it into your palms and you were pushing any and all combinations of numbers, desperately trying to find the code that would detach that thing from your hands.

Bumping your butt against the dusty front of Tucker's Jeep, you rested there, watching me peel myself from the vehicle. You leaned languorously like a pinup, strings dangling from your frayed denim short-shorts along your tanned, lean thighs, making me simultaneously uncomfortable and depressed.

You had curves. Woman curves. And I have to tell you, Jenny, even after all we've been through, I still think of you as a tiny, young thing. Six years old, asking me with the utmost amount of intellectual curiosity if Iceland had a vanilla section. It was difficult to watch you morph into a woman, sometimes because of how old it made me feel, but mostly because I watched you shift from "Prettygirl" to a stunning young woman. Your innocence and sweet nature were in sharp contrast to that dangerous body you were acquiring. All I could do was picture your future heartbreaks. I wanted to keep you in a closet, locked away from the boys who had the power to turn you into something harder, jaded, and worn.

You have always been my walking proof of time, the tangible evidence of life inevitably moving forward.

"Ooh, you had to get a ride!" you sassed, practically dancing with excitement, shaking your head, sucking your cheeks, lips pursed. I recognized in your face the one that used to meet me at my locker before dance practice. "Are you mad?" you asked. "I'd be mad. Mama didn't even text you back and—hey, listen: she saw you texted."

Family documentarian, historian, and amateur paparazzo, that's the smarty-pants known as Jennifer Cooperton. Always on to what the grown-ups were doing. We had to start spelling things over your head before you were four. If there was a secret to be found, you sensed it, rooting it out like the furriest cat finding the party guest with the most sensitive allergies. This is why your mother wouldn't let you have a blog.

"Wait until I'm in the loony bin before you start writing trash about your mother," I remember her saying. "I know you're scribbling it all down somewhere. I'm not stupid. *Dear World: Life is so unfair and my mom's mean and please send help because this is child abuse, how I can't have a Coke with my breakfast. Send.*"

Tucker groaned as he stretched his large frame toward the sky. "Your daddy ready?" he asked you.

"He's coming."

Tucker and Henry had their furniture restoration business going for about a couple of years at that point. Smidge would tease them that they spent their weekends antiquing like old ladies, but often they were out there searching for a credenza or a china pattern Smidge had fallen in love with online. I can't even count the number of times she pressed a printout into Henry's palm as she kissed him good-bye, whispering, "Fetch me this."

And, you know, he usually did.

"Danielle Meyers!"

Slight with a dark tan, always in jeans with holes at the knees and a white T-shirt, wearing the same belt he'd worn since the seventh grade (something he liked to brag about), Henry often looked like he'd just walked off the set of a teen-rebel movie. He even slicked his hair back on the sides, which shouldn't look good on any man, but always worked for him. He smelled of almond oil and beer.

"You sure did pack a lot more than Smidge," he noted in his soft drawl as he helped Tucker with my second suitcase.

"Well, she wouldn't tell me where we were going, so I brought everything," I said. "From bikinis to snow boots."

Henry had gained a little weight around his tummy, which finally made him look old enough to be someone's dad. It looked good on him, like he was happy.

Henry patted Tucker high on his back. "Thanks for going to pick up Danielle," he said. "I knew my wife wasn't going to get her anytime soon, so I appreciate it."

"Tucker, you liar! You *were* there to pick me up!"

Tucker lifted his chin, looking away in mock pride. "Maybe," he said. "Maybe I did tell a small untruth. But it made you feel special, so it was worth it."

And another successful superhero moment hits the history books.

# THREE

Once Henry and Tucker took off in search of something vintage, you and I walked back up to the house. You hooked your arm around my waist and dropped your head onto my shoulder. The heat of the sun soaked your thick, blond hair, which had that impossible shine of youth. Your hips kept knocking into mine as you walked, once again proving you were no longer a little kid—your center of gravity was lowering, and you were still getting used to your new body. You smelled like cheap perfume, which meant you were rubbing magazine ads against your forearms again.

"Oh, hey, I got you something," I said as I remembered, pulling back to reach into my purse.

"Yay."

I handed you a small bottle of Chloé perfume. "Hide it immediately before she finds this and throws it at my head."

Smidge had been known to suddenly declare the most random, innocuous things offensive, tacky, or dangerous. There was the time she outlawed cheese, the month she banned hip-hop, and the unforgettable winter she tore all the carpeting out of her house. *With her own two hands.*

Smidge would then change her mind in what would appear to be just as abrupt a decision. She'd never just admit she might have been wrong or made an irrational decision. There was no regret, no remorse. Rather, it was always a choice to go in the other direction, as if she'd done some consulting from a more learned advisor.

"I guess listening to a little hip-hop won't kill anybody," she might have said. "If it's the good kind with Kanye West in it. Y'all, that man knows what he's doing."

As if he'd called her himself and talked her out of the ban. "Shorty, why you trippin'? How can Kanye fix this?"

Smidge never did change her mind about Capri pants. I learned that the hard way when she cut mine into shorts while I was wearing them. *While I was wearing them.* In her backyard, surrounded by guests, a barbecue in progress, your mother attacked me with a pair of scissors she'd grabbed from the kitchen, shrieking, "This is for your own good!"

Perfume became contraband when Smidge was on a tear about the way things smelled, often stopping a conversation midword to flick her head to the side and sniff.

"What in the *hell?*" she'd mutter to herself, glaring at any unfortunate nearby stranger. Everyone was a suspect as her senses were continually assaulted.

She'd gag on the smell of gasoline, strawberry milk shakes, and chewing gum. One day she stared into her backyard for almost half an hour, positive she'd found a skunk. It got to where even the idea of certain smells were upsetting to her; the thought of someone striking a match made her queasy.

But Jenny, you were not having this perfume ban. I have to admit I got a bit of a thrill watching you stand up for yourself, recognizing injustice when it encroached on your own body.

"It's not like I'm always around her nose," you said to me. "If she's so sensitive, she should just wear one of those surgical masks, like an Asian lady at the airport."

Still, I made you promise to keep the bottle safely hidden in whatever place you were keeping your secrets those days. You swore you would, tucking that small, golden bottle into your shorts pocket, patting it gently as you shot me your mother's smug expression. "I love you, A.D.," you said.

Remember when you called me that? For Auntie Danielle?

You wandered away from me, headed toward the backyard, your head down as you rapidly thumbed keys on your phone, somehow already in the middle of another conversation.

Standing at the front door, I prepared myself for the familiar sound of your family's chaos. I always had to take just a second before I stepped inside.

It still seems impossible only three people lived in that house. Three people and that old dog and I know somewhere there was allegedly a hamster named Quiche Lorraine, but I hadn't seen it. The amount of electricity, energy, and sound surrounding that place made it seem like a hub for a family of ten, or maybe a squad of fifteen cheerleaders. Perhaps some kind of adult day-care center. A television was on in almost every room, with each set tuned to a different channel, even if nobody was watching. In the kitchen next to the microwave, an iPod rested in a speaker system, blasting twangy songs I never recognized.

The house was always impeccably clean. What it lacked in serenity, it more than made up for in order. Your mother arranged her cereal boxes by hue. The refrigerator bore no magnets. All cords were sheathed in a tube the same color as the wall behind it. So loud and yet so empty—like everybody had been kidnapped. Or perhaps all just got up and left.

The Rapture.

That was it. What it will look like after the chosen ones have been summoned, when people disappear. Since I'm certainly going to be one of the heathens left behind, I always said I'd beeline it straight to Smidge's during End of Days, as her cabinet had the expensive snacks.

I didn't live that way. I couldn't. I need quiet, even at the expense of a mess. I don't mind being buried under piles of laundry and stacks of papers as long as the background noise is either the television or the radio—not both. Never both. Being in Smidge's house was like living inside a slot machine. The bedlam made me uneasy, like I needed to grab the counter with both hands to steady myself.

"Smidge! I'm here!"

From the back of the house, I heard my best friend shout back, "Good! Come get this!"

I headed toward her room, sidestepping the old basset hound camped out in the hallway. "Hello, Dr. Phil," I said as I gently tiptoed over his enormous floppy ears that stretched almost halfway across the floor.

Smidge was wearing a pair of white shorts and a blue tank. Her thick hunks of dark curls were pulled back into a low ponytail, covered by a floppy sunhat. One slender arm rested along a bookcase as she slid a cobalt flip-flop onto her foot.

She tottered there, head nodding toward the small, leopard-print suitcase on the floor beside her bed.

The rest of the room was pristine. We could have just as easily been standing in an IKEA display, or the bedroom of a child hampered with severe allergies.

"Just that one bag?" I asked. Smidge normally carried enough pieces of luggage to outweigh her by a factor of two.

"Yes, smarty-face," she said. "I'm traveling light!"

When she raised her arms in celebration I noticed she'd lost weight since I'd seen her last, around six months ago, when she flew out to my apartment for an overdrunken event we called Danielle's Definitely Divorced Weekend. I don't remember much of it, but I know somewhere she had pictures of me wearing a black veil, hugging a palm tree, simultaneously crying and laughing. I look deranged. She claimed it was her favorite picture of me.

Catching my stare, she pulled her arms across her chest into a defensive hug. "What?" she asked as though issuing a schoolyard challenge, her chest puffed up and chin tilted.

"Nothing."

Her eyes remained slits as she warned, "Better be nothing."

Then, just as quickly, all the toughness melted from her face. "Come here, yay!" she said, dancing into my arms for a long hug. We remained that way until I heard a toilet flushing in the master bathroom.

"Who's here?" I asked.

Smidge scrunched her face and shrugged as a way of an apology. I needed no further answer.

Vikki Lillian was a woman instantly recognizable by her big teeth and even bigger parrot necklace. A woman for whom I had absolutely no patience. As she came lurking around the corner, I watched her decide to act like she was surprised to see me.

"Oh, hello, Danielle," she said, all singsong and gooey. "Well, didn't you just about frighten me?" Her face held that fake shock as she tangled her fingers into her hideous necklace. The parrot was green, sitting on a branch, half the size of her hand, and I couldn't help but wonder if summers ended with her finding a bird-shaped white patch across her splotchy chest.

She rocked on her heels, fixing her gaze Smidge's way. "I was just here to see if Smidge needed any help while y'all go off gallivanting on y'all's trip. With Jenny or Henry or the house. Y'all are sometimes gone for so long and this house is so big, I know you'll need help keeping it up when y'all are gone for who knows how long."

Sometimes hearing that accent, no matter how many years I'd been surrounded by it, with some people it still sounded like someone was plucking a banjo. *Ping, pawng, y'all y'all.*

"Isn't she sweet?" Smidge asked, not meaning it in the slightest.

"That's nice of you," I told Vikki. "But Smidge has a housekeeper."

Smidge smacked her thighs. "No, I don't!"

She did. Her name was Tamara; she was forty-six and always entered through the back door, even though your mom would insist she came through the front. Smidge wasn't embarrassed to have someone working for her; she just didn't want Tamara getting the daily credit when she only came once a week.

"It's not like company's coming over to see if my sheets are clean and my towels are in the closet," she'd say. "When people say my house is clean, it's because I wash the damn dishes every day and know how to use a broom. That praise is mine."

"She doesn't have a housekeeper," Vikki corrected me, so happy to think she was up on something.

Smidge gave me her wide-eyed warning to let it go.

"I told Vikki I'm good here," she said, "but she just keeps on insisting there must be something she can do!"

Vikki shook her head, presumably to dislodge all the self-righteousness she was about to need. "Y'all are just so lucky," she said, "getting to drop everything to go wherever you want, whenever you want, without feeling bad. I just don't know how y'all do that. Well, I mean, I guess you've got Henry to help, and with Danielle here not having any kids or a husband. All alone, you might as well travel. That's what I'd do if I were like that with nobody in my life. Nothing else going on, why not see some Chinese people?"

Vikki had started hanging around Smidge about a year earlier, when Smidge's knitting club dissolved after everyone finally admitted they were unable to knit and purl at such high levels of intoxication. People were starting to get testy with one another, leading Smidge to make a declaration that she wouldn't hold more than three women on her porch at once. I have to admit it's not that bad of a rule. Despite the lack of an invitation, Vikki kept coming every Tuesday night, and eventually Smidge felt sorry for her. "I think her husband hates her," Smidge confessed to me one night, whispering into the phone as if Vikki was within earshot. "He's probably afraid she'll chomp on him with those horse teeth of hers."

After that, Vikki always seemed to be there, acting like she'd always been there, like it was normal for us to be a threesome. Even if I'd just traveled hundreds of miles to get to that porch.

Vikki loved being a shadow to Smidge, like her sole purpose was to stand around waiting for the moment Smidge needed someone to agree with her. But the joke was on Vikki; Smidge already knew she was right about everything. Smidge let Vikki have just the smallest perception of the wonderland that could be her friendship, without anything tangible to take home. I don't think Smidge would have even lent her Fiestaware.

Smidge interrupted here with one of her singing segues, a habit of hers that never failed to suck all the attention in the room straight over toward her. She usually did it to change the subject, but sometimes it was to make a conclusion. She could draw out that word until it sounded like she was frozen, trapped in the middle of singing "Do Re Mi."

"*Sooooooo!*" she sang. "Let's hit the road, Danny. I wanna stop at Sonic for a cherry limeade."

And that was it. No *Bye, Vikki*. No *Thanks for stopping by*. Smidge acted like Vikki was already gone, a doll dropped as she wandered into another room.

Some decent part of me knew I should have at least a pang of sympathy for Vikki as I watched her slink out of the house, but it was hard to feel for her when she insisted on bringing these situations upon herself. And the parrot necklace made me irrationally angry. Did she sleep wearing it? She must have. She probably showered with it.

That's when you appeared in the doorway, arms crossed in front of your budding chest, head swiveling at us like you were an audience member on *Jerry Springer*. "Y'all are mean," you said to us, your tiny little mouth a bracket of disapproval.

Your mother snorted. "I learned it from you."

# FOUR

You followed us all the way to the driveway asking your mother for some extra cash. "What if something happens while you're gone?" you whined. "What if Daddy forgets to feed me and I need emergency pizza?"

Even though we all knew you'd be fed and safe, Smidge made a big production out of slipping you a twenty. "Give me Odd Hugs," she said, once you'd stuffed the bill near the perfume-shaped lump in your pocket.

You two began the series of contortions that was your Odd Hugs ritual—repeated awkward embraces that mocked affection while still technically counting as touches. A leg lifted here, an elbow bent into someone's side there—your mother was fond of pulling faces while she leaned toward you. You preferred making chicken wings out of your arms while asking, "Like this? Like this?"

"What's that smell?" she asked you after your tenth Odd Hug. "Why do you smell like a brothel?"

You kissed her on each cheek in a mock French fashion,

quickly noting, "Y'all better get going before Vikki packs a suitcase."

Your mother said, "Love you, stinky," and we drove away.

Smidge wanted a road trip, a back-to-basics, paper-map-and-fast-food, feet-up-on-the-dashboard, singing-Madonna-songs girl trip. We headed east, toward a destination only Smidge knew, even though she was making me drive her large, green sedan that I liked to call the Pickle. We wouldn't hit Mexico going east, but we would eventually hit the Atlantic.

*Where there were cruise ships.*

"How about a hint?" I asked again.

"Unh-uh," she said. "I wanna see your face when we get there. And I don't want you to ruin it with all your thinking. No brains! Just driving." She took a second before she added, "I love you. You are my prettiest friend."

"Thank you."

"Pretty, despite those flesh sticks you call fingers. You knew we were leaving; you didn't have time for a manicure?"

"I type a lot, Smidge. You know manicures are wasted on me."

She grunted. "Never gonna get a new man wagging around those skin stumps you've got going on."

This was not the time to stand up to Smidge. I would never be so dumb as to say to her something bold like, "I think I know what's best for me." If I ever lost my brain and told her something like that, I already knew what would happen.

First, her head would jerk back, like someone had shot her between the eyes with an invisible bullet. Her dark, thin eyebrows would search for each other, straining to meet just above her freckled nose. Then her sharp chin would drop to her pale chest, already flushed patchy-pink with outrage. With her right hand slapped to the back of her head, she'd fluff those bundles of chestnut hair, outraged that I'd offended her right down to her secretly gray roots.

And then she would speak, which is when it's over. Once Smidge's singsong, Southern-soaked voice got into your head, once it flowed past your ears and IV-dripped deep into your bones, there wasn't much more to do but obey.

"*You* know what's best for you," she'd say, not as a question, but a shocked statement. "I'm sorry. Did you just say *you* know what's best for you?"

Smidge would turn indignant, about to say the very last word on the subject. Pressing the fingertips of her left hand with the perfectly painted index finger of her right, she'd count off with her bony fingers, getting to the heart of exactly what she felt was wrong with me.

"No husband. No kids. You ain't got a house."

Smidge wouldn't say the word *ain't* around most people, but I'm hardly people. I'm a constant. I'm expected, like ground under your feet when you get out of bed. Smidge never saw me as someone else, this other human. I'm an extension of her. I'm extra Smidge. So when she called me out, it's because she saw something she didn't like about the entity that is Us.

Usually it was better to deflect her hits and blows one by one, like Wonder Woman using her steel cuffs. But in a situation where she's listing my flaws, it doesn't matter why I don't have those things. I don't have them. And to Smidge, having those things would prove I'd done something right with my life. Husband. Kids. House. They're the merit badges earned by grown women.

I suppose I could have tried the truth, something like: "Well, I got separated before we ever had enough money to even think about buying a house, and real estate is rather expensive in Los Angeles. I'm only newly divorced, not that I'm counting the months, or anything. But I've been pretty busy with my career to have kids, with or without a boyfriend or husband or even a nanny." Perhaps I'd end with a very quiet, very quick: "It's also possible that I have different goals for myself than you have for me."

But saying all those words would risk too big a fight, so what I'd say instead would be a very levelheaded, "Smidge. You know you're the only one who knows what's best for me."

"Cor-*rect*," she'd say, leaning over to rub my arm while handing me a glass of wine she'd somehow magically make appear via her powers over the space-time continuum. Then, unable to keep from having even more of the last word, she'd cluck, "Honestly. What would you ever do without me?"

We were about thirty minutes out of town, driving past a whole lot of nothing, when we passed an empty road lined thick with trees in bloom.

"That's a pretty road," I said, pointing. "Look at all those purple flowers."

"You don't know that road?" Smidge asked, crinkling her forehead until she cut her freckle number in half. "That road's famous. Some man did this thing where he would film every person in this parish walking down this one street. Every year he'd come back and do it again. I think it's in some *faincy-paints* museum."

"That sounds cool."

Smidge's eyes widened. "I can't believe you don't know this!" she said, her excitement growing. "Every year for like, sixty years now or something, he comes back to film them again. Everybody. From babies to old people. They say if you missed the day the man came to town and didn't get filmed walking down that street, it's like you didn't live here. Like you didn't count."

I could picture the scenes. Bodies shifting from tiny to big, sometimes disappearing, sometimes new ones showing up. People moving away, coming back, making families. "I bet that's so neat," I said. "Watching all those people grow up on camera."

"They call it Big Count Road," she said, nodding. "In fact, that's how the Count on *Sesame Street* got his name."

"What? Seriously?"

"No!" Smidge yelled, pushing my arm so hard I swerved the Pickle and had to wave an apology to the driver in the next lane. "How could any of that be true? You're so dumb sometimes, Danny, I swear! Oh, my God."

You might think the tendency to believe the things people say is a normal human function, even considered a trait of nice people. It should be a sign of decency, humanity, perhaps something to honor and respect. If you were talking to Smidge, you'd find out you were wrong.

She thought my trusting nature was something to be exploited, mocked as often as possible. Smidge wasn't the only one who delighted in telling lengthy tall tales, seeing how far she could get before I started to question the validity of her story. James used to do it all the time. The worst was when he and Smidge would conspire together, ganging up to breathlessly share something they'd witnessed on the way home, and how they couldn't believe I'd missed it: a dog walking a cat; a kid floating above his front yard, clutching a giant birthday bundle of balloons; Carmen Electra in a wig store.

Smidge was particularly pleased with herself on this Big Count Road speech, probably because she made it all the way to mentioning a Muppet.

"Do you how hard it would be to film every single person walking down that street every year?" she asked. "And how long did I say he'd done it, sixty years? With what kind of old-timey editing equipment was he doing that? How old is that man? Jesus, Danny. All those brains you've got, but sometimes just no smarts. I'm gonna have to call that idiot ex-husband of yours and brag about that one. I bet James misses this so much."

"Yes, won't that be nice? The two of you talking about how stupid I am for believing in you."

"The Count," she muttered. "On *Sesame Street*. My Christ."

When we got to Sonic, I made her pay for my lunch.

———————

## FIVE

Once we were back on the road, Smidge let out a giggle as she remembered something.

*"Soooooooo,"* she sang. "Guess what I'm fixing to tell you: what had happened to me last Friday night."

Smidge held her gigantic cherry limeade with both hands, bouncing the already nearly empty Styrofoam cup on her knees, both feet kicked up on the dash. The sugar was working, obviously, but I think the vacation was starting to get into her blood as well.

"Tell me what had happened," I drawled.

"First of all, I made the mistake of going out with Vikki, who was so boring. Here's how boring: so, so, so, so, so, so boring."

"Six sos!"

"Six. Maybe even seven."

"That *is* boring."

"Yes. And it's your fault for going out with that guy who had rapist hair when we were supposed to talk on the phone, leaving me to fend for myself with Vikki. In fact, all of what

I'm about to tell you is your fault, so I hope you're ready to start feeling guilty."

Rapist Hair was originally named Lane, but when I e-mailed Smidge a photo of him she replied with just: *Rapist hair. Do not date.*

She was right, of course. Not about the hair, but the dating part. He started strong. Tall, good chin, dark eyes, but he had a terrible habit of intentionally making bad jokes and then acting offended when I didn't laugh at them.

It got worse. Once inside his apartment, I saw he had an iguana. I would like to receive some kind of medal or certificate for not screaming while running from the building right then and there as if he were an actual rapist. Instead, I waited at least ten minutes before pretending there was an emergency that would somehow render me unable to contact him for the rest of my life.

Nights like that sometimes left me thinking, *"Maybe I'll just move in with Smidge. Be her Boston wife. Jenny can think of me as some weird aunt and I'll live in the back room and clip coupons in front of a dusty, old television while having an intimate one-sided relationship with Drew Carey on* The Price Is Right, *where I yell at him about the rising cost of olive oil."* There was something about it that felt so much easier, letting her make all my decisions. Just melt into someone else's life and disappear, no longer worrying about what I'm going to do next.

Funny how you can be so wrong about something.

I propped my elbow to rest my head in my hand. "Let's focus less on what's my fault and go back to your complaints about Vikki," I said.

"*Ugh,* Vikki. Six so-borings! All she talks about is that dog, I swear to God. She got a dog, did you know that?"

"No."

"Some kind of shit-zu. Looks like someone took a pretty dog and melted it down. Named it Barksy. Like she's *two*. Now, what kind of grown-up names a dog Barksy? Honestly. And she can't stop going on about the damn thing. 'Barksy jumped up on my bed. Barksy ate a carrot. Barksy got stuck in the pantry.' I wanna be like, 'Vikki. Just have a baby. I will steal one for you, if I have to, just to make you shut the hell up.' She is turning into one crazy woman, Danny. I can't take it. Okay, so she's got raisiny ovaries. Lots of people have problems. Just fix it."

One had to be careful in telling Smidge personal information, as she'd find a way to fit it into one of her rants like a piece of trivia. Fun facts everyone knows, no big deal. I'd think Vikki would prefer I wasn't privy to the workings or nonworkings of her reproductive system, but to Smidge, if it were really a secret, she wouldn't know about it. In her mind, if you're talking about it to someone, obviously you don't mind someone else knowing.

"Smidge," I gently scolded.

"What? You've got the ovaries of a Golden Girl, too, but at least you put them to use most nights. Can't wait to find out which derelict will end up being your baby's daddy."

With my right thumb and forefinger, I reached out to the front of Smidge's tank top and flicked the very tip of her tiny nipple. She instantly doubled over, howling and laughing, clutching her chest.

"I earned that."

"Yes, you did."

"*Soooooooo*. To numb the pain of Vikki's dogologue, I started drinking. The next thing I know I have had a bottle of wine. And a *half*."

That's usually an alarming amount of wine to anyone else the size of Smidge, but my friend never met a blood alcohol content she couldn't handle. I'd seen her drink marines under the table. Marines at a bachelor party. In a strip club. In Patpong, Thailand.

Smidge fiddled with her sunglasses as she talked, playing with the hinge in a way that was definitely going to cause them to break. "And it's fine, all that wine," she said, "because Jenny's at her friend's house for the night, and Henry's out with Tucker, and I suddenly realize that all I want to do is get into bed and watch an old movie. Without Vikki. I just want my bed and some Turner Classic Movies. I start wanting it so bad I'm practically salivating. So I'm cleaning up, doing the dishes. *Washin' up a little hint*, you know? I put on my *pajamas*, trying to give some clues. The ones with all the happy tacos on them? Those are pants that say, 'I am going to *bed*.' But this girl's just standing in my kitchen, chatting away. So now I'm fixing to kill this woman who thinks I actually want to hear about her dog-baby, because she will not take the *hint*! Crap. I just broke my sunglasses."

Smidge leaned forward to scroll through the radio stations, unable to find one that wasn't pure static. She banged the knob with the palm of her hand, silencing it. Then she turned her attention to the remaining sips of her cherry limeade. She slid the plastic straw through the lid, causing a haunting sound that made my spine shiver. Yanking off the lid, she tipped her head back to pour the last sweet drops onto her tongue. Rooting for the maraschino cherry at the bottom, she jammed the straw back into the cup and hacked at the packed shaved ice.

"*Soooooo,*" she continued. "Vikki finally goes home, and I get into bed and realize, now that she's gone, I should celebrate. With a drink!"

"Oh, dear."

"'Oh, dear' is right," Smidge said, "because dumb Vikki made me drink the last of my wine before she left. I had to drive my bike over to the Liquor Stop Gas Shop for a bottle of red. I am in my house shoes and pajamas—"

"Looking like a crazy person."

Smidge dug her fingers into the cup to scoop ice into her mouth. "Like I rode away from the sanitarium," she said as she juggled the minuscule frosty cubes over her tongue. "On my *bike.* Anyway, I end up buying a six-pack and I've got it in my basket and as I'm headed back I start wondering if it's too late to catch Sweet and Lowe's show over at The Pantry."

The Pantry was a dark bar with a huge back patio and rows of damp, musty wooden benches adorned with piles of over-flowing ashtrays. Nightly, a band crowded onto the matchbox of a stage and played so loudly all conversations were held just shy of screaming. You never went home from The Pantry without a damaged larynx.

"Smidge. Tell me you didn't go to The Pantry on your bike in your house shoes!"

I was only mostly sure that "house shoes" were the same thing as slippers. I understand what the people of Ogden say and do, but it's neither my native tongue nor my first instinct when it comes to communicating. For instance, I would never say "I drove my bike," even if it were a motorcycle.

Smidge patted me on the hip. "I parked my bike up to a post like I was hitching a horse, hid my six-pack in a bush by the back door, and waltzed into The Pantry just in time to hear Lowe sing 'Midnight Train to Georgia.'"

I would never think to do these things, to wander around looking for fun while intoxicated and wearing pajama pants. If I tried half the things Smidge could get away with, I'd no doubt be arrested within twenty minutes. But in the end, it was always just another funny story for Smidge.

"I'm kind of jealous," I admitted.

"You should be," she said. "Because the lovely Lowe had me come up onstage to help her sing."

I gave her a brief but challenging stare. "She *had* you?"

"I mean she was already up there singing, and there was a second microphone, and space on the stage and—I don't know. It happened. Plus, Sweet has a crush on me."

I could imagine Smidge standing onstage in her taco-covered pajama pants, hair twisted into some bedtime knot, belting away like she was the one they all came to see. Most likely, the only people in the bar who weren't cheering her on were the ones who never even noticed Sweet & Lowe had a surprise guest.

"Anyway, I take a bow, the crowd goes wild. Obviously. Then I head over to the bar to finish my drink, and who's sitting there but your buddy Tucker Collier? And guess what he said?"

"'Can I request some Skid Row?'"

"He said, 'If you could kindly do me a favor and stand still for a moment, I need to call your husband to inform him that you are neither dead nor kidnapped.'"

Smidge had left her house wide open with all the televisions on. Just like I'd always imagined was possible, Henry came home to find that busy, empty house and assumed someone had snatched his wife.

"Had he already called the police?"

"No. Once he knew Tucker was on his way to The Pantry, he figured he ought to find out first if I was there. If I had been kidnapped I could have been dead before he even bothered to check on me, so I'll make sure to be mad at him later for that. But the moral of this story is, my husband must really love me, because I don't know why else he hasn't killed me yet."

Henry loved Smidge in a kind of old-timey way you rarely see men love women anymore. Not just in the way that he looked at her like she was always telling the most fascinating story, or how when he came home from work, the first thing he did was bend down toward her until his head rested in her lap and she rubbed the back of his neck with her hand. It wasn't in how they made each other laugh, or how he would cook until she begged him to stop feeding her. It wasn't in the way he brought home flowers every Friday.

Henry's love was in his patience.

We all endured Smidge, but the rest of us shared the burden, spread it around a bit. Henry was the only one who was her husband. The one man in her life. There are statues less patient than that man. Even a statue would have found a way to mobilize his marble-stone mouth just to tell your mother to shut her crazy ass up.

But Henry, he just nodded. Rocked his head and absorbed her words. The more Smidge consumed, the more he doted. Sometimes I wondered if his insides were riddled with ulcers.

"*Soooooo,* Tucker calls my husband and tells him that he found his wife. Henry goes to bed. Once the bar closes I figure I'd better get home. I do, on my bike, *somehow,* and when I wake up the next morning I get a phone call from Sweden."

"Sweden? Like the country?"

Smidge threw back her head and cackled. "Yes, Sweden! They were just looking over their recent online orders, and they wanted to know if I meant to purchase a chair shaped like an egg."

"What did you say?"

"What do you think I said? I *immediately* answered, 'Uh, yes, ma'am. I did!'"

"Oh, no!"

She pulled at her eyelids with her thumb one at a time, trying to keep her mascara away from her tears. "Well, I'm sure I wanted it when I bought it!"

"An egg chair?"

"And *then* my credit card company called to also make sure I meant to purchase a brand-new laptop computer."

"Smidge!"

"I know! So what I am telling you is that last weekend I made a two-thousand-dollar drunk dial on my credit card. Which is why I am now asking you to drive faster, because I want to make sure I am long gone and far away by the time Henry finds out."

"You are a dead woman," I said.

We drove in silence for a while as I tried to imagine what would happen if one day everybody decided Smidge should be forced to do what *we* said for a change. Just for one day. What if she ever had to answer to anybody? I don't think she could handle it, living under rules that weren't hers and hers alone.

I was just about to ask her which one of us she'd let be the boss of her, when I noticed she'd fallen asleep, a thin, red line of cherry stain on her upper lip. Her hands twitched as the empty Styrofoam cup tumbled to her feet.

_____

## SIX

While Smidge slept I stopped at a gas station for a fill-up, taking a moment to check my messages. Even though I had told all of my clients I was on vacation for at least two weeks, I knew there'd be an emergency. Sure enough, there was an e-mail from a client who desperately needed me to "fix the flow" in his kitchen.

*I am convinced we have the refrigerator against the wrong wall. Mark insists—GET THIS—that we currently have it on the wall that is the most pleasing to his arm when he reaches. Please come tell us where the fridge should go, because I think it's why I keep giving up on making breakfast. McDonald's is easier than fighting over how to reach for the eggs. My stove sits untouched. My fridge only has mayo. We miss you! Help us! Take us shopping and whip us back into shape!*

*Your cheerful yet soon to be diabetic client,*

*Sean*

*PS: "Pleasing to his arm"!!*

I couldn't wait to tell Smidge about this e-mail, because I knew she'd give her smug smile and say, "This is why your job is sad balls."

We didn't always take our vacations with just the two of us to a place where we could rest. Since these trips originally came out of Smidge's grief over her father's early passing, at first we tried to make them have importance. It's as naïve as it is noble how we thought we could leave a place better for having had us in it. Eventually we learned that our lofty goals were covering the guilt that came with the privilege of getting to travel, and not every trip needed to be a charity event. But back then we were young, and hadn't yet experienced "sad balls."

Sad balls came about the summer we volunteered to go to Guatemala to help a local organization rebuild structures damaged from a large earthquake. It had been almost a year, but there was still rubble in the streets, bridges destroyed, roads unpredictable and dangerous. Parts of the country were quite unsafe. We never felt in danger, however, since we were clearly marked as relief workers. Our nights were spent in the heavily policed tourist zones, our days hard at work carrying lumber, digging holes, and lugging buckets of water from rickety wells consisting of not much more than a hose, a PVC pipe, and a bucket.

I believe that was the trip where I asked Smidge if maybe we could start a tradition of doing the backbreaking, morally fulfilling vacation every other year.

Smidge was in her element when we worked on these projects. Her smile never left her face and she would often extend our trips by a day or two, having gotten attached to a particular group of people. She couldn't leave them until the last board was nailed, the final bag of sand carried. She worked well under pressure. In a situation where leaders were needed and nobody questioned the bossy one, she was a natural. She might start with grunt work, but by the end of the second day she usually had her own crew and her own side assignment.

In Thailand they painted her name on the back of a bench to thank her for helping to repair a damaged hospital in Phuket. I have that picture framed in my living room. Smidge is standing in the middle of a group of smiling Thai men coated in the same thick red sand as the roads, their grins toothy from ear to ear, all standing at just about the same height—including Smidge—arms locked around one another. An elephant stands in the background with his head down, looking like he was banished from the happy clique. Smidge has one leg wrapped around the other, like she's about to lead a kick line. Her head is thrown back in laughter.

Toward the end of our stay in Guatemala, our guides took us to visit an elementary school. We had lunch with the children on their hillside campus overlooking a breathtaking mountain that shot high into the perfect blue sky. Smidge and I wondered how anybody could focus enough to learn how to read at that school—we knew if we went there we'd never stop staring out the window at the magnificent view.

After lunch it was time for recess. One of the teachers tossed a pair of soccer balls onto the play area, sending the children screeching with joy. The girls chased one ball while the boys chased the other. Smidge and I were soon gasping for breath as we ran alongside them. A young girl of six or seven with a wide nose and dark, serious eyes held my hands, pulling me with purpose. The grass had long worn away in the field; the shuffling of fifty pairs of tiny shoes sent clouds of dirt into the air. I was sweating and coughing; my eyes stung from gritty bits of earth.

*"Tortuga!"* said a round-faced eight-year-old wearing a worn pink sweater over a thick, patterned skirt. She pointed at me as she repeated, *"Tortuga!"*

That means *turtle*. That's how they saw me. Slow as a turtle, hunched over and openmouthed. *Blanca tortuga.*

Once recess ended, our group headed out to go back to the work site. We watched one of the main guys locate the two soccer balls and kick them back toward the van.

"Hey!" Smidge shouted. "You're not taking those, are you?"

I can't remember his name, but he looked like Sean Penn. To be honest, a lot of the guys we met in Guatemala who had left everything to work with charities seemed to resemble Sean Penn. They were either Sean Penn look-alikes or they spoke German.

"Yeah," he said. "It's a rule. We can't leave any toys here."

He walked away not knowing enough about Smidge to lock those balls in a safe place.

"That is just mean," Smidge said. "How much could these things cost? I'll buy them some new ones."

She trotted back over to the children, who were standing in lines outside their classroom doors. Balancing a ball on each hip, she looked like a proud mother about to announce her twin babies.

Neither of us knew much Spanish, so I'm not sure what the kids were yelling when they broke their lines to surround her.

"Okay, now," Smidge started to say, but then a ball was ripped from her grip. "Hey!"

The second one immediately followed, and for a moment I couldn't even see Smidge through all the dust kicked up by fifty children tangling over possession of two balls. It wasn't a game they were playing. This time it was a fight.

"Those are to share!" I heard her yell. As she was getting elbowed out of the crowd, she turned to me with a look of desperation. "What is Spanish for—" She abruptly turned back toward the kids and yelled, "*¡Compartir! ¡Compartir!*"

The kids continued fighting, pushing, running, and yelling until the teachers got involved. The children were lined up and severely scolded as Smidge returned the soccer balls to the van.

"I see now why you have a rule," she said, chin tucked in defeat.

To his credit, fake Sean Penn never said a word the entire drive back to the work site. He just chewed on a toothpick, as if nothing had happened.

Smidge was in the backseat, staring out the window in shock, her face slack. "I didn't mean to do that," she said. "I just wanted to help."

I rubbed her arm. "It's okay. You were trying to do a good thing."

"I need to learn Spanish," she said.

"Probably not. I mean, it's not like you're going to get asked back. Not after you gave them sad balls."

From then on, "sad balls" stood for trying to do a nice gesture, only to end up accidentally causing a shitstorm.

I would have never guessed in a million years that the king of all sad balls was about to smack me right in the face.

# SEVEN

_____

About seven hours into our road trip, just outside Birmingham, Alabama, Smidge abruptly yelled, "Okay, we're pulling off here!"

"How can you have to pee again? We just stopped like—"

"No, no, we're here!"

"What do you mean, 'here'? We barely left Louisiana!"

We were in some place called Anniston, Alabama, and I was confused. It was just a little suburb, and as Smidge directed me off one street and onto another, I started getting suspicious. What could be at the end of this map? Judging from the lack of anything you couldn't find in your typical small-town-off-a-highway, I was concerned our destination might not be an airport.

"Okay, park here," she said, just past a hotel.

It was a parking lot near what appeared to be a furniture store. "Are we doing something for Henry?" I asked.

Smidge laughed, pointing at something on the other side of the windshield. "You still haven't seen it! Look up."

I craned my neck to look out the window. Towering above

us was a giant office chair. It was bigger than the building, probably thirty feet high.

"Smidge, what is this?"

"Duh! It's a gi-*normous* chair!"

"I can see that."

Smidge was already out the door and on her feet. "Come on! Grab your camera!"

I did what I was told, but I felt a growing knot of anger in my stomach. I'd been looking forward to this vacation. I'd even figured out how I would enjoy the cruise ship, if that was where she was forcing me to go. I was going to pretend we were an old lesbian couple on our first trip away after the kids were grown. It wasn't ideal, but I could have worked with that, had a little fun with it, maybe made Smidge rub my feet by the pool, just so we seemed more legitimately like lady lovers.

I'd been busy and I'd been sad. I needed our vacation, our escape from our lives. I wanted to be far, far away. But there we were, staring at a giant chair, still in the *South*. You can't vacation in the South when you're from there. And listen: I'd rather walk from here to Los Angeles than step one damn foot into Florida.

Smidge looked elated standing underneath that gigantic chair, like she'd reached an important milestone, as if we'd walked the entire Great Wall.

It might have been just another prank. Maybe she was about to tell me there were plane tickets taped to the bottom of that chair.

"Can you take a cell phone picture for Henry?" she asked. "You probably have to go way back to get everything in the frame."

"Smidge." My voice warbled as I tried to hide my impatience.

"I'm gonna tell Henry I bought this chair, too." She posed, one hand behind her head, leaning sassily against a thick leg beam. "That's why we're here! Because this is the funniest thing I've ever thought of."

"That's it?"

"That's it! Well, and you're looking at the World's Largest Chair, so you can cross that off your to-do list."

"We're not going anywhere else? I packed half my life into a plane so that I could drive to a giant chair and take a picture of you?"

"Yes! I mean, fine, we can drive to Atlanta if you want and get a drink."

My jaw clenched tight as I hissed through my teeth, *"Smidge."*

I wonder how many people have forgotten that her real name's Farrah. She never seemed like a Farrah. Nobody called her that, not in as long as I'd known her. Not even her father called her that, and he named her after his sister.

Your mom had what she referred to as a "sad puberty." She was a big girl, too big for her small size. I've seen the pictures she threw away before you were born. She had a stomach that would sit high up over her shorts, like she was playing make-believe pregnant lady with a basketball stuffed under her shirt.

Her mother named her Smidge. It originated with "Just a smidge more," as in, that's what she would always eat. "Just a smidge more than a normal girl should." Than a thin girl would. Your grandmother's relationship with your mother was a complicated thing.

Smidge's mother once said to one of her friends, "I don't know how that pudgy thing shares my genes." She didn't care that Smidge was standing right there. "But that's my daughter. Squat and stunted. The Smidget."

Smidge dumped all that weight once she turned twelve and discovered the glamour and camaraderie that came with preteen eating disorders. After Smidge got tiny she embraced the nickname and grew a personality to match it. By the time I met her she was small, sassy, and proud. I think she liked how the name made her seem like she was already everybody's best friend.

Sometimes when we got drunk I called her Smidget Jones. Occasionally I got away with calling her Midge. Smidgeriffic. Smiddy. Or simply Smeh, which is what I used when I ran tired of words and just needed her to give me a beer or a hug. I said it like a sigh. "Smeh."

*"Smeh, I need you."*

*"Smeh, I love you."*

To which she would reply, *"Danny. You know I love you, too. I love you the mostest."*

But the woman standing underneath the World's Largest Chair, I was not calling her Smeh. That woman was Smidge, and about thirteen seconds from being Farrah.

"Do it, Danny. Go take a picture!" she shouted.

"No!" I threw my cell phone to the ground like a petulant child. I was done with feeling like I was the only one not in on the joke. I didn't want to be the last to learn the truth again. "This can't be about the chair, I know it. What is going on? Why aren't we on a plane? Why aren't we having fun somewhere with drinks that have umbrellas or taking pictures of churches and *real* monuments? What are we doing in Alabama, Smidge? Can you at least tell me that?"

"Fine!" Smidge clenched her fists and practically doubled over. "I have taken you to the middle of nowhere so I can tell you that the cancer is back!"

I felt it first in my knees. They went numb, liquefied, stopped working entirely. My lungs paused, leaving me frozen in time.

Her cancer was back. *Her* cancer was back, as if it was something she used to own, something she had sent off to boarding school. But it wasn't supposed to be here ever again. Not after she beat it. Not once we called her a survivor. We had a party. We wore T-shirts. There was a cake. Once you've eaten your survivor cake, that's supposed to signify an ending. That time was supposed to be over.

So how was it here again? Why would cancer rear up like a phoenix? *This* should be the twisted joke. I wanted her to bust into a grin, shocked that I once again fell for something that couldn't possibly be true. *You can't get cancer twice, silly! That would be so unfair!*

I'm sure I don't have to tell you that your mother didn't start crying. Even in that moment she wouldn't let her face get wet. Rather, she was slapping a pillar of the gigantic chair's leg, batting at it like a vending machine that stole her money. A tiny little lady battling an enormous piece of furniture as she invented curse words for this situation, barking in furious gasps.

"I just wanted to see this . . . suck-crap chair because . . . I'm trying to get some . . . goddamn things done before I'm . . . shitballs dead!"

"Smeh," I said, but I could hardly hear myself. "Smeh," I tried again, but I knew if I kept talking, I'd cry.

Smidge threw herself back against the chair leg. She swallowed and punched her thighs before staring me down. "My stupid cancer is back," she said. "And now I'm going to be dead just like my daddy. I can't believe it. Fucking cancer. Fucking cancer, Danielle! Again!"

*Cainsir.* That's how she said it. Hospitals and needles and vomiting and tests and *no, please, not this again.*

I forced a question past my lips. "What can I do?"

All the little muscles in her face relaxed as she resumed control. "I'm glad you asked," she said, as she folded her arms across her chest. I was right; they were thinner. "I have a job for you," she said, all business.

"Anything."

"Can I get that word in writing?"

"Why, what do you mean?"

"Get me to a drink, and I'll tell you all about it."

I stumbled over to my small friend and pulled her in tight. I hugged her as hard as I could, until I worried I was pressing tiny tumors into her heart.

"I still need you to take a picture of this chair. I mean, we drove all this way."

# EIGHT

I'd known Smidge longer than I'd known how to use a curling iron. I know that's a fact, because Smidge is the one who taught me.

I was fourteen when my dad moved us from Brooklyn to Ogden. I remember being so pissed off my first day at Neville High. All my preconceived notions of what living in the South was going to be like were bouncing around in my head, notions that were mostly acquired from television shows. I assumed everyone would own a horse; they'd all get into their cars by jumping through the windows. I figured everyone I'd meet would have a lump of tobacco jammed in his cheek.

My mother takes some of the blame for this. Right around the last time I ever saw her, she told me she was leaving and had absolutely no desire to haul her ass down to a "po-dunk, racist-ass, shit-kicking, cousin-fucker town just because your father thinks he owns me."

You never met my mom. I don't really talk to her all that much. Never to her face, anyway. I sometimes talk to the idea of her, when I get really frustrated. I talk to the memory of her, ask why she didn't care to find out what happened to me once I left Brooklyn. I ask her if she started doing drugs and that's why she forgot about me, or if she reinvented herself and became a happy homemaker with three kids and another on the way. That last one I could almost understand. Maybe for her it's just too painful that even though she eventually got it right, there's a little girl in her past for whom she got it spectacularly wrong.

My parents were very young when they had me, as it wasn't something they were planning on doing. They got married because that's what you did, that's how a man was a good man to a girl who was suddenly going to be a mother. They got married and tried to pretend they were in love with each other. It never caught on between them, never tricked their emotions into believing it. Therefore, I was pretty much a sentence they were serving. My mom got out early for terrible behavior.

She defected from the family, declared herself a "roving artist," a woman who only wanted to be married to "Our Lady America." I'm going to go ahead and guess that's an area that never went past the five boroughs.

Because of her reasons for not wanting to live even in the same state of the union that I was going to be in, she had me concerned that the citizens of Louisiana were restricted to ultrasnobby ladies with abusive husbands, men unironically named Bubba, and people who still owned slaves.

The first time I did meet an actual man named Bubba, I was heartbroken my mother had been at least slightly correct.

I was all alone, thrust into this small Southern town, attending a school filled with people who talked like words were made out of taffy. They pulled and squished their sentences into any old form they wanted. These people said "might could." As in, "You might could find a more podunk town than this one. But I sure do doubt it."

I was so far out of my element, I was positive I'd never meet anyone who could understand me, who would want to be my friend.

That's when I plopped down into the desk next to Smidge's on my first day of biology.

I remember her eyes as she gave me the once-over, how big and wide her pupils looked. She was wearing blue mascara, which I'd never seen anyone actually use before. She looked famous, important. Smidge had a way about her that could make you feel extremely self-conscious. When she's in front of you, you don't see her; you see her looking at you. People are always tugging at their hair when they're under her gaze, fixing themselves, straightening their shirts, surreptitiously wiping their noses, adjusting their necklaces. You don't know what she's thinking, but you have a feeling it can't be good. Her stare bores right into your secret shame and gets your brain screaming, *She knows! She sees my lies! I knew I shouldn't have worn this padded bra!*

Smidge was barely fourteen the day I met her. She always looked younger than everybody else. Did you know she had a fake ID before she was sixteen?

She was chewing gum with her front teeth. The pink wad crackled briefly before disappearing somewhere into her surprisingly large mouth so she could ask, "What's your name, new girl?"

"Danielle." I remember the word barely made a sound, I was so nervous. "I'm Danielle Meyers."

"Well, Danielle Meyers, if you are going to be my friend, we have *got* to do something about this hair."

Coming out of her mouth, the word *hair* had two syllables. *Hay-ir.* She grinned, leaned over, and held my sad strands in her left fist as she shook her head in pity. "Poor hayir."

She was always bold when talking to a stranger. It never occurred to her to have a boundary, or attempt something that resembled a tactful approach.

"If you had toilet paper stuck to your shoe, you'd want me to tell you, right?" she once asked me. "Even if I didn't know you, you'd want me to say something. Well, imagine your hair was that toilet paper. Because it was."

Not much changed about our relationship after that first exchange. Smidge fixed my hair that afternoon and became my self-declared guardian forevermore.

I was smart enough to know not to contradict her about that. It's a lot like having a lion for a best friend—everything is really fun and exciting until the lion is unhappy.

Did you know your mother once stopped a woman in a mall and told her she should get a mole on her face checked? "That thing is ugly," she said. "And God wouldn't have made it so hideous if he didn't want people to come up to you and tell you to do something about it." I was there that day, hiding behind a sunglasses kiosk, mortified down to my very last blood cell.

And do you know, one year later that woman with the mole showed up on your doorstep with a homemade sheet cake and a dozen roses, thanking your mother for saving her life?

Nobody ever stopped Smidge from talking, because she somehow had the ability to always end up being some kind of right. It was maddening.

---

I was sliding a dark walnut bar stool out from under the bar for Smidge when she gently pushed me aside.

"I'm not dying *today*, Danielle. You can cool it on the coddling."

I tried to cover. "I just assumed you were too short to reach the bar without some help."

"I'm not buying that," she said. "But I *will* buy your first drink."

In the hours after Smidge dropped the bomb on me, we had silently driven to Atlanta, quietly checked into a hotel, robotically changed outfits, and then practically sprinted to a rather swanky, dark bar in midtown. We didn't have to say why; I knew neither of us could handle whatever we were about to discuss without a drink. I'm glad we found a quieter spot in a corner, pressed up against the bar near a mirrored wall, watching the place grow crowded.

The regular patrons were standing together in easy-to-recognize groups. There were the overly boisterous office workers who'd been here since happy hour, ties loosened and pumps off. The young married women early into a girls' night that would end badly, their shot glasses aloft as they focused on temporarily forgetting all the young children they'd left at home in the shaky care of their husbands. Awkward body language gave away the couples on first dates, unsure how close they could sit despite—or because of—the noise level.

The walls around the bar were glassy and black, twinkling with ever-rotating dots of lights, making everyone look just a little more glamorous. For a second I was homesick. The upscale atmosphere reminded me of a place James and I would have gone to in Los Angeles after a movie or for celebratory drinks with friends.

I studied Smidge's face, thinking maybe I could find a sign, some hint as to how advanced her cancer was. What would I do if I were faced with the knowledge that my time was quickly coming up? Would I want to sit here with my friend at this trendy bar in Atlanta, ordering a martini? Wouldn't I want to be home with my family?

It might seem wrong that I could think of my own life, my own decisions, as I was waiting to find out the details of Smidge's illness. But everyone sees this disease through their own mortality, looking back over their shoulders, wondering, *Would I be ready for this?*

Cancer is selfish. It rips through its victim's body without the slightest hint of remorse. Then it spreads, jumping to anyone who hears the victim's story, infecting those people with fear, guilt. Cancer is at its most selfish when it comes to the spouses, the families, the friends. Because that's when it mutates again. For them, it's not their cells it destroys. It's their dreams.

"Okay, so I'm just going to start talking," Smidge said, smacking the bar with an open palm like a contestant on a game show. "I can't take it anymore, Danny. You have *got* to get that look off your face. I am not a pound puppy."

I tried, turning my eyes turn downward, forcing my focus

onto the bowl of wonton crispies left for us by the bartender. I picked at one, wondering how long I could waste time pretending I was deciding whether or not to eat it.

There was another pause as Smidge took a healthy gulp of her drink. She leaned back, eyes closed in boozy bliss. Finally, she said, "These taste *much* better when you're dying."

I tried to laugh but my breath caught in my throat. "Are you sure you're supposed to be drinking?"

"Lord," she said, rolling her eyes. "Here we go. I'll tell you something funny. They say alcohol *reduces* the risk of some cancers." She shook her head and rubbed her nose with the heel of her hand.

"If that's true, I don't understand how the cancer could come back. With the amount of preventive drinking you do, a relapse should be scientifically impossible."

"That's my girl," Smidge said, giving my elbow a gentle squeeze between her thumb and forefinger. "That's better. Thank you. Now drink a lot of that." She wiggled her fingers toward my drink. "I've got a proposition that'll sound better if you are nowhere near sober."

"A proposition? I don't recall you ever having a *proposition*. You mean I'm about to get some orders."

Smidge had all the information and I was trying to get a foothold on the situation. Just how she liked it.

Her dark eyes sparkled in those twinkle lights as she leaned in and said, "When I die, I want you to take over my life."

I think I laughed.

"I mean it, Danny. Consider it what I'm leaving you in my will. I'm giving you this life. You come in and finish the job."

Then she made these jazz hands, like that was it. That's all I needed: case closed.

I opened my mouth to say something, but filled it with a slow intake of air instead.

"*Soooooo!*" she sang. "Great. I wonder if they serve food here."

I grabbed her arm before she could raise it any higher toward the bartender. She tightened up, wrestling herself from my grip. For an allegedly sick lady, she was notably strong.

"Hey!" she shouted, outraged.

"Are you being funny?" I asked.

When Smidge knew she was trying to get away with something ridiculous, she would talk down to the person who was growing wise. This method worked especially well when she was haggling over a price tag at a flea market, or if she wanted extra work done on her kitchen for free. She had a way of making it sound like she figured all of this out a long time ago: *"Oh, let me explain where you probably got confused."*

There was the time she accidentally ran a red light and hit someone. Fifteen minutes later, the guy in the other car was *apologizing* to Smidge for not looking both ways while he was legally traveling through the intersection. He practically begged her not to file an insurance claim.

Part of her power lies in the accent. Americans think that British people just *sound* smarter. Maybe bossiness in a Southern accent comes across as *"Duh, dummy. Get on board."*

Smidge puffed out her chest, practically shining a spotlight on herself as she made a big production out of sighing, looking around for all the other people she assumed would be sympathizing with her, as here it was, so difficult to deal with my mental incapacity.

"I am dying," she said, emphasizing each word. "We covered this."

It's this next phase of the tactic—where she repeats only the parts that are emotionally heavy, getting her victim all jumbled up in empathy—that allows logic to take a backseat.

"So after I am gone, once I am dead," she said, "once the cancer wins and I am deep in the ground, I want you to live out my life. You finish raising Jenny. You be with Henry."

"Live out your life? Like run your errands? Raise your kid? Sleep with your husband?"

"Yes to all three."

"Come on, is this a joke?"

"No, ma'am," she said. "I ain't playing. I am dead serious." Then she laughed, having heard herself. "Okay, right now I'm *only* serious. Later, I'll be dead serious. And then you'll be Smidge 2.0."

Like it was nothing, no big deal. Just take control, sliding over in the seat like the designated driver of her life. The godparent to her day planner. I still hadn't come close to processing her being sick again and now she was asking me to do something that sounded absurd, not to mention possibly illegal.

"Don't think about it too much," Smidge said, waving a hand in front of my face. "Because then you'll screw this up. It's a smart plan. Look, you don't have to do this forever, just a few years. Until Jenny gets to college."

"Just live with them?" I asked. "Be a nanny, kind of?"

She shook her head. "No, that won't be enough. Henry

needs a partner. Jenny needs a parent. They need you to fill my spot. Be a mom, be a wife, be a good woman."

"A good *woman*?"

"Get that look off your face. You know what I mean. It'll be like it's me, but you're doing it. Do it right and finish the job."

"I think they'll notice it's not you as soon as I try to fit into your clothes."

"You can get your own clothes."

"Oh, *thanks*."

Smidge rocked from one side to the other, a sign of discomfort. She knew she didn't have me yet; perhaps it never occurred to her that I might have reservations.

"You're out of your mind," I said. "Is the cancer in your brain this time?"

Smidge cocked her head like I'd slapped her, but she was grinning. "I like that you're getting a little angry. It means you know I'm serious."

"You're seriously sick. I'm not going to have sex with your husband and have Jenny call me Mom and walk around your house like your ghost is commanding me to make your lemon bars every Labor Day weekend."

"First of all, I'm really glad you know you'll have to keep making those lemon bars."

"Smidge, this is the dumbest, the stupidest, the—"

"I can't just be *missing*. I can't just *disappear*, Danny. Too many people are counting on me."

"And nobody's counting on me? I have a life, too!"

I hated how sometimes when I stuck up for myself I sounded like a kid sister complaining she didn't get as much candy as her sibling.

"Look. I've thought about all of this, and if you just shut up and let me talk, it'll make sense. Just make sure they . . ."

Smidge stopped here, her eyes filling up with what appeared to be real tears. Her face began to twitch as her words turned to mumbles, the corners of her mouth pulling down. She sucked in a deep breath to knock that emotion out before forcing herself to continue. "See that they get breakfast every day and look nice and . . . that Henry doesn't get fat and . . . Jenny only dates nice boys and— Excuse me."

Smidge jumped off her bar stool and quickly wove her way through the crowd to the bathroom.

I didn't follow, mostly because she would've pushed me out the door and told me to leave her alone. But I wanted her to have a moment, so she could come back with a huge grin on her face, boasting that she'd just gotten me good. I was still holding out for a prank. I needed Smidge to take it all back. *"Even better than Big Count Road,"* she'd brag.

Maybe anger and resentment weren't the first feelings most people would have if their best friend had just asked them to take over once they die of terminal cancer, but I had previous experience with Smidge stretching things out of reality, exaggerating the extent of the situation. Smidge could be rather dramatic. Maybe she's saying "cancer," but she really means a kidney stone. Instead of willing me her life, maybe she just needs me to babysit for a month.

And honestly, it wasn't the first time she had tried to hand her daughter over to me without much of a warning.

You were about seven when your mother called me one morning, calmly informing me that you were on a plane headed straight to my apartment, where I was to continue to raise you for the rest of your life.

You wanted to have all your clothes in your favorite color, but when Smidge refused to buy purple underwear, somehow you figured out how to use fabric dye and tossed your entire wardrobe into the washing machine with a box of purple. I still think it was rather clever for someone who was only in the second grade.

Smidge was icy calm as she informed me she had just shipped her offspring to California, so much so that I wasn't absolutely sure you *weren't* sitting on a plane somewhere in the sky, sobbing in the bulkhead. Tiny purple fingers wiping away tiny purple tears. I made your mother put you on the phone, just so I could ask, "Where are you right now? And has your mother packed any kind of suitcase? Do you see one, Jenny? Look carefully."

One time Smidge called in the middle of the night so hysterical I was immediately terrified someone had died.

It was two in the morning West Coast time—meaning four her time—and she was shouting into the phone, "I don't know where I am! I'm lost and sad and I need you to come and get me!"

I was fifteen hundred miles away. Which 911 do you call for that? Mine? Hers? If hers, how exactly do you dial some other city's 911? Only because of Smidge have I had to ponder such questions. When normal people have an emergency, their first response isn't to call the one person who at that moment is at the absolute farthest point.

"Smidge!" I shouted back as I wandered through my dark bedroom. I made a vain attempt to find something to pull over myself, meaning some sleepy part of my brain knew there was a slim chance I might have to walk straight out of my apartment and drive to wherever she was. "Where are you?" I asked.

What Smidge lacked in tears she made up in volume. "I don't *knoooooooow*!" she wailed. "Everybody's mean here and they won't let me *driiiiiiive hooooooome*!"

This is when I stopped looking for a pair of pants and started looking for a glass of wine.

"Who's everybody?" I asked into the phone, my confusion making me sound like an old, lost lady. "Where are you? What is happening?" I tried to keep from sounding too judgmental as I asked, "Are you drunk?"

The missing answer in her answer told me all I needed to know. "This party is the worst!" she shouted. "Everybody here is an asshole and they're all laughing at me right now."

"Where is Henry?"

Then the *skritch-shluck!* of a phone sliding down someone's shoulder filled my ear. Smidge returned even louder, sounding like a walkie-talkie wired straight to my brain. "Who cares?" she shouted. "I told him if he didn't give me the keys, we were getting a divorce, and he didn't give me the keys so I hate him and that's it. The end."

Most likely Henry was standing right there, listening to her diatribe, Smidge's keys safely hidden in his left palm.

"Can you describe where you are right now?" I asked, like she was a little boy trapped in a cave or a well. Like I'm talking a trauma victim through a hypnotherapy session.

"Some guy's house," she said. "He can't decorate for shit.

He's got stuffed monkeys on his shelves. What kind of psychopath decorates with baby toys?"

"Well, I guess I can see why you're so upset."

"*Thank* you. Now come get me."

"I can't come get you, Smidge."

She began her tearless wails again, her voice raising an octave as it warbled, "Then you aren't a very good friend and I hate you."

*Hatechoo.* That's how she says it. Like a vicious sneeze.

She wouldn't remember it in the morning, but I would never forget it. As drunk as she was, and as little as she meant she hated me, what was real in her anger was how far away I was and how impossible it seemed to her that I couldn't just come right over and take her away from all those people who—thankfully—wouldn't let her drive home. I never forgot how useless it made me seem. What good was I in her life if I couldn't be at her beck and call?

And then there was the swimsuit incident in Puerto Rico.

Smidge usually wore a one-piece to hide the scar on her chest from when they removed the tumor, but this time she'd just completed a six-week boot camp and wanted to show off her impressively toned body.

We were flat on our backs, poolside, when she pointed at a mole on her left flank.

"You see this?" she asked me.

I leaned in. "Yeah." It was brown and shaped like a tulip, blurred edges and oblong.

"It's cancer," she said.

I sat up so quickly I spilled my drink.

"Damn, I should've known you'd get scared!" Smidge cackled, wiggling a hand like she was trying to erase what just happened. "I was kidding! I'm sorry. I'm sorry!"

I wiped chunks of boozy ice from my thigh as I scolded, "Now, why would that be funny?"

"I don't know. The mojito made me say it, Danny. Don't be sore."

When it came to Smidge, sometimes she was definitely kidding, sometimes she was kidding but she wanted you to pretend she was serious, and sometimes she was seriously out of her mind. It made it hard to know exactly when it was time to take action, or if it was a better idea to wait a few minutes, long enough to accurately assess the situation.

I couldn't summon the courage to ask Smidge just how bad the cancer was until an hour or so later, once we were back at the hotel room, safely away from the public. When she realized I had some doubt, her response was to hurl various items from her suitcase directly at my head. They were mostly clothes; soft, squishy things I could easily catch or watch pathetically float to the floor like exhausted streamers. Every once in a while she'd find something with better aerodynamics. Her toothpaste comes to mind as a particularly effective missile.

We squared off on either side of our hotel bed. Smidge wore her taco pajama pants and a yellow camisole. I was still fully dressed from the evening, what with all the defending my body from personal injury I'd been doing.

Smidge had weaponized every item from her suitcase save for a bottle of whiskey, which she then grabbed like a baseball bat. While it made me momentarily nervous, I knew it was for drinking, not battery.

One of our traditions on these trips was to pack the bottle of wine we'd bought on the last one. But in China we feared the bottles of so-called Chinese wine, and opted for what we saw others copiously drinking: Johnnie Walker Red.

Smidge sat at the edge of the bed, whiskey bottle tucked between her legs. Her hair had fallen out of its ponytail and strayed in wild bunches in front of her face. She quietly stared at her hands.

"I wasn't thinking about how you're just now finding out about this," she finally said. "I should be nicer about giving you some catch-up time."

The mattress creaked underneath me as I sat down beside her, causing the much-smaller Smidge to roll toward me, just slightly. "I'm really confused," I admitted.

"You're in shock," she said. "I confess I was hoping to take advantage of that. Have you saying yes before you got a chance to wrap your big brain around it. But I need you to hurry up so we can get to the important stuff."

I took a deep breath, and as I held it I imagined Smidge's lungs, how maybe she couldn't take that same breath without thinking of what was going on inside her. I don't think I've taken a deep breath without thinking of her ever again.

Smidge twisted the top off the bottle before lifting it to her mouth for a swig. "I didn't get much of that martini," she said. "This feels good. This'll be my new drink of choice. Danny, let's start being whiskey drinkers."

"Okay." I sounded miserable, which seemed to spark Smidge in another direction.

"*Soooooooooo!*" she sang. "What's going to happen is that nobody's going to find out what we're doing. This is our secret."

I snorted. "Yeah, right."

She nudged my hand with the bottle, trying to force me to take it. "Drink on it. We're not telling anybody about this."

"About what?"

"Any of it. The plan, the cancer, the future. Only these walls will know what we're doing, otherwise it won't work."

I pushed the bottle away. "No. That's insane. We have to tell Henry, at least. Doesn't he get a say in whether or not he wants me to be his wife?"

Smidge nodded, her jaw locked. "I need you to remind me of something. I don't think you've ever been through cancer before. I think that might be true. Is that true?"

The carpeting in the hotel room was beige with navy squares. I focused on counting how many squares my bare toes were touching at that moment as Smidge continued.

"Well, since I'm thinking you might not know what having cancer is like, I'm going to tell you a little something. People think having cancer immediately makes you some kind of hero. 'Oh, you're so brave,' they say. 'Oh, bless your heart,' they're always wailing. From afar. Way afar. They're not coming over to make food for your kid when the smell from a can of tomato sauce makes you vomit for half an hour. Nobody's rushing over to help you wash your sheets after you find your scattered pubes in them one morning. No. Just words of encouragement, like I'm walking a tightrope and they would love to come up there and help, but *darnit*, I'm just so far away!"

I quickly count twenty-six squares touching my toes because I know there's a chance Smidge is referring to me. "What about Millie Mains? Didn't she wash your laundry every day?"

"Oh my God, are you really going to make me feel guilty about Millie Mains right now?"

"No, I'm just saying—"

Smidge shook her head. "You're talking about the girl who was hoping I'd die so she'd get into my husband's pants, but I'm the ungrateful bitch? I get it."

"Is that true?"

"I need a glass."

I knew it wasn't true. Smidge just liked her story better if she had gotten through her cancer all by herself.

Finding a glass from the faux marble wet bar, she poured herself an inch, leaning against the counter with her free hand like a weary bartender. She was still shaking her head, lips pursed, like I was this *thing* she had to deal with, a fool in her face.

She talked into her drink, staring at the liquid like only it understood. "Surgery, chemo, radiation," she said. "I wasn't being 'brave' or 'strong.' That's bullshit. I didn't have a choice. I was too scared to do anything other than what the doctors said. It's brave when you opt to do the hard part. So this time I'm opting hard."

I could tell these words were rehearsed, but I didn't know if this speech was prepared for me, or if this is what she'd been telling herself. She didn't seem to notice me there anymore. She faced the window, the lights inside the room kept her from being able to see anything other than her own reflection. I watched her stare herself down.

"It's stage four," she said. "It's spread already. In my ribs, other places. They didn't want to tell me how long I have, but I pinched the doctor under her arm until I got her to admit it's probably less than a year. Do you know they stage cancer in Roman numerals?"

There were thirty squares along the left side of my foot, fifteen squares along the right side of my foot, and too many things I didn't want to hear bouncing around in my head. Every time I thought it couldn't get any worse, more words came out, hitting me like fists.

"What did the doctors say you should do?"

"Some bullshit I ain't doing."

"What do you mean?"

"I mean I'm not going through chemo again. No surgery. Nothing. This is it. I'm not going to lose my hair again. Last time I looked like one of those just-born kangaroo inch-worms, all wet and pathetic, blind and helpless."

"Smidge!" I grabbed the comforter in my hand and gripped it to keep me from shaking her. I was seconds from taking her by the shoulders, turning her upside down, and treating her like a human Etch A Sketch. I'd rattle her until all the cancer fell right out. Then we could stare at that pile of unwanted, parasitic, life-robbing mass and watch it lose all its power, writhing and suffocating on the floor between us.

"There's nothing to do, Dans," she said. "They told me I could try surgery that'll remove a few ribs and hack out more of my lung. But it wouldn't give me too much more time, and I'd be stuck in a hospital bed for six months. I'm not spending half my remaining life in a hospital bed. I'm spending it with you."

These are the years when we're supposed to be taking our bodies for granted, just starting to feel morning aches and pains, not thinking of your parts as failing, as killing you. She's still supposed to be invincible.

"Last time I didn't feel like I had cancer," she said. "The doctors and tests and X-rays all forced me to acknowledge it was happening. The surgeries and the rounds of chemo made it clear. I remember thinking, 'Well, let's just get through this.'"

Smidge stretched her legs, pointing and flexing her toes.

"This time it's different," she said. "This time I feel it everywhere. It is weighing me down, and I have been in the worst pain. This is no way to live. It hurts to breathe. It hurts to be me. I hate feeling pathetic. And finally: my skin is disgusting. Cancer sucks. The end."

"Why is this happening?" I asked, as if there'd be an answer I'd accept. "How?"

"They shipped me with defective parts, I guess."

It wasn't fair that Smidge had to come over to the bed and hold my fetal shape while I cried. She shouldn't ever have been the one to do the comforting. But I was grateful she wrapped herself behind me, pushed back my hair, and clucked into the top of my head like I was her child. I slammed my eyes tight, attempting to keep that moment preserved. I needed it then, because I knew I was going to need to be able to bring back the feeling of that moment for the rest of my life. It was right then I felt our time start to run out.

"Maybe I won't die," she whispered. We were like heartbroken teenagers again, just like in high school when some boy wronged us in some way that seemed world crushing. Weeping and exhausted, clutching each other by the bones.

"Maybe I'll scare death away," she said, like it was all just a ghost story. "I'll be mean to it. But, hey, listen. I'm not getting treatment. And I'm not wasting time having to deal with everybody doing exactly what you're doing right now. They can cry later. I want my last days to be happy ones. So you get to sleep on this tonight, but tomorrow we get to work, missy."

I don't know how or when I fell asleep, but at some point I woke to find Smidge sitting at the edge of the bed, appearing to be counting the very same floor squares I'd tallied earlier.

The sound of my stirring pulled her from her thoughts. She turned, her face instantly waking, everything pulling in different directions at once, as she shifted from "neutral" to "on," like someone had pressed her power button.

"You look like shit," she said, not unkindly. "That is some serious cry-face you've got going on."

My eyelids were swollen thick; I could see them hovering at the top of my line of vision. My lips were equally puffy, like my mouth had just held a convention for bees. The back of my throat was raw from swallowing down too much information, and my stomach burned with all the things I didn't know how to say.

"You were talking in your sleep," she said. "Something about medication, so I'm sure it was me you were talking to."

"I don't remember."

"Well, it got me thinking, and I want you to know something. You know how you told me sometimes after people die, they come and visit you in your dreams?"

This happened with my grandmother, who showed up in my dream the night after she died to hand me a pinwheel and tell me always to finish my oatmeal. In college, a professor of mine was in a fatal car accident. I saw him in a dream the following week, where he informed me that he hadn't gotten around to grading my paper because he left it at Kermit the Frog's house, but that he called Kermit, who said the paper was a solid B. I remember that dream because I woke myself up by complaining, *"Man, fuck that frog."*

"Yes," I said.

"Well, if you don't say yes to this, Danny, after I'm dead, I'm coming for you. When you sleep. I will haunt you. I will destroy you."

Smidge could sound like a Southern gothic lady from the past when she wanted to, summoning her ancestors who would cast spells on me from the depths of the swamps and savannah, potions of evil created from the essences of mint juleps, eye of nutria, a scrap of seersucker. Smidge was being as serious as her diagnosis, and I knew there was only one response that would keep us together. Any other answer might result in the immediate, abrupt termination of our lifelong friendship.

"I'll do it, Smidge."

It's what I said, even though I knew it wasn't going to be true. But I told myself I could fake that promise, at least for the time being. I could go along with it for as long as it took her to realize she was asking me to do the impossible, the ridiculous. She wouldn't be able to keep this a secret. She'd have to tell Henry, and once she did, there was no way he'd go along with it. It wasn't like hiding an egg chair; her body would eventually tattle, even if she didn't. She'd get sicker. He'd notice. How could she ask Henry to be with me once she was gone? Did she really think her daughter would accept me as her mother once she couldn't be there anymore?

Smidge was the bossiest person I've ever known. I just couldn't picture her giving up status as the number one person in your lives. I'd more readily accept she'd hired a team of engineers to make a robot version of herself that could give you commands and answer questions, rolling around the house like a sassy Roomba. "Quit doing that! Put that over there! Go change that shirt!"

"Say it again," she said to me. "Say it with the word 'promise' in there."

"I promise I'll do it." My voice sounded ragged, like my throat didn't want me to lie, afraid of what she'd do if she figured out I was just trying to appease. After all, it was the throat she'd choke first.

"Okay. But remember: if you don't, I will *haunchoo*," she hissed, adding a pinch to my thigh, no doubt instantly entering us into some kind of voodoo contract.

I might have made the immediate future a little less stressful for Smidge, but I had just agreed to have that woman endlessly torment me from the afterlife.

# NINE

---

"Smidge, this year's vacation was kinda bullshit."

We'd finished driving back from Atlanta, having spent the morning acting as if the night before was well in the past. I guess we'd moved on, a decision having been made, and we were attempting to engage in behavior that seemed normal. Consequently, our ride home mostly consisted of singing along to the radio, eating greasy curly fries out of takeout bags, and creating small dramas and situations for the passengers in the cars that passed us by.

Playing "Did You Hear About?" with our old classmates used to be one of our favorite pastimes.

*"Did you hear about Amber Parkins?"*

*"The girl who scribbled Billy Robbins's name all over my favorite notebook in the tenth grade? Tenth-grade asshole Amber Parkins? Tell me."*

*"She got fat and sells her underwear on the Internet for money."*

The game didn't have any rules, per se, except for one: no matter what the fake future for the person would be, the first three words were always "*She got fat.*"

Due to various online social networks our game had lost its luster; there was no mystery in what happened to the people we hoped suffered endless years of obesity and beyond. Creating elaborate prisons for those who had wronged or slighted us was pointless. Within two or three clicks we could see: she had kids. Sometimes she wasn't fat. Smidge tried to create an offshoot called "Today Their Evil Children," but it was never as much fun. I didn't have kids, so I didn't care, and Smidge always ended up crying whenever she seriously thought about childhood obesity. That woman loved making people from her past into 700-pound, bedridden pizza lovers, but if you packed one extra pound onto a minor, you'd have to physically stop her from calling Child Protective Services.

"I do owe you a vacation," Smidge said as we grabbed our suitcases out of the back of the Pickle. "I promise to get one more in before this year is up."

I didn't want to know if she was referring to a calendar year or *her* year.

"I still have a couple of days before my flight home," I said.

Smidge turned to me, brow furrowed. "Oh," she said. "That's not happening."

I followed her inside the house. "I have to go home, Smidge."

"You'll see. You'll be too busy and you won't have time to go home. You need to be here, now."

"No, I have clients and—"

*"Jennifer Ellen Cooperton! That had better be an ugly-ass wig you're wearing!"*

I might have been temporarily off the hook, but the tone in Smidge's voice had me instantly frightened for *your* immediate future. Because, yes, Jenny: this was the day of The Haircut That Almost Got You Killed.

Take the excitement that comes from simply being a thirteen-year-old girl, then add to that the overwhelming freedom of two days without your mother's constant supervision, and basically what happened was: you went crazy and hacked off a stunning amount of your lovely blond hair. In order to make sure you wouldn't just be grounded, but grounded in a way that would make it into the record books, you then dyed one side of your hair black. And *then*, since none of the women in your family liked to do anything without going to unnecessary extremes, you shaved sections of the black side into seemingly random stripes and squares.

Jenny, your hair was a carefully constructed flag of teenage rebellion.

You looked like a before *and* an after photo, taped together. Turned to one side, you were a pretty, healthy, lovely girl possibly on her way to church camp. Spin you the other way and you became the sullen, angry skater punk who kept voodoo dolls of that pretty church camp girl hidden in her locker.

"Mama, it's no big deal," you said, but I heard the trembling in your voice. You were scared. I bet you'd tried to ready yourself for this moment, but we came back much earlier than you thought. You didn't know we'd come back wiser, sadder, older, exhausted, and a bit resigned. But not too resigned or exhausted to hate that haircut. Even Smidge's cancer was saying, *"I'll just step back and wait for you to deal with this idiot kid for a second."*

You had taken your first, defiant step across the threshold

into the hormonal-land-mine-ridden field of teenage girls. And Jenny, your mother did not like it.

I'd seen Smidge's parenting technique range from screams to fits. She never gave you more than a firm swat on the behind, and even that was reserved for near-bodily-harm incidents back when you had the added protection of diapers. I know she didn't really believe in beating a child. But I don't think, until that moment, she'd ever stopped to consider her thoughts on beating a *teenager.* Somehow that seemed different. More necessary. It just made sense. A baby doesn't understand why someone's whacking at her. But you weren't a baby, and you had done something so stupid. Why shouldn't she knock some sense into you? I could tell Smidge was weighing her odds in a physical encounter with you. You guys were practically the same size; it seemed a fair fight.

Not wanting to be in the position of having to be a witness at a hearing or a trial someday, I tried to head out of the room, in search of anybody else who might have been in hiding. Henry, for starters. I didn't get three feet away before Smidge stopped me.

"Danny," she said, her voice oddly calm and stilted, fake chipper, like she was recording an outgoing message for her voice mail. "I would like you to handle this."

I stared at her hand, wondering how it had latched itself onto my arm. *Burrowed* into my skin. "Handle what?"

"Jenny. And the hair."

"Why would I do that?"

She bugged her weird, fake-friendly eyes toward me and shouted, "Jennifer, go to your room!"

You and I both jumped, but then you turned and sped off,

the half of your hair that still had the ability to move trailing behind you like a rhythmic gymnast fleeing in terror.

Smidge's face had the look of someone who's just been jilted by a con artist. I couldn't get my arm out of her vise grip. If I wanted freedom, I was going to have to chew off my own limb.

"I need you to go in there and take care of this situation," she said. "So that I do not kill my daughter. Although, what are they gonna do—give me the death penalty?" She chuckled.

There was something about ordering me around while simultaneously punishing her daughter that made Smidge positively gleeful. Her murderess smile had turned into an amused grimace, like she'd just been handed a human dollhouse. I might as well have been eight inches tall, her giant hand wrapped around my plastic torso as she bounced me over to your room.

I'd never punished a child. I don't have any siblings, so I had no idea what was supposed to happen when a parent goes into a bedroom to scold a kid.

After his divorce, my dad stopped punishing me entirely. If I messed up at school I took care of it, and I never did anything bad enough in my social life that would warrant getting grounded. In fact, if I'd done to my head what you had done to yours, my dad would have calmly asked, "Was that for school, or something? Are you in a play?"

When I was much younger, my mother's parenting style could have best been described as one of detached interest. In her defense, she didn't know she didn't like kids until she had one. She was so young she probably had a hard time finding the difference between what I wanted and what she wanted. My mother was an intellectual, an artist, a thinker of big ideas and wild opinions; not really all that interested in messy diapers or stacking blocks. The mundane life of a toddler must have driven her to fantasies of self-mutilation, just to have something interesting to talk about.

*"My kid reached out and grabbed a giraffe on her mobile today. That's the biggest thing ever to have happened in her life so far. It's so depressing, considering how much life she has left that I'm in charge of monitoring. So I decided to cut off one of my pinkies, for I intend to erase myself inch by inch until I no longer have to be here."*

I was five years old the first time she told me just how much she wasn't interested in young people.

"I'm sorry," she had said. "I know you were trying to tell me about the new swings at school. But I can't seem to force myself to care, Danielle. Can you understand that your mother finds children to be boring? Will you please learn one interesting thing to talk about with me? Or try to speak your child-babble in Spanish. At least then we'd be doing something enriching."

That led to my horribly misguided decision to start a book club with my mother. I thought that maybe if I'd come to her like one of her peers, a thinking female who drinks wine and makes art, she'd see I was just another human being who loved her and wanted to spend time with her. The most grown-up book in my collection at the time was *Lord of the Flies*. I don't know what bad adult had gifted a six-year-old that literature, but there it was on my pink bookshelf, sitting underneath my ceramic elephant piggy bank.

I sent my mother a formal invitation to our book club meeting. I'd crafted it with construction paper, spelling out the word *book* in macaroni. I drew sparkly crowns and smiling houseflies around the borders. I saved a box of grape juice I wanted to use for my wine. I settled into my bed one night, ready to dive into my intelligent, thought-provoking book club selection.

*Lord of the Flies.*

Even the wisest, most world-experienced child might have difficulties understanding that novel. I was only six. I remember sitting at the foot of my bed desperately trying to comprehend these disgusting boys and their weird way of talking. The only character I could relate to was Piggy. He was stuck outside this world, trying to get in, trying to be heard.

Consequently, I was so traumatized by the description of his death, my mother found me at the foot of my bed in tears, heaving, having my own fit of *ass-mar*.

"What is wrong with you, Danielle?" she asked. She often said my name at the end of her sentences, as if she had to remind herself just who this person was who resembled her around the eyes, and walked into her kitchen every morning in pajamas.

"Piggy!" I shouted. "Piggy died!"

"Sure," my mother said, dismissively. "That was a given. But what about the conch?"

"The conch?" I didn't know what she was saying, because I hadn't yet heard the word spoken. I was pronouncing it like *konch*, but she was calling it a *kankh*, making it sound like the dirtiest of words. "You mean the shell?"

"Yes, the *shell*, Danielle. You're completely ignoring the fact that the conch shattered at the same time Piggy died. That conch represented their last attempts at civilization, at common sense, at morals. That's the real tragedy. I can't believe you didn't see that."

Toward the empty space where she had been standing in the doorway, I mouthed, *"I hate you so much."* I couldn't put voice to those words. She never heard me say how I felt.

Standing outside your door, faced with my first moment of motherhood, I had a swirling terror in the pit of my stomach that I was about to say or do something that would scar you forever. I'd accidentally toss you off a shame cliff and your head would shatter like Piggy's. Somehow, despite my best efforts, my voice would find that deadened disdain my mother's took when she spoke to me, letting me know I'd ruined her dreams as early as initially failing to abort myself inside her uterus.

You were flung across your bed; facedown on that puffy green-and-pink comforter, crying into your forearms, shuddering in misery. Your hair dangled in stripes of black and gold, making your head resemble a discarded pom-pom.

Standing in a teenage girl's room during a tantrum is not unlike auditing Acting for Drama Majors. You're technically sitting to the side; you don't have to participate, but you can't help feeling all the emotion in the room. I could practically see squiggle lines of hormones coming off your body, floating into the air, sailing over toward my face. If dogs were around, they'd be whining. If cats could wander past, they'd instantly go into hissing fits. It's just too much passion, too much angst, so much sadness. Over a haircut.

As I searched for something to say, I worried that if I waited much longer you'd begin slamming your face with your own palms, martyring yourself on your bed, not just to punish me but to punish *the world* for making you be alive in it.

"Your mom made me come in here," I said, establishing blame early on.

You muffled your reply into your elbow. "I don't care."

"You know how much hair means to her," I said.

Your head slowly rose and lowered, the world's saddest bob.

"More than it means to normal people," I added.

You'd gotten to that part of the cry that was mostly shivering and gasping, so I gingerly took a seat at the edge of the bed, waiting for you to finish thinking about how hard everything in life is and why do they make it so unfair and why were you ever born and thirteen is hard.

Then I told you a secret. "The worst haircut I've ever gotten in my entire life your mother gave to me."

That got your eyes poking out. Your sweet face was wet and shiny, sweaty around the temples from hating everything. Pink-cheeked and blotchy, cry-face had reduced your eyes to puffy dots. I didn't say it then because it wasn't the time, but your little, hot head emerging from your arms reminded me of how you looked the day you were born. Angry, damp, and purple, looking for someone to blame.

"Your mother is never going to admit this, by the way," I said. "She heard people just flat-out tell me how terrible my hair looked. She'd roll her eyes and nod at them, like she'd been saying the same thing and I refused to do anything about it."

"She's so unfair," you whined.

"She really is. And that was awhile ago. She's seen pictures from that time; she knows how bad it was. She still hasn't apologized. She pretends it didn't happen. She'll do that with this, too."

"No, she won't. She'll bring it up for the rest of her life."

You either didn't see me or didn't notice how I winced.

"She always thinks she's more important than everybody else," you moped.

I knew I had to bring you back from mother-hate, because Smidge was expecting a full report and I couldn't lead with, "Well, she's done crying and now she blames you for everything."

"I don't know if that's it," I said, most unconvincingly.

"It *is* it. She's so mean." That got you worked up into a new round of heaves and whimpers.

"She just has a lot of conviction," I said. "And pride. She knows she gave me a bad haircut. You know what she said when I last brought it up? 'It was the *style* at the *tiiiime*.' She insisted it would have worked on me if only I believed in it. Like a haircut and a fairy are exactly the same."

You turned your head to the side to wipe your face. "What did it look like?" you asked. "Your hair."

"Oh," I said, trying to sound like I was searching for the words. I reached out and stroked your head, pulling on a few strands. *"This,"* I said, grandly gesturing toward your severed locks.

You laughed as you swatted at my face, catching me under the chin as you sat up, folding your knees.

"I hate it," you said, playing with the toes of your socks. "My hair. That's really why I'm crying. I've been crying since last night when I did it. I was going to tell Mom that, but she freaked out before I could even say anything. But I know it looks bad."

"Kind of a light term for this. It looks like you were hazed."

You gave the most miserable mumble. "I know."

"I think your mother wants me to beat you up."

"You should."

"I can't hit a crying girl. That's just mean. But look at you: can't we just say I did *this* to you?"

You placed both hands on top of your head and pressed down, as if you were trying to shove the hair back inside your skull so it could spring back in a new style, like snakes from a trick can of peanuts.

"I just wanted to look *different*," you said through clenched teeth. "My old hair made me look like a baby, and Aubrey's a grade older than me and—"

You halted right there, knowing you'd accidentally said too much.

"Aubrey?" I asked. "That's a boy's name?"

"Don't tell Mom. She'll kill me if she knows I cut my hair for a boy."

This was turning out to be quite a time for secrets in my life.

"Do you think he's going to like your hair? This Aubrey?"

"No. I just thought . . . he's cool, and I didn't think he'd like me if I was cute."

"Well, you know," I said, "mission accomplished."

You kicked your legs out in a tiny tantrum. "Now Mom's going to start on all the nicknames."

"There will be a lot of nicknames, I'm afraid."

"I don't know what to do. I don't want to be grounded! Ugh! I hate everything!"

I recognized we were hitting a critical moment. I had to keep you from spiraling out. You were a ticking time bomb; my clippers were halfway through the red wire and you were sitting there, holding up the green one, taunting, "Are you sure?"

"Maybe you could write your mom a letter of apology?"

That is what I said to a thirteen-year-old. It came out like a sad, weird question, totally showing my cards. I had no idea what I was doing and was just trying to keep from saying anything real.

You spotted my weakness immediately, your torso twisting like you were agonizing through your own personal exorcism. You flung back onto your bedspread and wailed, "A letter!"

I should've cut the green wire.

"Well . . ." I started, but you were writhing around so much you'd think I'd just dumped acid straight onto your skin.

"I'm so sure!" you yelled. "You write letters to Santa or your congressman. Not your mother! Like she's the editor of my life, or something?"

I can tell you now that I didn't have a random coughing fit just then, Jenny. I was covering up the fact that your teenage angst caused a giggle fit I desperately wanted to hide. It made me remember I was never going to be thirteen again, and I was just so happy about that.

"You're right," I said, trying to control my breath from

shuddery chuckles. "That was a dumb suggestion. Don't write a letter. I'm sorry."

I got up and adjusted the blankets around your tortured body. I figured since I was leaving you just as I'd found you, there was no real harm done. I never called you an ungrateful brat or a crybaby, so I was already doing better than my mother would have done in that situation.

Smidge was waiting for me in the hallway with her coach face on, sizing me up like I'd just gotten cut from the softball team. Eyes narrowed, mouth bent into an unimpressed frown.

"That was fast," she said, her interrogation beginning with a statement.

"Well, that's just how I mom," I said.

"Did you beat her?"

"No."

"Did you tell her she looks like shit?"

"I used other words, but yes."

"Is that why she's crying?"

"She's crying because she's thirteen. And because she doesn't like the haircut."

"Good," Smidge said, pushing me aside as she headed toward your room. "Then she won't mind when I beat it off her."

# TEN

I found your father hiding in the backyard garage. Henry might have defined it as "working," since he was busy sanding a table while Tucker hunched over a workbench, rewiring a lamp. Those boys could call what they were doing whatever they wanted; I knew they were hiding. The dead giveaway being they were down to one beer, which they were now sharing just to avoid going anywhere near the house.

I slid inside the garage, shutting the door behind me in an attempt to absorb a few minutes of quiet. The men watched me, smiling. We were equal parts chicken shit and independent observers, able to step away from the situation. Not even Henry could be asked to genuinely care that much about his daughter's haircut, which is why I nominated him to go in there to bring us back some beer.

Tucker seconded. "It's your house, man."

"Such betrayal," he said, clutching at his heart. "And here I thought I was among friends."

"I'd also like a soda, if it's not too much trouble."

I'd be lying if I said I never thought about Henry, if we'd

be a good couple. We make each other laugh, and Smidge always says we're the same kind of patient. But Henry's so quiet it can be hard for me to keep a conversation going with him. He often seemed miles away, politely nodding whenever I paused for breath. I assumed we'd grow bored of each other; the kind of relationship where we retreated to separate rooms to read books we will not swap. Meals eaten while watching television programs.

I wasn't sure how Smidge thought she could just snap me into her place, that I'd be loud enough or big enough to occupy her space in his heart. He holds her everywhere.

I'm not saying I'm jealous, but I *did* find him first.

Not that your mother had a reputation, but I don't think anybody assumed she'd only been with one man her entire life. Smidge could be surprisingly old-fashioned. She made sure to go out with enough boys who would want to brag about dating her that nobody ever confessed how platonic their relationship actually was.

We were still in college the night your mother pointed toward the slender boy in jeans and slicked-back hair leaning against the bar at The Pantry, the one who was ordering three beers that—unbeknownst to her—he had plans on taking straight to our table.

"Who is that boy?" she asked, her fingernail pointed like it could shoot a web on command. She asked with decision, with finality, and I knew that despite what I was about to tell her, she had found her next big thing.

"That's my date," I said. "That's Henry."

Smidge leaned back. "What?" she asked. "That's the guy we're meeting here tonight? Oh, *nuh-uh*. He is not your date."

I sighed. "And why would that be?"

"Because he's now mine. I'm sorry, but that guy is not your type. He is exactly what I've been looking for."

These were about the craziest words I'd ever heard her say, which is how I knew she meant them. I'd never seen her instantly smitten with someone, but she couldn't stop staring.

"Smidge, I kind of like him," I admitted.

"Yeah, but you don't even know if this is a date, which is why I'm here, remember?"

She was right, of course. Henry was in my English lit class, and we'd struck up a conversation when we both showed up too early one day. He asked if I ever went to The Pantry. When I told him I did, he said he'd maybe see me there that next weekend.

Since he didn't really *ask* me, but instead described a possible bump-into, I felt like I needed Smidge there in case he turned out to have a girlfriend or a group of friends with him. I didn't want to look desperate or confused.

"But he waved when he saw me," I said.

"Oh, honey," Smidge said, "the wave might have been toward you, but that boy was looking right at *me*."

And he was. I still haven't seen two people ever fall more instantly in love.

"Why did you two come back so soon?" Henry was asking me in that garage, clearly having had his entire day, if not week, ruined by our immediate rearrival.

"Smidge wanted a short trip," I said. "It was a surprise to me, too."

Tucker adjusted himself in his chair, sliding the legs roughly along the concrete, purposely making himself heard.

"Guess you didn't fight her too hard," he said into his hands as he worked.

"I packed lots of outfits," I said defensively. "I'm not happy about this recent development."

"They still fighting?" Henry asked, glancing worriedly toward his home.

"You could go in there," I said. "Maybe try to calm them down."

The withering look Henry shot me indicated he thought I was kidding. But I desperately wanted Henry to step up and stand by his wife's side as they dealt with their daughter. I wanted him to be indispensable, strong and stern, solemn and calm, powerful and heroic enough that Smidge would realize she needed Henry for everything she was about to face. She needed her husband to be her partner, not me. Henry has always been there for her.

She knows she can't say the same about me.

Years ago, if someone had asked me how I'd behave if my best friend was diagnosed with stage II lung cancer, I'd have been telling them to immediately place a bet on me winning a gold medal in the Friendship Olympics, Hard Times division. Smidge and I had been through so much, I didn't think there was anything I couldn't handle.

I was wrong.

You probably don't know this, Jenny, because a lot of that time was sheltered from you, but I was a shitty cancer friend.

I'm still embarrassed when I think about my behavior over the two years Smidge went through treatment. I try not to think about it, and it's a testament to Smidge's character that she didn't constantly bring it up. It's the kind of thing you'd think she'd hold over me. Yet, in all the mean things she'd spat over the years, it was usually about the ugliness of my visible features, not what I had going on underneath them.

When she was sick, when things were really bad, I couldn't find a way to separate her from me. All the tests and hospital visits, the surgeries, the late nights where she was sleepless, sick, and destroyed from chemotherapy, it felt like it was all happening to me. I was catching her cancer. I could feel my cells mutating, replicating, poisoning me right along with her. I was miserable, and I knew I just couldn't handle it.

I can only imagine Smidge was as shocked and disappointed in me as I was in myself.

I gave no good excuse for avoiding her, but I offered many, bowing out of Smidge's next blood test, or another round of chemo. We e-mailed each other as I tried to keep up with everything, calling Henry to ask if there was something I could do, knowing full well he'd tell me everything was fine, and that I shouldn't worry too much, and to stay on my side of the country tending to my own busy life that was falling apart in its own way. James and I were already having problems.

You were mostly staying with your grandparents, then. Henry's parents rented a nearly furnished condo so they could pick you up from school and take you to practices, be there while you did your homework. You called it Grampy Camp. They were so good at keeping you entertained, of making this time feel special, not sad.

When your mom was at her worst, when she got down to ninety pounds and they thought maybe she wouldn't make it, your grandparents took you on a road trip to the Grand Canyon. When she was still in bad shape a week later, they just kept driving. You went up through Nevada, and over to California. You went up every roller coaster and down each waterslide Southern California had to offer. That's when you got to pet a baby tiger and hug a dolphin.

You even spent a weekend with me. We went to Disneyland and later the beach, where you didn't want to get your face wet because you'd gotten a butterfly painted on your cheek that you were trying to preserve.

"I wanna surprise Mama and say it's a tattoo," you told me.

You went home after eight weeks, most of a summer, once Smidge had turned a corner and put on some weight. Once she was safely out of the woods.

I don't know if you ever figured out the truth about that summer, but I have a feeling nobody's ever told you that you weren't just having Grampy Camp.

One night Henry found Smidge on the floor of the kitchen. Around three in the morning she'd woken up hungry for the first time in days. She was trying to make a peanut butter and jelly sandwich, when she was hit with a wave of pain that lowered her to the floor. Eventually she fell asleep. Henry found her still clutching a jar of grape jelly. He gently woke her, pulled her into his lap, and fed her off a spoon, her weary head tucked under his chin. Neither of them was crying, no words about how terribly unfair life can be.

Smidge's church organized a spreadsheet so people could come by with food or books, magazines and casseroles.

Millie Mains lived down the street from you and had that dog you said could count to five. She was young—a teacher, I think—and you thought she was the prettiest grown-up you'd ever seen because she had orange hair. You know she's the one who brought you those stuffed animals, right? Did someone tell you that?

Millie would come by in the mornings to pick up all your family's laundry and then she'd leave it folded and clean on the back porch at the end of every day. She always tied the bundle with a green ribbon, sometimes topped with a small stuffed toy. For two years, every day, Millie Mains washed your laundry. Once Smidge was better, Henry got down on his knees and built that woman a new back deck.

Your daddy is a good man. And your mother was being hateful insinuating that Millie Mains was trying to get into his pants. Still, maybe Millie would be more interested in this life-altering arrangement than I was.

After Henry left to find beverages, Tucker and I stayed quiet. He was keeping himself busy with the lamp, but I'd brought nothing to do to pass the time. I found that moments of silence made my brain shift to pondering unanswered questions, so I started pacing, stopping only to lean against various corners of the garage.

"You're making me nervous," Tucker said. "It's like you're waiting on a baby to be born or something. Or posing for a photo shoot." Tucker gestured to the chair next to him. "Sit down, California. Tell me what's been going on."

"With what?" It was funny how I'd known Tucker almost as long as I'd known Smidge, and yet sometimes when I sat next to him I could feel like a stranger. He often seemed to be trying to figure me out for the very first time.

"I don't know 'with what,'" Tucker said, peering at me from underneath the brim of his cap. "That's why I'm asking. Tell me about your fancy life. How 'bout you start there?"

There were so many things I wasn't supposed to talk about, I'd almost forgotten there was anything left I could say. No longer nervous, I took the seat next to Tucker and pulled up to his workbench.

"It's not that fancy." I watched his solid, callused hands wrap around a complicated-looking metal piece of electronic equipment I couldn't identify. Dirt and varnish were shoved so deep underneath his fingernails it was like he was sporting a reverse manicure; all the paint was on the wrong side.

I enjoyed watching him work—how his left leg would bounce quietly, making the stool rattle under his weight. It was impressive how much his lower half was in motion while the rest of him remained still and calm, working with screws barely the size of the blackened curve of his fingertip. I don't know who can resist watching a man work with his hands.

"You got quiet again," he said, his voice low and steady.

It was like being at the dentist: the foreign tools, the squeaks from his metal stool, all the questions I won't answer truthfully.

"Work's been good," I said. "That's kind of it."

"No fella." A question spoken like it wasn't one.

"A *fella*?" I teased, eyes wide and in full drawl. "Golly, I don't know! Lemme just check up under my hoop skirt for a cricket's breath!" I dropped my head and stared between my knees. "Nope! No *fella*!"

"You like that I say 'fella.'"

He might have been right.

"What about you, Tucker? You got a dame?"

"No. No dame. And for the record, I like your Yankee voice too."

"I don't have a Yankee voice."

"If she calls a Coke a 'soda,' she's a Yankee."

Even if my chess club days hadn't ruined my chances of dating Tucker back in high school, we never seemed to be on the same kind of schedule, even once our two-year age difference didn't seem as vast. He went away to college at Loyola, and almost always had a girlfriend, a few of which I'd met when we'd all get together for Mardi Gras or spring break.

One Christmas he brought home a girl he'd been seeing for a few months. To this day, hers remains the loudest voice I've ever heard.

"I just remembered Loud Loud Shane," I said.

Tucker's leg stopped jittering as he dropped his tools like a man instantly regretting having eaten too much food. "Lord," he said, pinching the space between his eyes as if he could hear her now. "That girl. When she talked, pieces of my inner ear would crumble and fall out of my head. I do not miss her voice."

"How did she get to be so loud? Did she grow up on an airstrip?"

"To this day whenever I hear an ambulance I am reminded of being with her in bed."

"I thought Smidge was going to punch her in the face that time—"

"—when we were playing Uno," Tucker finished, his eyes glassy and distant with memory. "That was when I knew I had to stop seeing her. She was not a nice game player."

"Really mean. She called Henry an assface!"

"Well, he did make her draw four like a total assface."

"Poor Henry," I said.

"Poor Henry," he agreed. "He's got that crazy wife and a daughter who's apparently turning into a punk lesbian. The man spends his day shopping for antiques, arguing with blue-hairs over ottomans. I say if he gets some sort of satisfaction winning a card game based more on luck than skill, then hell. He can make me draw sixteen; it's the least I can do."

That was before Tucker was engaged to a girl I never got a chance to meet, back when he was working at his dad's law firm. I always thought he was going to make an amazing law-yer, what with his skills at having the last word.

They were a few months into planning the wedding, mov-ing into a house in the part of Ogden that was populated with young couples turning into young families, when she got a job opportunity in Germany she either couldn't pass up or didn't want to. She also didn't want Tucker to come with her. The breakup changed him. When life didn't go according to what he'd planned, he let the rest of his plans fall away, too. He quit his dad's firm to work with Henry. He didn't try to date any-body. Tucker stopped doing anything the way people assumed he would, but he never looked like he felt he was missing out on anything. I guess because he didn't look like he felt much at all.

Tucker kicked my foot. "It's good to see you again," he said. "You remind me that I wasn't always so old."

"You've always seemed old to me."

"Don't confuse wisdom with age, young lady."

The garage door banged and shifted at the handle. Real-izing Henry's arms must be loaded down with beverages, I jumped to help.

"How long you think you're staying around?" Tucker asked as I reached the door.

I told him the truth. "I don't know. I have to go back eventually." I just had to figure out how to get Smidge to understand that.

Henry entered looking stunned and disoriented, like he'd been staring into the sun for ten minutes.

"You okay?" I asked. "Did you break up the fight?"

"I'm okay," he said, brow furrowed as if he was working out a math equation. "Nobody got beat in there, it seems," he said. "So that's good news."

Tucker asked, "Then why do you look like you just witnessed a murder?"

Henry took a few seconds before answering.

"I know this might sound crazy, and I guess it's a recent thing, but . . . I might have developed a legitimate phobia of my own daughter."

# ELEVEN

I think of Smidge as family not just because we're close; when I was younger, her family ended up adopting me like I was a runaway. In turn I later played the role of mother when the one they had gave up on the job.

Once my father and I had been in Odgen for about two years, it was pretty clear my mother wasn't going to have a change of heart and suddenly appear on the doorstep with a suitcase filled with presents and apologies. Dad worked long hours, often overnight, and wanted me to be adult with him so that he could be less parental.

I cooked my own meals. I did the laundry, set out the trash cans, made dinner complete with reheating instructions on the plate in the fridge for when Dad came home. When he was on the graveyard shift, we'd often have an hour or two between when I got home from school and he left for work. Sometimes I woke up extra early to catch him at the kitchen table before he went to bed. We'd sit together, each with a cup of coffee, reading our respective books, sharing a plate of buttered toast. Sometimes he'd sign a permission slip for

me or I'd remind him of an upcoming doctor's appointment.
Those breakfasts were more like bookkeeping sessions than
family meals, but I loved them. I was proud my dad never
thought of me as a baby. I liked that he knew how I took my
coffee. After I turned sixteen he never said a word if I had my
own six-pack of beer in the fridge. I didn't have an allowance;
I had a part-time job. Sometimes I used that money to buy
us pizza, my treat. Not out of sacrifice, but responsibility. It
meant I was grown-up.

I should have seen it coming, but I was still surprised when
my dad told me one Sunday morning that he was done, too.
He was moving to California, curious if he'd look better in
tennis shorts and a polo shirt. I was almost seventeen. My
father was thirty-four and feeling antsy, like the best years of
his life were quickly coming to a halt. That's amazing to me,
picturing my dad that young, thinking, "She's raised enough.
I've got to find a life for myself now."

He wasn't inviting me to California with him. He was
informing me that he was leaving. He had come into some
money, an inheritance, and was leaving me a chunk of it.
That would be the arrangement. He would pay for my living
expenses until I was eighteen. He said that's how old he was
when he was on his own and raising me, so I actually had it
easy by comparison.

Louisiana has a lot of laws that let minors do a lot of
grown-up things. You can drive a car, have a job, and get
married much younger than one would think is a good idea
for a kid. When you're too young to drink in Louisiana, you
quickly learn words that give you adult privileges—like *eman-
cipation* and *hardship*—words that equate you with farmers

and slave hands. You can drive a tractor if you want to; you can live in a carport. You can be your own person at an age when you have no idea who you are. But at least I had finally run out of parents to abandon me.

Or so I'd thought.

Life with Smidge started with lots of sleepovers. Eventually I stopped going home to change. Once my father figured out I wasn't at the apartment he was paying for, he cut that off. Then I was a full-time resident of the Carlton household. Nobody ever seemed to mind.

It was perfect that first year. Smidge's parents both worked, so we had the run of the house. Mr. and Mrs. Carlton put in long hours in a way that made them seem exotic. I don't know what Mrs. Carlton did for a living, but it had her wearing some of the most beaded and sparkly dresses I've ever seen. I once asked Smidge if her mother was a professional pageant contestant. She replied, "No, ma'am, just an overdressed drunk."

Louis Carlton, affectionately known as Lou-Lou to his oldest and bravest friends, owned the upscale restaurant inside the Chesterfield, the nicest hotel in Ogden. He'd come home every night with stories of politicians or musicians passing through who'd sat at his bar for a drink or stopped inside his restaurant for dinner and directions. The Chesterfield was proof there was life beyond Ogden, that people got out of this town and lived exciting, vibrant lives.

Left with the run of the house, Smidge and I would down Shirley Temples spiked with a dash of vodka and consume endless hours of terrible television. As soon as the days turned warmer, we would lie out in the backyard coated in baby oil until we were the color of Hershey bars as we made our plans to take over the world. Smidge was confident she would run some kind of empire; I had dreams of working for a news station, ultimately leading to my own hour on CNN. The only thing standing in the way of our destiny was our reality.

Senior year of high school, Smidge's family fell apart. Since it's your grandparents I'm talking about, I don't know if it's right for me to tell you what had happened, but know that it was rather public and quite scandalous, and resulted in Smidge's mother having to move out.

I'd started feeling like it was my fault; that I was the reason any parent left home. I worried if I stayed, Smidge would lose her father, too, but she wouldn't let me go anywhere. "Daddy's not going to be able to handle this," she warned. "We'll need you." She was right.

After Mrs. Carlton and her fancy dresses left, things got bleak. Mr. Carlton, once barrel-chested and boastful, withered to a skinny, solemn man. He was home all the time, no longer interested in the life at the restaurant. He soon sold it for next to nothing. He didn't care. He talked quietly, called us "girls." It was like he'd screamed the life out of himself. Smidge's mother took everything great about that man, stuffed it into her suitcase, and moved it with her to Florida.

That's when your mother started calling her the Lizard. And for the record, she made me call her that, too. I'm pretty sure Henry told you we all called her that because she collected lizards. Another untruth.

After the Lizard left, I used all my grown-up skills to fill in where she left holes. I cooked meals, cleaned the house, did the laundry. I taught Smidge how to hem her jeans. I am one-hundred-percent positive she would never cop to that, but it's true. Using some of the guilt-money my father was shoving into my bank account, I made sure the pantry was stocked, and I never let Mr. Carlton go through the uncertainty of answering a ringing phone. It was the least I could do to repay them for letting me take refuge during my lost and lonely time. They helped me finish growing up. They showed me that sometimes people stay with you even when their instinct is to run as fast as possible in the other direction.

Mr. Carlton died of a heart attack long before you ever got the chance to meet him. That's when Smidge and I started taking our trips, one almost every year, in order to see all the things he never did.

When my dad first moved me to Ogden, I remember tearfully telling him that I would never forgive him for displacing me, for making me start all over. He ripped my life to shreds. But then I found Smidge, and I didn't want to go anywhere else. Not without my best friend.

It was Smidge's idea to stay in Ogden for college. I was okay with it because I could barely afford in-state tuition. Your mom claimed it was so we didn't have to be apart, but I knew that wasn't exactly the truth. She was scared to leave the safety of her city, the place where people knew her so well she didn't have secrets. Smidge probably felt if she'd left for even a second, there was a chance somebody could do something she hadn't sanctioned, and she wasn't interested in getting shafted ever again.

Smidge had only enough strength inside her to cut one person out of her life forever, and that was her mother. I think that's why as soon as she felt safe with Henry, she didn't hesitate to ask him to ask her to marry him. She told that sweet, patient, handsome man to find them a nice house with a big yard and get her pregnant with a beautiful daughter as soon as possible.

As with anything Smidge wanted, that's exactly what she got.

Smidge developed her own sense of how to do things, of how to run a home. Once she was married and had you, she distanced herself from anything I had to do with her learning it in the first place. She did it with an abundance of pride and protection. This was *her* family, and she'd never leave it.

The more Smidge fell into married life, the more she focused on raising a baby, the more I found I wanted exactly the opposite. Plus I often felt like the fifth wheel; there was no reason for me to be a part of your family's firsts.

Eventually I just wanted out, to get away, go somewhere big where I could be anonymous. I had become too fused to my best friend, this woman who was no longer able to be my second half. I needed to move to a place where I could find out exactly where Smidge ended and I began.

I moved to Denver. Then San Diego. Then a weird year in Phoenix that led to a job in Las Vegas, which turned into a career in Los Angeles. A strange career, but one that earned me more money than I could have imagined possible, considering it required little more than my laptop and spreadsheet software.

Smidge might have called my job "sad balls," but my business card said I was a homemaking consultant.

Not a nanny, not a chef, not a designer. Not a decorator or a landscaper. I can barely keep a plant alive.

I knew how to make a house function. How to cook, keep a place clean, and schedule multiple hectic lives. I was good at finding sales, at stretching a dollar. I could declutter even if I chose not to in my own life. I could make a family run smoothly. I looked at everyone's strengths and divided the labor so everyone felt useful and appreciated. I could teach a teenager how to cook a simple, one-pot meal for a family of six before his or her hardworking parents got home from work. I could help a family overcome a seemingly insurmountable debt while keeping them from being reliant on outside labor—nannies, accountants, personal assistants, housekeepers, gardeners, and sometimes marriage counselors. I could do it in person, or I could do it online. I was helping to restore order.

It started small. My friend Rainey knew a couple struggling to stay sane while caring for their newborn. I organized their kitchen, created a monthly meal plan, and set aside nights where friends of theirs volunteered to come over with a cooked meal. Soon the word spread among their friends that there was a way to help the new family, and before long there was a visitor each day at the door offering to help with the dishes, the laundry, to get the car washed, to run a simple errand while already on their way to do their own shopping.

Rainey was a professional blogger. Her website specialized in self-help and personal growth, and she often wrote about little things women could do to make a big difference. Rainey asked me if she could feature what I'd done for the young family on her site, and if I ever thought about using my talents to start a business. When I didn't understand how that was possible, she insisted on creating my website.

It seemed absurd that anyone would want to hire me out to do these things, and even crazier that there would be an audience who wanted to read stories about the people who hired people to do these things. I was never much into reality shows. I didn't get that involved with strangers' lives. Until suddenly, that was my job.

Rainey was savvy. She knew how to make everything look beautiful. She had a way of turning my work into something soothing. Calming. Whether or not I was making your meal plan, just looking at a photo of one tacked to somebody's refrigerator made it seem like everything was going to be okay. Rainey gave me her old digital camera, showed me how to style a room for taking photos, and how to post those pictures on my site. She talked me through my own blog, instructing me to diligently keep my copy short and my identity perky. I was to be a West Coast Mary Poppins, without all the nannying.

She bet me fifty bucks that I would be able to quit my job in retail within five years. I handed Rainey her cash in just over half that time.

Thanks to Rainey's connections, including a PR firm that boasted a roster heavy with professional bloggers and unique specialists, my website, HowToGetYourHomeBack.com, got over half a million hits a month. I lived off the revenue from ads, sponsors, and my personal clients. I was featured on a few talk shows and magazines. I was known as the House Whisperer. I was sort of like a semi-expensive domestic stage manager. Sometimes I even wore a headset.

It was a very weird way to become almost famous. It happened very quickly, and I wasn't prepared for how busy it would make me.

Sometimes I felt my domestic consultancy job was only possible because I lived where people were willing to take advice from complete strangers about how to live their lives. If I'd tried to have clients in Ogden, I'd have been treated like an abortion doctor in the sixties, running under the cover of night, entering through the back door, everything I said or did a solemn secret. The gossip alone!

*So it seems that Mary-Lynn is using some kind of hippie nurse to teach her how to wash her towels.*

Perhaps one could imagine asking a domestic consultant to take over her life after she's gone, but Smidge would've scoffed her head off if I'd ever suggested she needed any of the services I provided. I'd never once dared to give Smidge a word of advice when it came to running her own family. She had a way of doing things that was set in stone; her rules were to be obeyed without question.

I had to assume she was only suggesting this arrangement because she was in shock over her diagnosis, grasping at straws. I could understand that. I'd be panicking, too. I needed to get her to take a step back, to tell me what was really going on. I wanted to get her to talk to me about what her doctor had said and what her options were.

But what I really wanted to know was what I could do to fix her *right then*, because I made a silent promise to myself and to your mother, back when I was sitting alone in that stupid bar in Atlanta, that this time around I wasn't going to be a shitty cancer friend.

I'm not sure how an entire week passed without us talking even once about her illness, especially since we spent those days pretty much attached at the hip. We ignored any topic that might become sensitive as we spent our days shopping, gossiping, taking you to get your hair changed back to something normal. We fell into a pattern.

We were settled on the back porch one night, holding our half-empty wineglasses, listening to the Willie Nelson album that she insists on listening to (but I do not enjoy), and watching the sky turn lavender, when a coughing fit hit her. It seemed to start from the center of her stomach, knocking her in half with absolutely no warning. As her body rocked, Smidge held her wineglass aloft, saving precious cargo from going overboard during her tidal wave. It wasn't like someone clearing her throat, or a reaction to swallowing the wrong way. This was a chunky, watery cough, something angry inside of her. It was the first time I'd heard it, and it was alarming.

Soon she calmed down, the blood pooling back from her face, her skin settling into a more normal peach. But I could see in her watery eyes, and the way she was biting down the left side of her lip: she wasn't prepared for that. That kind of coughing might have been new for her, too.

When she sighed it sounded like a bicycle pump, an achy wheeze that required all her effort.

All cancer is unfair, but the kind Smidge had was an extra special kind of unfair, the one people would always use as a disclaimer when discussing her illness.

*"Lung cancer, but she never smoked."*

*"She got it young. Very rare."*

Smidge had lung cancer with an asterisk. Carcinogens saved up for only the *very-est special-est.* People always marveled at how healthy she was, how she took care of herself, even running a couple of marathons right after you started kindergarten. Smidge transformed herself from a skinny stay-at-home mom to a toned lady-who-lunched.

It didn't matter that the collective number of cigarettes we'd all smoked in our lives couldn't fill a pack. It didn't matter that Smidge was only thirty-one and the mother of an eight-year-old. She wasn't a coal miner. She didn't sleep on a pillow of asbestos. She was just living her life, and then she got cancer.

Your mother hated all the medical attention almost as much as she hated being in the hospital. She hated the tubes, the tests, the decisions, the conferences. She hated being sick, being weak, and most of all she hated being in need of other people. So she got angry. She eventually got so furious she burned all those cancer cells right out of her body. Her fury spiked her internal furnace to one million degrees and she raged that sickness away in less than two years like it evaporated.

They say seven years is how long you have to be in remission from lung cancer to be completely cancer free. Smidge made it to just past three.

There was a clanging sound coming through the house, headed right toward us like a runaway train.

"Smiiiidge?"

The voice came from behind my head, causing an involuntary spasm in my shoulders. Vikki was just as pleased to see me, though you'd never know it through her fake face.

"Hey, there, weary travelers!"

Even in the darkened light of the back porch I could see the wine stains on Vikki's exposed teeth as she smiled her mostly insincere greeting. She was drinking from a yellow plastic cup shaped like a beer stein that read *Neville Seniors '92* in red letters right above the words *This Is How We Do It*. Under her other arm a bundle of ropey fur trembled and yipped.

"Hey, Barksy," Smidge greeted the wiggling pup. "What is up, Vicksburg?"

Vikki released her dog and plopped her ample hips between us. As she angled herself some room, she patted each of us on a knee. "I hope you ladies have fun adventure stories to tell, because I need to know it was worth what Jenny went and did to her head."

"You saw that?"

Vikki grunted. "Bless her heart. It'll grow, Smidge. Hair does that."

Suddenly we were moving, the swing bench activated by Vikki's flip-flopped feet. It didn't take long before it was too much for me. The closeness and the movement felt like we were all on a bad date, trapped on a carnival ride. I moved to a nearby easy chair, folding myself against the cushions.

As Smidge showed Vikki the picture of the giant chair I had taken with her cell phone, I couldn't help but stare at Vikki's purple sundress and the many ways it had failed her. The top bunched so low on her chest I could see white arcs poking just above what must have been the start of her nipples. As she rocked the bench, her knees pushed the fabric from under her dress, making her look like she was expanding and receding. Growing and shrinking like a giant, breathing grape.

Wherever elastic touched her skin she was puffed and sunburned, like she'd spent the day at the beach drinking straight from the ocean. Her parrot necklace stuck to her chest in the heat, but it had gone askew and the bird perched on her left shoulder, poised for flight.

Each of Vikki's toenails was painted with a yellow blob of a smiley face. I heard the ice settle in her cup and realized she was drinking her red wine on the rocks.

Barksy sniffed my ankle, bobbing his moppy head to mash his damp nose against my skin. He gave a disappointed snarf and then settled beside the screen door.

"Well, that sounds like a fun time," Vikki said.

"I owe Danny here another vacation," said Smidge. "This trip was more just for me. I kind of took over everything."

"I bet you did. You're such a good friend, Smidge."

"I know."

Like I wasn't even there.

# TWELVE

The next time I failed at being Smidge's understudy, it was an accident. I didn't know I was being evaluated. I thought I was alone, going through the motions of something I'd successfully accomplished just short of ten thousand times.

Making a bed.

I was putting new sheets onto the guest mattress, and had just smoothed out some of the wrinkles with my palm when she let me know I'd screwed up.

"You tuck that sheet under at the bottom so it doesn't pull up when you're sleeping," she said. She had one hand gripped on the doorframe, the only thing keeping her from walking over and doing it herself.

"I'm just going to kick it out as soon as I'm under the covers," I told her. "I don't like sheets tucked in around my feet. Feels like I'm in a body bag." And then I tucked the sheet in just as she wanted it.

"Too soon," she joked.

At that point it seemed I hadn't slept in a month. Whenever I eased myself into bed, my muscles twitched and pulled, begging for some sort of rest. I'd been so stressed I hadn't even had a chance to note how stressed I'd been. My body, however, was well aware it hadn't stopped being on alert since I stood underneath the world's largest chair weeks ago.

"I know you want to go home," Smidge said, staring at the floor, fiddling with her wristwatch. "But maybe you could think about staying. I don't know what's going to happen. I mean, I know what's going to happen, but I keep having these coughing fits."

I felt weak at the sight of her vulnerability. It's true I'd been thinking of home, of how I was supposed to be back by now. The bills piling up, the clients I wasn't visiting. The day before, I'd received an e-mail from someone asking me if I wouldn't mind drafting up a budget that could include an additional nanny—her third—because she wanted a "sleepover nanny" who could take care of the kids once the installation of her sixth—and detached—bedroom was finished. *I literally have no idea how to figure out how much money we have. What would I do without you? Love and hugs, and when you get back I am taking you out drinking.*

I felt that familiar panic upon reading that e-mail, a feeling that I was winging it with every new message, with each client's additional problem. It was always a juggling act, and I knew it was only a matter of time before someone figured out I had no idea what I was doing. I was making a guess, my hunch, and turning it into a decision that was to be followed. Even when my clients were at their happiest, I could still feel like a fraud. I figured it was because I usually didn't stay with them past that one problem. They disappeared, for the most part. Occasionally I'd get a holiday card, or someone would ask for an additional month of consultation. An extra room to organize here and there. Coming up with things to write about made me nervous, too. I didn't feel like I had much to say, but I knew if I didn't update I'd lose money, I'd lose clients. I juggled, but with my eyes half closed in anticipation of disaster. It's why I didn't have an assistant. I knew another person around would expose my weaknesses even sooner.

Going through my recent batch of e-mails, I had to pass on a client because I didn't have time to travel to San Francisco. Normally I would have fit that job in over a weekend, but I knew I couldn't get away. I was searching for quick fixes, little questions I could handle. A consultation over e-mail for fifty bucks a pop was about all I could do in my little amount of time that wasn't taken up by Smidge.

She was taking over, even if I didn't think I was going to allow her to have so much room. How little does she think of my life that she can just knock everything off my plate and hand me hers?

Then again, it seemed wrong to help a stranger over a friend, and I had to remind myself that even though I had doubts about my work—sometimes I felt I didn't deserve to be where I'd gotten in such a short period of time—the truth was, I had made something of myself, something Smidge seemed to ignore completely. The fact that she insisted on telling me how to do everything down to making a bed proved she either had no idea what I did with my day, or absolutely no respect for it.

My life didn't look like the one she chose, and nothing like the one I'd originally planned. Somehow, she felt that gave her the right to choose a new one for me.

"When did you come up with this idea, anyway?" I asked her. "For me to do this. Why me?"

She brought her hand to the light switch. "I saw it in a dream," she said. "You know I'm always right about my dreams. Remember how I knew Robert was cheating on you?"

Senior year of high school I fell in love with a guy I thought was perfect until Smidge had a dream that he had been making out with the girl he tutored in Spanish and then that turned out to be true.

Once she had confirmation, Smidge spent the next three months going around our high school offering psychic services. She'd storm up to people in hallways, sometimes yelling at complete strangers. *Don't take the bus home today! If you are on that bus, it will crash! I fell asleep in trig and now I know things! You're welcome!*

"What was in the dream?" I asked.

A smile found its way to the corners of her lips. Frail and serene, like my fairy godmother was about to grant her super-best wish for me.

"You were on the front porch, standing next to Henry, and y'all were watching Jenny get into some car, like she was going on a date or something. Henry put his arm around you, not saying anything, which he does when it means something. And—I don't know—it just looked right to me. Like that was it. In the dream I knew somehow that I was gone, and this was the future. The future that's supposed to happen."

Then I was in the dark. Smidge had flipped the light switch, shutting the door behind her as she left. Through the walls I heard her find Henry. *Sooooooo!* she sang, changing the big subject.

I could imagine Smidge wrapping herself around her husband's back, arms hugging his arms, her chin on his shoulder as she peeked over him to see what he was reading, maybe teasing him about how long his hair was getting, something she must have wished could be their biggest problem.

Days could stretch on with their lack of answers, but nights were even worse. I was alone with all those thoughts rocking from one side of my brain to the other like those mineral-oil motion lamps that tip and turn, an endless current of worries. I wanted to fix an unfixable problem, I knew that. I also wanted to help in places where I'd been specifically forbidden. I knew Smidge needed someone else besides me. I wasn't enough for her, and even though that knowledge tore me up inside, I felt it was my duty to get some assistance.

---

The next morning Smidge seemed ready to start talking seriously about the things she needed me to know in order to take over her life. I'm not sure what brought it on, but I wasn't about to question her in the middle of her first lecture as we stood in her hallway.

"I have made a list," she said, punching a fist as she declared her latest achievement. "Let's get to teaching you how to be me."

"Okay."

"Item one: how to fold a fitted sheet."

"This is where you're starting?" I marveled. "*This* is the most important thing you can think of right now?"

"Yes. Look, I know you just ball those sheets up in your arms like you're making a giant wad of cotton candy to stuff inside your linen closet," she said. "And that's not how it's going to be around here. Not in this house."

Smidge reached into her linen closet and plucked a perfect bundle the color of a fir tree. She then shook it loose, a queen-size flag unfurling. Like she was about to claim me for her country.

"I know you have a housekeeper," I said.

"What if you have to fold one when she's not here? You'll just leave it in a to-do pile for your help?"

"That to-do pile is called a hamper."

"I knew it!" Smidge said, rising to her tiptoes in sanctimony. "I knew you didn't teach those helpless idiots how to fold a fitted sheet. This is why people get divorced, Danny. No offense. But if you can't stick around long enough to figure out how to wrangle a bit of elastic bedding, then how's anybody supposed to make it to their second anniversary?"

"Yes, I can see how these topics are directly related."

She pursed her lips. "You go ahead and stay snarky, but I'm right. From wedding to bedding, you got to learn how to do it." She fiddled with the fabric in her hands, prepping it for instruction. "See, I put my hands in the corners? Now the right hand goes to the left and you fold the corner in your right hand over the one in your left."

What was happening in the space between Smidge's arms looked like an origami dance, as if she were making the world's biggest cootie catcher. I wasn't any good at folding those paper toys when I was a kid, either. I couldn't get the edges sharp enough and I was bad at figuring out how to make the corners meet. In the end, it would look more like a sick bird than any kind of four-pointed fortune-teller.

Smidge continued instructing, faster than I could have possibly understood. "Okay, now you reach down, pick up the front-hanging corner, bring that up. Fold this guy over those two corner guys you've got here."

Her arms opened, she slid a hand through, and then her arms closed again. She bowed with a flourish and came back up, smiling, her dance completed. It was all so fluid and mystical, she could've been performing a religious ceremony. Despite her constant narration, the words didn't seem to match what her body was doing, flipping and folding, weaving around.

"I think we should tell Henry," I said.

"Okay, now here comes the part where we lay it flat."

She wandered away to lay the sheet out on the closest flat surface—the desk in the office. She reached over everything on the table to make space, pushing pencils and spine-bent paperbacks out of the way. She stared intently at the sheet in front of her, head tucked at an awkward angle. I realized she was doing that to keep from looking at the framed photos along the back of the desk, an arc of frozen memories. Family pictures. Standing in front of Alcatraz, huddled together in the wind. A close-up of Henry laughing with a pink smear of birthday cake icing clumped to his chin. You in your softball uniform. The newest addition was Smidge leaning against that giant chair. The picture gave me the chills because while Smidge might have been smiling, her eyes were looking past the camera. They were searching me. Even now, in its frame, safely jumbled with other memories, that picture taunts, *"Whatcha gonna do, Danny?"*

"Let's tell your family," I said.

"Can't break them down now," she said, shaking her head, her voice not much louder than a mutter. "I'm not going to be selfish, rob their time with my moaning. I'm dying either way, so why prolong their sad parts?"

"Smeh, they want to be here for you."

"No. Think of what the Lizard did. She broke our family, and then she had the nerve to be crying about it, trying to be the focus when the entire town knew she had skanked around with the mayor."

"This isn't the same, and you know it."

"Isn't it? She made us have to deal with her pain, her suffering, her, her, *her* all the time. No matter how much we loved her and wanted her to stay, guess what? She left anyway. She wasn't strong enough. She made a mess and then disappeared forever. I ain't going out like that, Danny. No, ma'am."

I wanted to tell her that, while we can get through this together, that maybe I will do whatever she wanted, she didn't have to make us do this alone. We needed to tell her husband. I could use Henry's calm, level head for just a second.

I had a brief flashback to the day I was about to sign my first set of divorce papers; I was terrified and lonely. I needed Smidge to tell me it was all going to be okay. Despite two phone calls and six consecutive texts, she did not reply. Instead, Henry called.

"Smidge left her phone on the edge of the bathtub, it seems," he said. Henry could sometimes sound like he was trying to solve a puzzle, often ending sentences with "it seems," or beginning them with "turns out." He talked through his thoughts, trying the internal words out loud to make sure he'd processed everything he was thinking. "She's at the movies with Jenny," he told me. "Otherwise I'm sure she'd be looking for it. Maybe she is looking for it, but it's here. She would have Jenny call it, if she knew it was missing. So I'm guessing she doesn't know it's gone yet." Then he asked, "Are you okay?"

I told him how I was staring down a stack of papers that said there was nothing I could do to save my marriage, documenting my intent to have the state of California come in and sever it, to rip it apart in front of everyone, to put in public record that I was finished being married to James and he was finished being my husband and that was it. We were done. Signed and stamped, gavel-dropped, *done*.

"I put my pen to the first place where I'm supposed to sign," I told him. "But then I couldn't stop shaking. Then I couldn't breathe and I lost all feeling in my legs. Either I'm having a panic attack or I'm dying, so I called Smidge."

"You know she probably would have just made you more upset," he said.

"That's true."

Henry sniffed as I heard him shift the phone in his hands. I pictured him sitting on the lid of the toilet seat, staring at the cabinets filled with zit creams and moisturizers, the mason jars stuffed with cotton balls and Q-tips, the boxes of open eye-shadow samples and shreds of perfume-scented magazine pages. The sink would be snaked with a stringy collection of twelve-inch auburn hairs. The shower curtain would be jerked to the side, possibly still damp from when Smidge ended her call and apparently took off running.

I could just imagine Henry looking over the state of this

bathroom and asking himself, *"How did I end up having to deal with so many damn women?"*

"Thanks for calling, Henry," I said. "That was nice of you. You don't have to stay on the phone. Tell Smidge to call me when she gets home."

"Let me ask you something," he said. "Do you have a life insurance policy? Some kind of money that goes somewhere after you die? Your next of kin?"

"Yeah, I do. Why?"

"Well, just in case you *are* dying right now, you might want to sign those papers quick so James can't get a penny of it. Especially since he's the one who killed you."

My signature is shaky on my divorce papers, but it's from laughter.

Smidge had folded her fitted sheet into a tight rectangle. She presented it to me like an award. "Ta-da!"

"I want to tell Henry," I said again.

"No," she said. "I can't do that to him. And if you go behind my back on this one, Danny, I will mess you up. Do you understand?"

She tossed the folded linen at my head.

"Now you do it," she said as she left the room. "Call me when you get it right."

"I thought you were trying to teach me!" I shouted toward the hall. "How am I supposed to figure out what you did?"

*"Google it!"*

The tension in her response hit the little hairs along my earlobes. Before I could say another word, she slammed her bedroom door.

It is no small confession to say I have regrets about how things went down with your mother, Jenny. This moment here I'll remember, because I should've done more. I should've forced her to talk. I think it's when she really needed me, and I was still too scared of her to step up to the plate. All I could hear in my head was this frantic, urgent voice, incredulous with judgment.

*This is her last request.*

That's what I kept thinking, mostly because it seemed impossible. How could someone like Smidge ever have *one* final request? There would always be more. This is Smidge. Smidge *wants* things. Random things, big things. *Your* things. How could this be the last thing she'd ever need?

We make our loved ones' final wishes sacred. We find the exact lake to scatter their ashes, erect park benches under their favorite trees. We name buildings and avenues, libraries and highways after the deceased. We create scholarships and gardens and sometimes even laws. We need enormous monuments to fill the space they left behind. Maybe sometimes it can't just be a statue. Sometimes you need the real deal. Another life. A living memorial.

At the most, Smidge was asking me to give up five years. Five years she couldn't have. This is the kind of thing siblings do for each other all the time. It wasn't Smidge's fault she didn't have a sister to step in to help. Of course I was the next logical choice. Who else could do it? It wasn't like the Lizard was going to be asked back after all this time.

*Unless . . .*

Unless I could find the Lizard. Had *Terms of Endearment* taught me nothing? No matter how estranged a mother and daughter could get, this was how they'd patch things up. Maybe I wouldn't even have to tell her about the cancer to get her here. Mother's intuition could kick in and save me from spilling a secret. If the last person Smidge would ever expect to be there for her could show up and stick around, maybe she would see it was okay to tell everybody else.

Smidge told me to get on Google. I was just searching for something a little bigger and more elusive than housekeeping tutorials.

It didn't take long to find her. She had her own website; she was running what looked like both a pageant class and a photography studio. Lots of pink and sparkly graphics, the word *princess* used several times. I clicked Contact and wrote what I hoped came across as a breezy yet intriguing e-mail, asking her to write back when she got a chance. Yes, it had been a while. Still, could she possibly contact me. We could use some catching up.

It wasn't until I hit Send that I realized I'd been holding my breath. I knew I was doing the right thing, but it still felt like playing with fire.

# THIRTEEN

---

As someone who's been an actual shitty cancer friend, I can tell you with absolute certainty that if you're going to know someone going through cancer, it's best to do it with a tertiary friend. There's just a lot less pressure.

Michelle Stevens was a girl I knew from that hot-yoga class I stopped attending once it gave me a worrisome skin rash. Not long after that, she was diagnosed with breast cancer.

I mostly heard about it from friends of her friends. Talk of Michelle's cancer spread through acquaintances via Facebook updates and the occasional fund-raiser tweet. I'm pretty sure I gave money toward something.

I hadn't thought about Michelle in a while, but I do know that she survived and for some reason her number was in my cell phone, so the next morning I walked the half mile from Smidge's house to the coffee shop to try to get some advice without the threat of Smidge overhearing.

Michelle answered the phone, which solidified my hunch that at one point I'd donated at least ten dollars to that fund-raiser.

YOU TAKE IT FROM HERE 127

She gave a jubilant "Hi, Danielle! It's been a while!" but was then interrupted by a child yelling in the background. Something about a pillow.

"It sounds like you're busy," I said.

"No, just hold on." After a moment I heard her calmly say, "Lily, Mommy needs to use the phone for a second because her friend has called her. Do you think you could let Mommy talk to her friend for a few minutes, and then we can set up your pillow for nap time? Would you mind?"

A voice answered, "Okay, Mommy. That sounds reasonable."

Everybody else seemed to have a lock on this parenting thing.

"Okay, sorry, about that," Michelle said. "Mini-meltdown with the mini-people."

"I won't keep you, I just . . . well, I have a friend who's sick and she's . . . sick like you were."

"Oh."

She only said that one word, that one syllable, but still her voice was packed with empathy, sympathy, and disappointment. She'd never even met Smidge, but she'd already expressed more emotions for her than I did for Michelle—and I used to do Warrior II beside her every Tuesday, Thursday, and Sunday.

"I was wondering if you had any advice. Treatment-wise."

She sounded uncomfortable as she started with "I'm not her doctor, so . . ."

"Sorry, I don't mean doctor stuff," I said, losing my ability to describe anything that might approach oncology. "I'm looking for advice that isn't necessarily medical. Anything that helped you. I mean, overall. I hesitate to use the word 'spiritually.'"

"Oh, I got you," she said, sounding pleased. "And yes. Move to California. That's what I did."

Michelle said she didn't normally believe in homeopathic remedies, but when her husband insisted they take a place on the beach near the water, she wasn't about to complain. The sun and laid-back attitude of the neighborhood eased her stress levels. She no longer dreaded waking up, because she knew that even if she couldn't move an inch that day, if she never once got out of bed, she still had an amazing view. Watching the sunset with her family became their daily ritual, and has remained even now that she's cancer-free.

"It makes you appreciate time," she says. "The time you once had, the time you have right now, and the time you have left. And since I'm already sounding like some kind of hippie, which I am not, I will quickly add that I also went to a healer. Don't make fun of me. I can't believe I just admitted that."

I tried to imagine Smidge in the same room as a healer. Would that be inside a yurt or a hut? How many seconds would she hold out before mocking that healer to tears?

"I don't know if my friend would go for something like that."

"Believe me, I thought I would be the last person to meditate, take supplements, or own a juicer. But when you're sick enough, you'll try anything. And I have to admit, some of those things made me feel better. I still start my days with a green smoothie. Maybe you could ease her into that."

I heard Lily tell her mother that a reasonable amount of time had passed and maybe she could say good-bye to her friend on the phone now.

"I'll let you go," I said. "But thanks."

"Is your friend in Los Angeles?"

"No."

"Well, if you get her here, I'll take her to my guy. He's pretty amazing, just as a person. It's worth it. It's been forever since I've seen you. I heard what happened with you and James. I'm sorry."

Lily promptly began a screaming fit.

"I'll let you go," I said again.

"Okay, well, you call me," she said. "Let's catch up, I mean it."

I would think once you've survived cancer you no longer have to be nice to near strangers. You get a free pass to skip fake intimacy. No more forcing tenuous connections with the acquaintance characters in your life's play. Smidge kept her social obligations, but I assumed it was because the more people she knew, the more she could control. But what did Michelle get out of making plans with me for when I got back to Los Angeles? She was busy. I was busy. We'd be getting together just to have gotten together, to go through the motions of people who know people. It was like putting your day in a costume and making it act like someone else's life. *Today I lunched with my friend Michelle I know from hot yoga.*

"Lily!" Michelle shouted, not to me. "That is not okay, and you are going to sit in the punishment chair right now. You go sit down."

The screaming instantly stopped. "I'm sorry, Mommy."

"I know," Michelle said. Then to me: "I have to go, but hey, you're a good friend for asking about my cancer."

Neither of us had used that word yet. "I don't know about that," I said. "I feel pretty bad about it, actually."

"I think you wouldn't be calling me if you didn't really care about her."

"No, I meant you. I'm sorry I wasn't around when you were sick."

Michelle laughed. "You weren't? It seems like everybody was. And no apology necessary. I wasn't taking attendance."

If I had cancer, even though I might tell people to stay away and not bring me anything, I would definitely be taking attendance.

As I hung up the phone I felt a shove from behind. I lost my footing and stumbled, but before I could fall I was encircled at the waist by a strong arm. Tucker's low laugh buzzed in my ear. "Excuse me, ma'am, excuse me, excuse me."

"You almost knocked me over!"

"Well, I didn't. So calm down," Tucker said, as he pretended to straighten me out, pulling at my shirt, brushing back my hair, like I was a mannequin he had toppled at a department store.

"You're wearing sweatpants," I informed him.

"You caught me in my escape clothes." He pulled a pair of sunglasses from his waistband and lowered that ubiquitous ball cap over his eyebrows. I briefly worried about the state of Tucker's scalp. "That's what I call my running pants," he explained. "I can't go running unless I pretend I'm being chased by the good guys, so I just like to think of the whole endeavor as training for being on the lam."

"I like how you think you're the bad guy."

"If the New Balance fits."

"Is this coffee shop your supersecret lair? Is this where you keep all your evil cappuccinos?"

"It's my reward. For each mile over three I get to go up a size."

"And today?"

"Extra-extra-large, baby. Supersize latte, full-fat."

As he reached past me to open the door, I caught a quick smell of him, of tired, sweaty man. The salty-sweet tang that lingered around the curve of a neck, the underside of an arm, all the places where your head might rest afterward.

Tucker waved his hand in front of me to fall into a bow. "M'lady."

"Oh, no, I'm just leaving," I said, even though for some reason I didn't want to leave. Which is why I knew I needed to leave. Part of not being a shitty cancer friend is not hiding all day, semiflirting in the corner of the coffee shop. "I have to get back to Smidge."

"She says jump, you ask how high."

"It's a little more complicated than that."

"Right."

"Good luck dodging the cops on your way home."

"See, that's your problem," he said. "You think the good guys are cops."

Once he was out of my sight I exhaled, feeling my shoulders drop.

He made my shoulders tense. Around him, my body seemed to put itself on hold, like it wanted to be ready for whatever was going to come next.

I chose to ignore that.

My head was tilted back to reach the final few drops of milk from my bowl of cereal when Smidge entered the kitchen with an announcement.

"We have a real problem," she said. "Besides this bitch-beast of a headache I woke up with."

From under the last of my breakfast, I asked, *"Mllh?"*

She pressed her palms against her eyelids, causing her faded red sweatshirt to ride up enough to expose a small strip of her pale stomach. "My husband won't stop humping me," she said.

Jenny, sometimes I'll have to pretend I'm talking to some-one who isn't you, because in order to get into the whole truth I'm going to share some things you might not like to hear about your parents. This is probably one of them, and I'm sorry. But this whole part was your fault for getting older. You reminded all of us that we were aging, and something about that made your father want to prove his virility and youth through bedtime frolicking.

I apologize for using the words *bedtime frolicking*. I went through about ten other phrases, but couldn't find anything that didn't sound like I was describing your parents having sex.

"It took forever to get him to admit this was about him having some kind of old-man crisis," Smidge said. "He just kept rolling over on top of me, trying to act like he thought I was sexy, which I know isn't true right now. Look at this."

She hitched up the hem of her sweatshirt, accidentally flashing the bottom of her C-shaped scar. The surgery that robbed her of part of her lung left a mark that was knotty and gray-pink like a mouse tail. It snaked up and around her back, making her look like she survived a shark attack.

Which is exactly what she told the gawkers on the beach the summer we vacationed in Maui.

Smidge wanted to wear a bikini and get some sun on her "survivor scar." A young newlywed couple couldn't help but stare. It was massive, breathtaking. One wanted to assume it was fake because it looked so real. There was no mistaking that slow shake of a head, like witnessing a tragedy. You could tell what the couple was thinking. *Such a pretty girl, so ruined by whatever happened to her.*

I thought Smidge was asleep behind her sunglasses, face-down on her towel, magazine tossed aside. But she was watching them watch her, because she pointed at her scar and told the couple, "Shark attack."

"Oh, no!" That was from the girl, who immediately reached toward her husband's hand until their wedding bands overlapped, as if somehow he could protect her from everything now that they were married.

Smidge got to her feet and posed, jutting her hip to reveal the entire length of the scar.

"Right there," she said, pointing at the deep blue water just beyond, where the waves were rolling in, splashing boogie boarders and bobbing swimmers. "That's where he got me. And why we came back here, right, Danny?"

From underneath my massive sunhat and layer of sunscreen that could technically be labeled SPF-Apartment, I immediately fell into my role, nodding solemnly, sagely, like I'd seen too much and learned too little too late. "Was a bad day," I said, almost in a whisper.

"Okay, Quint, dial it back," she muttered before returning to her audience.

"That's where that shark tried to kill me," she said. "And now I'm going back to kill him."

She glanced around like she was searching for some kind of weapon. I handed her the only thing within my reach—a rolled-up *InStyle* magazine.

The quick, disappointed glare she threw told me she was going to give me hell for handing her a paper weapon for a water fight, but she couldn't break character then. True to her nature, she acted like I'd just handed her a massive harpoon. "Thanks!" she practically cheered, and then ran right into the ocean.

I tried to figure out what would be the best thing to say that would get the couple to lose interest or go away so Smidge could come back. Those waves were strong. The longer she was stuck in the ocean, the angrier she was going to be when she returned with a soggy mound of glossy print in her left hand.

"She'll be out there for a while," I said. "You'll probably hear about it on the news later."

Luckily for me, the couple had already started packing their things and left, presumably for some newlywed sex.

Smidge came back with a new friend she'd made out in the waves, a pretty surf instructor named Kai who gave us a three-hour surfing lesson in exchange for a few mai tais and a generous tip.

But there in the kitchen, Smidge wasn't trying to show me her shark scar. She was pointing out a dark bruise streaking across her stomach to her back, like she'd been kicked by a rodeo bull. This was a bruise better suited for a stuntwoman or an action hero, not befitting a lady who took to standing on chairs when she saw a spider.

"Wow," I said, fighting the urge to touch it. "What happened?"

"I hurt myself drinking *water*," she said, her face suddenly flushing with outrage. She rotated her hip to get a better look at the dark patch just above her waistband. "I was having a sip when I started coughing and then fell against the sink."

"Does it hurt?"

Her eyebrows relaxed toward her ears, her eyelids suddenly heavy from attempting to be so tolerant in the face of my stupid questions. She chose not to answer, saying instead, "The point is: I'm real sexy and I can't have Henry rolling on top of me all the time. Not just because it hurts, but I don't want him to see a bruise and start asking questions. He's already suspicious because I'm all squirrelly when he wants to get busy. What we need to do is get a project."

She winced as she jammed the edges of her sweatshirt into the waistband of her jeans. I reached out instinctively to help her, but there was nothing to do. I was standing there with my arms out, fingers spread, like someone watching her baby try to stand upright on its own.

"My arm hurts when I lift it," she admitted, whacking at her right limb.

"Where does it hurt?" I asked. "I mean, is it your arm or your shoulder or—"

"I guess you could say it hurts in my *cancer*," she said, effectively shutting me up.

Smidge then sang us to a new topic. "*Sooooo*, I am going to call Tucker. Tell him that Henry is driving me crazy and I want him out of the house. Make him—I don't know—build me a new garage, or something. Something that will have him busy all day chopping trees and hauling heavy things. Whatever will get him as exhausted at night as I am."

"I could call Tucker," I offered, but the second the words left my mouth I knew I said them with way too much enthusiasm.

Smidge was on it immediately. "You sure volunteered for that quickly, missy."

"No, I didn't."

Smidge coughed into her fist, the world's tiniest lawyer forming her closing argument. Wagging her index finger, she said, "Don't you get any ideas that involve Tucker Collier, do you understand? You are mine."

"I don't have any ideas, Smidge."

"Better not." Satisfied, she rolled her shoulders before giving a small shudder of a cough. "Danny, I have been thinking that we do not devote enough time, as a people, to the glory that is napping."

"I think you're right," I said.

"It's just a smart thing to do. Recharge. Animals know to do it." She raised her head toward me, but her eyes were closed. "Who are the people who *siesta*?" she asked. "Mexicans? The Spanish?"

"Actually, I think several cultures—"

"Well, I'm fixing to *siesta* up in here," she said, turning from the counter to bend forward at her waist. She dropped her head, stretching out her back. *"Poquito siesta por moi."*

It was 8:30 in the morning. She couldn't have been awake for more than an hour.

"Okay, you nap," I said. "And then I'll call Tucker for you."

"That sounds like a lovely idea," Smidge murmured. She must have been tired, as her voice hadn't been that sweet to me in a while. She was looking around the kitchen as if trying to determine which countertop would provide the most comfort.

I eased a gentle arm around her waist. Smidge folded herself into it, dropping against me. She fit so perfectly into my curves you could almost hear the *click*. Careful not to go anywhere near her bruise, I slowly walked her toward the couch.

Just as easily, we could have been back in college, Smidge coming home too late and too drunk as I guided her toward her future hangover, foot over foot. We could have been twenty. We could have been thirty. We could have been in Costa Rica drunk on what we thought was a mixed drink that turned out to be pure tequila. We could have been walking Smidge as we did when she was in labor. We'd been here so many times.

But this time, we were almost thirty-six and headed toward a couch so Smidge could nap before most people had finished their first cup of coffee.

It was too early to call Tucker, but I'd already picked the skin around my fingernails and chewed off the inside of my bottom lip. I needed to find something else to distract me. I turned to the internet, where hours can pass like seconds, when one question leads to ten answers and paths you couldn't possibly predict.

This is when I did something I'm not exactly proud of, but I would never take back.

I read through Smidge's cache. I clicked every website she'd gone through recently. If she wouldn't tell me what was going on with her, I'd let her internet history give me some answers.

She'd searched *non-small-cell lung cancer* and *adenocarcinoma*.

She'd searched *metastasizing*.

I selected pages at random and dove in.

*"Lung cancer is the leading cause of cancer deaths in women, and the second-highest cause of all deaths in the United States."*

I was looking for answers, not facts. I wanted the loophole, the excuse, the way out, the reason this wasn't one of those numbers. That *she* wasn't like all the others. How her cancer was different.

*"Almost a third of lung cancer patients never smoked, and one in five women with lung cancer never smoked."*

I felt like I was groping through darkness, clicking from one bleak page to the next. If Smidge had read all of this, no wonder she had no hope. No wonder she was past all this and on to her plans for what would happen after she was gone.

*"Survival rate hasn't improved in decades."*

*"Not enough funding."*

*"Not enough answers."*

After an hour of letting one page take me to another, I could tell you that her adenocarcinoma probably started in tissue of the outer parts of her lung, that it might have taken a long time to develop, and she probably didn't feel the tumor growing. Eighty percent of lung cancers are non-small-cell lung cancers like hers, and it's the most common lung cancer to affect women, often in nonsmokers. The survival rate can be good, but when it recurs, as Smidge's had, and spreads outside the lung (they call that "metastasizing"), the survival rate is about the same amount as my dear friend's nickname.

*"If you've never known someone with lung cancer, it's because they didn't make it."*

I got to where I could spell *adenocarcinoma* without checking. I could tell you that it is the most common type of lung cancer in people under the age of forty-five and the most common type of lung cancer among all Asians.

I became the equivalent of a human search engine with what was killing my best friend, but I couldn't find anywhere in the whole wide Web or world that could tell me how to make it stop.

Needless to say, by the time you skipped into the kitchen, I was grateful for the interruption. You didn't notice me, as you had earbuds in and you were bopping around to some song, having just come back from a jog around the neighborhood. Your skin was a refreshingly youthful pink, rosy and glistening with sweat. The back of your shorts and halter bra were damp and you were light on your feet in running socks with small white balls at the heel. Now that we'd bleached everything on your head back to blond, and cut the longer half, you found a way to wear your hair pushed back with a silver headband.

Your back was to me as you took a long gulp straight from the milk carton. Where you once had chicken pox, now you had hips. You had definition in your arms; perspiration had collected beneath your breasts, pooling in the curve of your lower back—you had lost the allover shine and stink of a kid.

You spotted me as you closed the refrigerator door. "Stare much, pedo?" You grinned, pulling your earbuds out by the cord. "I want food."

I took you to the Office, our nickname for Waffle House since you were six, when you declared it to be the best restaurant in the world, so much so that you planned on working there as soon as you grew up.

"I will be head waffler," you proudly proclaimed that day. "And they're going to put my picture over the door and start calling waffles 'Jenny Squares.'"

"Aim higher, darlin'," your mother had said.

I argued with Smidge that getting people to change what they call a waffle seemed a rather lofty goal.

We threw one of your birthday parties there. I flew in for it once I found out that they were going to let us replace one of the songs on the jukebox with "Jenny Squares," a number Henry had commissioned Sweet & Lowe to write. They played that tune at The Pantry for years after. They might still play it, for all I know. I can't go back to The Pantry. Have you been there? Do they still do the Smidget Special on Tuesdays?

We sat at the booth closest to the griddles so you could guess which part of our order would arrive first. You were never wrong.

"Here come your hash browns," you said, and within fifteen seconds they were placed in front of me, long before my eggs or bacon would arrive, in typical Waffle House fashion. Food comes strictly on a this-part-is-finished-cooking basis.

You hovered over an overbuttered piece of toast with two hands, your wrists bent inward, shoulders hunched forward, as if everything was just so much heavier when you are thirteen.

Suddenly I felt, for the first time in my life, completely uncool. You were sitting there with your distant stare and your weighted toast and I just couldn't compete. All of me was lame, every part. I was like your dorky aunt with a pilly sweater and a cat-shaped purse, someone who says things like "You'll understand when you're older," and asks unimportant, time-filling questions like "How's school?"

It was one thing to be intimidated by your mother. I knew why she could get inside my head and make me question myself. But to be nervous around you, to feel as awkward as the new girl by your locker, it threw me off. How could you have that much power and at the same time not care even slightly that you had it? Your lack of concern only made you stronger.

I found myself treating you like you were a sunglasses-wearing celebrity, and I was on your press junket. Despite desperately searching for topics, all I could think to do was compliment your shirt and ask if your food was good, working hard to keep myself from fawning: *What's it like to be so cool?*

"You guys weren't gone for very long," you noted while making brief eye contact, letting me know you were searching for information. I wasn't about to bend.

"I know." I craned my head back as if I needed something that wasn't just a change of subject. I asked, "How's school?"

*Dammit.*

You shrugged. "Why do people always ask that?"

"I know, right?" I said. "What is that, exactly? *School.* That's a lot of things. Classes. Teachers. Other people. After-school activities."

You busied yourself studying that bread you still hadn't eaten, staring at it like there was something to read across the front. Finally you chose to pull at a crust corner, breaking off a crumb to lick from your thumb. Your voice rose as you asked, "I mean, what is the *deal* with *school*? Eggs."

The waitress dropped a plate of eggs in front of me.

"Are you making fun of me?" I asked. "Did you just do a *Seinfeld* impression?"

"Yes, I am making fun of you, and I've seen that show. It's only on a million times a day, even though it's old."

"It's not old," I snapped.

"Old like you."

*"How's school?"*

"It sucks."

"How are things going with that boy you shaved your head for?"

"Bacon." You reached across the table to snatch a piece before the waitress finished placing it in front of me. "What's going on with my mom? She's been weird lately."

"Oh, you know your mom. She's just being your mom." I added a quick, "I bet they forgot your biscuit."

You had something on me. You knew it, even though you didn't know what it was you had yet. But you knew I was stammering for a reason. You slowly, deliberately, placed your chin into your right palm, settling in for a good, long stare.

It was my turn to examine toast. "A little burned," I meekly stated.

*I will not get itchy. I will not turn red. I will not let this child smoke me out. I will not remember the time she got me to accidentally tell her what she was getting for Christmas. I will not think about the time she got Henry to admit he was the Tooth Fairy. I will not—*

"Your eggs are getting cold," I said.

"So are yours," you countered, pointing toward my stomach, referring to the eggs *inside* my body. "At least, that's what I hear."

"Jennifer Cooperton!" I gasped as I placed my hands protectively over my hips, sheltering my ovaries from such insulting talk. "You are not nice."

"Mom told me how you're thinking of having a kid. Adopting? I don't know, I was only half listening. Did you catch baby fever? Is it because you're old? Is that what happens?"

I found a way to close my mouth before I spoke again. "Your mother thinks she's being funny. She wants me to have a family. A husband. A kid. The whole shebang."

You pushed your eggs into a pool of ketchup, rotating them until they were coated red. "*Tsh,* I don't want a baby. Or a husband." You continued to torture your food as you added, "Never ever."

"Why not?" I signaled for the check, intending to keep the conversation firmly fixed on you for the rest of our time there.

"Because it basically destroys your life. You never get to be what you want to be."

"What if you want to be a mom?"

"Then I hope I also want to kill myself, because that's what I'd rather do first."

I rolled my eyes. "You might think differently when you're older."

That's when you sneered.

But what else was I supposed to say to you? I knew I was saying all these things that people say to younger people, and I never thought I'd be this person, that I'd resort to these stock phrases, but also it was the truth. Not *my* truth, but some people's truth.

I could have told you about women I'd known who swore they'd never have kids but then met the right man or woman and from that second on all they wanted to do was stuff their house full of children and toys and pets and become a huge group of people who share the same last name and get discounts at amusement parks, who enjoy taking vacations in RVs and "roughing it" out in the woods, who gather around a worn-in sectional sofa to watch "their shows," who have game nights and compost piles in the backyard next to their chicken coops even though they live in a major city.

But I'd never related to those women, I didn't know how to communicate with them when it came to daily life, as mine never involved cutting up food for another person to eat, or wiping the butt of any living creature, including a cat. I wasn't convinced that you were wrong, honestly, but I felt like I wasn't supposed to give you that kind of life advice. I was really worried that anything I said would change your life permanently, and any stripping or pole dancing in your future could be traced squarely back to something I said to you.

"You're right, Jenny. I'm sorry. I won't ask you again how school is or tell you what it'll be like when you're older, because who the fuck knows."

I didn't mean to curse at you, but it brought you back to my side a little, like we'd shared a secret. You liked that your age suddenly didn't seem to matter, even though I knew it was the only thing I was thinking about. Your lunch had become a mess of swirled condiments and uneaten foods. Neither of us had had much of an appetite, for very different reasons.

"Thank you," you said. "I appreciate it."

"It's just that you could grow up to be a serial killer," I said. "And if that happens, I really don't think you should have kids."

"When I'm a serial killer I'll share my baby with you," you said. "We'll raise him together and make the worst baby in the world."

We shook on it.

## FOURTEEN

I decided to send Tucker a text rather than risk getting tangled up in a phone call. I let him know that Smidge had requested he find something to do with Henry, preferably a task involving heavy labor.

Within seconds I received his reply: *R u her assistant now 2?*

I craddled my stomach as I decided to ignore his text bait.

A pain had started in my gut, a burning just underneath my breastbone. It might have been anxiety, or it could have been Waffle House; I assumed it was a combination of both.

There was no response from the Lizard, but there were three messages from potential new clients, all referrals, asking about my availability. I wrote back asking if they could elaborate on what they were looking for, what brought them to me. It was a stall, but I needed a chance to figure out just how long I had before I absolutely had to be back in LA.

An e-mail from Lindsay Waters, a former client who was so high maintenance I ended up charging her extra just to keep myself from ditching her, caught my eye.

Subject line, all caps: *PLEASE URGANT NEED YOUR HELP!*

A married mother of two, Lindsay Waters ran a successful public relations business that focused on the music industry. She drove a car that cost more than most people's homes. Her actual home cost more than what people would consider an amazing lottery jackpot. Waxed, buffed, tanned, and coiffed, she had transformed herself into an image of a woman so perfect she was intimidating. She must have been, as I can't imagine how else a forty-six-year-old businesswoman could get that far in life without ever using a comma or knowing how to correctly spell the word *urgent*.

The e-mail was peppered with similar atrocities, apostrophes slicing into words where they had no business, a seemingly random system of capitalization when it came to verbs, and a newly invented word I vehemently disliked: *skutch*. I had to read it aloud before I could ascertain she was trying to describe "a small amount."

What was so "urgent" to Lindsay Waters was something about a diet she read about in a magazine, one that forbid wheat, sugar, and "diary."

I quickly scrolled through her included list of dietary restrictions before I finally reached the part of her e-mail that described her actual problem, which was filled with problems of its own: "Who should be in charge of cooking meals, or is it time to hire a cook and if yes than which budget should that come from—FOOD or labor?"

My stomach cramped again. I braced myself with one arm while I debated my reply. Just over a month ago this letter wouldn't have been much more than an amusing series of grammatical errors, one I would've forwarded to Smidge before launching directly into a helpful response. Her oldest son's food allergies would be foremost in my mind as I cheerfully suggested a few ways to incorporate her new diet into the family's daily life. I'd know the state of her finances enough that I wouldn't even have to go through my files. Her question answered and sent, I'd then record a billable hour into my ledger and go on about my day.

But as I sat practically folded in half trying to keep my insides from poking through to my outsides, thinking about what I used to call my life before this forced sabbatical, it was becoming clear that everything I was doing was absurd.

I am a woman who's never had to put a plate of food in front of a child, and there I was instructing a successful businesswoman how to arrange her finances in such a way that she could put her family on a diet. For the record, the last thing anybody in the Waters family needed was calorie restriction. You could line them all up fingertip to fingertip and they could still fit through a door while holding hands. The youngest girl was recently bragging about fitting into a pair of double-zero jeans.

Lindsay craved the appearance of control, and needed to be on the cusp of the "everywhere topic." She liked it when she could use the same words other women used when she was around them. *Diet, gluten,* and *playdate* were keywords of real mothers, the right kind, the ones who got to be labeled "mommies." Competent females who push the correct strollers, wear the same layers of expensive casual wear, who were never without a scarf or glittery flip-flops. Their thousand-dollar bags were filled with ziplock baggies of snacks, and designer-wrapped Kindles. Lindsay needed help to hang with the A-list mommy set, but it was imperative that she appear to be doing it with no help whatsoever.

When I first came into her life, the Waterses were two months behind on their mortgage. A warrant had been issued for her husband because of unpaid parking tickets. Their garage was filled with boxes and unopened postal bags from online clothing stores. After less than six weeks with me, they had a plan for their money, a schedule for their lives, and I got them to stop letting their eldest use the master bedroom. They'd had a lot of guilt about not being able to buy him a car, or pay for the college he wanted. He took advantage of that.

When I was faced with that kind of challenge I would often think, *What would Smidge say to these people?* Then the answers would come easily. I'd take whatever I heard in my head and tried to give the same advice in a much more tactful manner.

I told Lindsay and her husband that they had to think of themselves as the landlords of their home, and decide how their tenants should behave when they live rent-free. The rules should be simple: they pay for room and board through chores, giving back to the community, being decent individuals who don't scream or leave wet towels on the hallway floor.

Because of my website's popularity, I've sometimes been asked if I've thought about having my own talk show or self-help book. I know I'm not pretty enough for TV, or disciplined enough to write hundreds of pages. Besides, I don't claim to save lives. I'm merely the sanity police. My job is to come in and restore things when people are so blinded by their own guilt and selfishness that they no longer know how to operate a coffeemaker. Mostly I urge them out of their self-sabotaging behavior before they start blaming the universe for their problems. Not fixing a broken car leads to people needing to share a car, which leads to gas problems and people being late, and suddenly that person's asking, "Why did I get fired?"

I started out this business wanting to be helpful, and there are times when I know I've made a family get back on track, or saved the sanity of one overwhelmed woman who felt pressure to do it all, but more and more I was getting questions like "Can you teach me how to make a blog where I say interesting things?" or "If I wanted to throw a party with only yellow items, can you please give me a list of stores that sell yellow party things?" I don't feel great that I know the answer to the question about yellow party store items, but I do. I somehow became an expert on keeping up appearances. And because I *also* needed to look like I could do it all, I answered those questions, the ones I originally was trying to eliminate. I answered the dumbest questions. I even answered the ones that might have been questionable in taste.

A client asked me to write a letter to her husband, letting him know she was ready to start scheduling sex appointments so that she no longer felt uncomfortable when her girlfriends would gossip at brunch. She was the only one of her friends who was not having as much sex, and she wanted to publicly announce, through this third party that was me, that it was no longer okay.

The article generated a small flurry of activity, which helped with my ad revenue, but it changed things after that.

I wasn't running a website about families getting organized. It was a place where people could gossip about fad diets and whose kids were too skinny and whose weren't skinny enough. I quit checking my comments section when I saw the same few who would start feuds every day. I stopped so that I could pretend it wasn't happening, because I knew the bigger the flame war, the more clicks my site had. Those clicks allowed me to drop everything and go to Smidge's side for an undetermined period of time.

Part of what had happened to my website was my fault, but part of it was the culture. Yes, it was important to get everything right, but there was way more pressure to rub it in everyone's faces. Perfect pictures of kids, perfect table settings, perfect parties, perfect manicures. You get caught up in the cycle of the perception of effortless perfection and can't jump off that speeding train.

Your mother didn't want off that train. Mostly because she was the conductor.

It occurs to me only now that at no point did I debate telling Smidge's story as a way to make money. I normally didn't get through a day without wondering at least five times, "Is there an entry in this? Is there money to be made here?" When my existence became a commodity, I had to start thinking of my waking moments as potential income. But with Smidge, she was always my secret. My hidden family. She wasn't something I wanted to share.

Smidge had let only me in on her biggest secret, which was more power than anybody else had ever given me in my life. That made what we were doing—however uncomfortable and undefined it was at that moment—more important than anything Lindsay Waters could find so *urgant*.

I wanted to write back, *If this is truly your biggest problem right now, why don't you go hug your kids, kiss your husband, and thank whatever god you believe in that your life is pretty sweet? And PS: use spell-check. It's literally the least you could do.*

But I didn't. Instead I scrolled through my e-mail, searching for any sign that I might have missed from the Lizard. There was nothing. I tried again, writing: "Hi. Please contact me. It's important. It's about your daughter."

"Hey."

At the sound of Smidge's voice, I turned, dropping my phone. Smidge stood in the doorframe, dark circles under her eyes, a sleep line cutting across the left side of her face like she had been maimed in her sleep.

"Hey." I exhaled. "Sorry. You scared me."

"I slept for seven hours!" she complained. "This whole day is almost gone!"

"I guess you needed sleep," I said, retrieving my phone from the floor. For the first time in the decades I had known Smidge, I saw dog hair on the tile. There was an unswept Cheerio. *This* was the biggest sign that she was not okay.

"I had the longest dream." She absently scratched at her knee. "I need you to promise me that when you take over my life you'll give to charity every month. In the dream, Mark Wahlberg was there and he told me that since I never help people in need, that's why I'm dying. I did everything right, but I didn't think about those less fortunate. Now I am less fortunate, and Mark Wahlberg hates me. Which is kind of the most upsetting part."

"Did you tell Jenny I was trying to have a baby?"

Your mother liked to stall by fluffing her hair with her nails. *Fluff, fluff, fluff,* getting her curls to spring around her head like she could Medusa me out of the conversational topic. "No," she said as she worked up a combination of excuse and lie. "I said you were fixing to have a family and you were freaking out about it. I said the truth, so you can't be mad."

"That sounds like I'm pregnant."

"Pregnant with Old Jenny. That's what I'm calling her now, since she's a million years old and swings those wide lady hips of hers like a go-go dancer."

My stomach stung again, sharply, this time. I shoved the heel of my right hand under my rib cage and bent forward, my head between my knees.

"What's going on with you?" she asked.

"Nothing. Stress. I want to know more about what's going on with you," I said. "Medically."

"You don't need to know these things. I know these things. My doctor knows these things."

"Okay, you're seeing a doctor! That's news to me."

"I did need one to tell me I have cancer. It's not like I peed on a stick in my bathroom. Although that would've been much cheaper."

"Can I talk to him?"

"*Her.* And no."

"Why not?"

"Because why does it matter?"

I want a reason to know everything I already know about her cancer. I need her to give me just enough information so that I can justify the amount of internet research I've already done.

"Because I want to *do* something," I said. "I've been here for weeks now and other than rolling your sheets into balls and unsuccessfully grounding your daughter, I really don't feel like anything has happened."

"Okay, then. Now you're talking." She nodded, folding her arms across her chest. "Get dressed. We've got some errands to run."

I looked down to make sure I wasn't mistaken. But there I was, in a pair of jeans and a T-shirt. Shoes, even. "I *am* dressed," I said. "These are clothes."

"Wear something *nicer*," she said, backing out of the room. "I'll meet you at the door in ten." Then, as usual, just when I thought she was finished, she added, "Lipstick, too! And fix your hayir."

The bank was our first stop, to add me to her accounts. This meant letting me in on a secret: Smidge had multiple accounts, ones Henry didn't know about.

"It's funny that he doesn't know about this money, because he's the reason I even know how to save in the first place. He taught me. He said we needed to set a good example for Jenny, that ATMs aren't unlimited resources on the corner, like a water fountain at a park."

"Money faucets."

"Exactly. *Sooooooo,* sometimes I get money and I don't need to be telling everybody, especially my husband." She stared suspiciously at the bank representative as he clicked away from behind his monitor, like he was entering our dialogue into the public record.

"I don't understand why you need me on this account,"
I said. "Won't the money just go to Henry after you . . ." I
stopped myself, stammered into silence. "Can we have a code
word?" I pleaded. "I can't use the real word for what's going to
happen to you."

"Yes, well, I'm sorry to be straining your emotions," Smidge
said, patting my arm wearily, with as much condescension as
she could muster. "You're right; it's just so thoughtless of me.
Where are my manners?"

"Smidge, I'm trying. I really am. But I am *messed up*. We're
at the bank, and you are signing your secret money account
over to me. Why are you doing this?"

"Marsala."

"What?"

"The code word. For what's happening to me. *Marsala*."

"Why that word?"

"I think it's real pretty." She grabbed my fingertips and
gave them a tug. "As for the money, consider it your inheritance. No: it's your paycheck. All this should come with
a salary. Lord knows I would've liked getting paid for this job
over the years. Okay, so you're getting a husband, a daughter,
and a savings account worth thirty-five thousand dollars. You
have to admit: you can't say I didn't leave you anything, after
I marsala."

"As if there will be anything left after I pay off all the secret
credit cards I bet you have."

There was only the slightest of pauses before Smidge re-
sponded with "Touché."

As she finished signing the last form she told me, "We have
plans tonight."

"We have plans? You and me?"

"You, me, Tucker, and the horndog also known as my husband," she said. "Let's get Henry trashed enough so he'll go right to sleep."

"We're going out? Like with drinking?"

"Yep, and I am all rested up for it. Fifteen hours of sleep will do that to you. Jenny's going to a friend's house until late, so it's grown-up night. Promise me you'll do your hayir."

"I did my hair before we came to the bank! This is done hair!"

"Oh, Danny," Smidge said, scrunching her face so that one side of her mouth dropped to meet her chin, "I was worried you were going to say that."

After the bank and a pickup at the dry cleaner, Smidge stopped the car without warning. I hadn't been paying attention to the road, so I was unprepared to be sitting in front of Serenity Hilltop, the "fancy cemetery," as it's known in Odgen. People with money or even a slight modicum of fame find their way to spend eternity there. You have to *apply*. Whenever a new body is laid to rest, the entire town comes out. It's quite the event.

"I'll handle all the arrangements," she said as I stared through the passenger-side window at the imposing green hill peppered with hundreds of gray memorials. "I know I can get up here."

I tried to imagine myself soon standing on that hill, wearing black, weeping into a handkerchief. The whole thing still felt completely detached from my real life, like someone was describing the dream they'd had the night before.

*It was crazy. Smidge had died, and she had somehow finagled to get herself buried at Serenity Hilltop, and you were there in this amazing black dress, holding Jenny's hand and crying. And then a giraffe was getting buried in the next plot, and Smidge jumped out of her coffin and yelled at the giraffe for ruining her special day. It seemed so real at the time.*

"Why are you smiling?" Smidge asked as she whacked me in the back of the head.

"You'd be so mad if a giraffe tried to get buried here next to you."

Smidge puffed her lips in exasperation. "Focus, please. And get out of the car."

"Why?"

"Because it's happy hour."

Within minutes Smidge had set up a makeshift picnic on the lawn in front of the car. She was careful to have us sit where we'd be hidden from the main road or the welcome booth, so as not to get caught sipping the mini-martinis she had quickly shaken for us.

"That car cooler is the best idea I've ever had," she said after taking her first, slow gulp.

"Am I driving home?"

"Relax. I've got some water, and we ain't going nowhere for a while. You can't stop me from having a martini every afternoon at five. That's my new thing and I love it, so you can suck it if you think you can change that one."

The afternoon drink was a welcome change. I kicked off my shoes and stretched my toes into the soft grass. It was only once I leaned back onto my elbows that I noticed we were having our happy hour beside the tombstone of *HARRIET WEINERS 1902–1975, Beloved Mother, Grandmother, Devoted Wife, "GOD NEVER MAKES MISTAKES."*

"Is this weird?" I asked.

Smidge grabbed the martini glass out of my hand and tipped it forward until a small stream dribbled over the edge. "Here you go, Harriet." She handed it back. "Better now?"

"I do feel better, yes."

I raised my martini toward the hill in a cemetery-wide toast before taking another sip.

Smidge scoffed. "'God never makes mistakes.' Ain't that some bullshit? First of all, God gave some people the last name Weiners."

I dropped onto my back, lowered my sunglasses, and closed my eyes. Doves politely cooed overhead. The nearby bushes hummed with insect activity, the cicadas busy making their unmistakable throbbing pulse of a rattle.

*"Oooooooookay,"* Smidge sang as she plopped beside me, close enough that one of her elbows dug into the flesh of my left arm. The crinkle of paper in my ear forced my eyes open.

"What are you doing?"

"I told you there was a list," she said, unfolding a sheet of loose-leaf paper. She paused, staring at me curiously, and then slapped me across the neck.

"Urgh!" I choked out, clutching my throat. "Why?"

"Mosquito," she said, lowering her reading glasses onto her nose. "Now." Her accent made her sound like a cat: *"Ne-ow."*

"That hurt!"

She kissed the palm of her hand and rubbed it across my neck. "There," she said. "All better. Now remember these two words." She interrupted herself with a short cough. "*Bort* with a zero, *Jennifer* with a one," she continued. "The numbers are vowels." She coughed again, shaking her head.

I rolled over to my side. "Are you giving me your passwords?"

"Yes. Bort is also my PIN number, but when in doubt I probably used Jenny's name. Vowels are numbers."

"I can't believe you use *bort*."

"I thought you'd like that. I've had a lot of the same passwords since college. They make me think of you and how much I love you. Since I love you the mostest."

Bort stood for "bitch on red time," which was short for *I'm not nice this time of the month, and won't be for another three to five days.* Smidge and I started using it back when we were roommates this one morning when Smidge was angrily trying to call me both a *bitch* and a *jerk*, but it came out *bort*.

"I'm not done making all the funeral arrangements here, but when it happens I'll have written everything down for you. It's going to be a really nice ceremony, Danny. I'm sorry to be missing it. Take pictures."

She told me to convince Henry to buy a storefront for his furniture business, using the money from the life insurance policies she'd already taken out.

"The rest of the money goes to Jenny's college fund," she said. "Make sure she goes to undergrad, and don't let her waste time in grad school. It's just stalling real life."

Smidge's list was front and back on that page, and while she rattled off items like we were grocery shopping, I noticed her hands were trembling. She paused for a moment to cough, but blamed the fit on allergies.

"My half-a-lung shouldn't be rolling around in this grass," she said.

"Should we get back in the car? It's pretty hot out here."

"Speaking of the car. It's a piece of junk. Trash it. Don't let Henry keep you driving it like he did me. Tell him it makes you think about me and cry, whatever guilts him into letting you get a new one."

"I have a car, actually. Back in Los Angeles, remember?"

"Hunh," she said, as if she really had forgotten that I used to have my own life. "I guess you could use that one," she reasoned. "If you could get it out here."

"Well, *thanks.*"

"I'm serious about you making sure this family gives to charity every month. And on that note: start going to church. I was bad about it, and now I've got cancer, so do what the Lord says."

I'd never gone to church. It wouldn't even occur to me to think about going to church, unless someone was getting married or buried.

I said, "This part is where you're just testing me, right? This part's the joke?"

"I keep having these dreams, these realizations. My perspective has changed. You'll know what I mean once you're dying. *Which will happen.*"

"You mean you have regrets?"

This was a potential breakthrough moment for Smidge. If she could admit she'd made mistakes, perhaps we could veer toward the mistakes she was actively making, the ones involving me, cancer treatment, or the future of her family.

"I should've made sure people saw me in church. Because now here I am trying to prove I'm good enough to get my bones stuffed into this hill." She lowered her reading glasses and sighed into her chest. "Always make sure other people think you're better than you are, Danny. Your real life doesn't matter; only the one they imagine for you. You'll never actually live the life jealous people can dream up, but you can try to live up to it."

"Sounds like you've had a real spiritual awakening."

"Actually, I have," she said, staring into the distance. The fading sun set the wisps of her chestnut hair into a golden halo. "The world looks different to me now. I have answers to things I forgot I was pondering. I hear more, you know? Like I can really hear the insects in the trees. I can feel the air between us. Our connection, our pull to this planet." She drained the last of her martini and said, "*Now* I'm just messing with you."

"I assumed," I said, unfazed.

"But you still need to go to church. And not just any church, not some *we're more into the message than the man* church or whatever fake, dippy, barely legal, Bible-bendy church that's more of a glorified book club. You have to go to the one Daddy went to. You go to Second Baptist."

I pushed myself up onto my knees in protest. "No, Smidge, that place gives me the creeps. It's so big and there's so many people."

"Exactly. You aren't really at roll call unless people who judge you can see you. And the judgiest of Ogden worship over at Second Baptist. You take my family there, and for good measure you wear one of those giant hats. Raise your hand up and testify every once in a while, like my aunt Elsie used to. Be superchurchy."

"Please, Smidge. Don't do this to me. I will get hives."

"Don't think I won't be able to spy on you with my ghost eyes, so if you're not there I will know."

She continued through her list, moving into the "Do this or I'll haunt you" section. I was to make sure Dr. Phil went to the vet at least twice a year, that I renewed Henry's prescriptions, and purchased a real purse. "Not some kind of hobo bag like you're the crazy lady on the bus. No more contrasting patterns, or I will haunchoo."

Other things that would send Ghost Smidge into my life included letting her daughter try out for dance brigade. "She can be a cheerleader if she really wants to do something jumpy and popular, but there's no way in hell you can let her join the Whore Corps."

"It might be different from when we went to Neville."

"I will haunchoo!"

"Fine."

She may have been berating me, but she was also holding my hand. Her skin felt dry and thin. Her engagement ring, no longer perched atop her wedding band at the center of her finger, had loosened and dropped to the side. The diamond pressed against her pinkie like it was seeking shelter.

"If you let my veggie garden rot or get taken over by the squirrels, guess what will happen."

"You're saying you'll haunt—"

"Haunchoo!"

I practically dove headfirst into the bathtub once we got back to the house. I wanted to use my allotted extra "hair time" to decompress.

As the water splashed across my aching stomach, I thought about how this plan had already gone on longer than I could have ever thought possible. More unbelievable was how it was starting to feel real. I was actually thinking about how I'd handle carrying out Smidge's wishes, picturing myself in her house, sitting with her family at church. Although I confess I probably wouldn't be too overly concerned with the purse I carried.

Smidge hadn't once asked for my own opinions on how to run her house smoothly, so if it had nothing to do with my skills as a domestic consultant, why should I even be involved? Couldn't Henry handle these things on his own? Renew his own prescriptions. Take his own daughter to Second Baptist. Make sure the rosemary is trimmed back. Promise never to use soap on the cast-iron skillet.

A cold blast hit me as the bathroom door opened. Before I could say or do much more than splash and screech, as if I'd just summoned him myself, Henry was standing above me, eyes widened in terror. "Oh!" he shouted, his voice high and ladylike, his fingers covering his eyes in honest shock.

"I'm in here!" I shouted, which was the most obvious statement I could have made at that particular time.

"I'm sorry!" Trying to leave, he accidentally slammed the

door into his own forehead, which made him have to open the door once again, only to see me sitting up in confusion. If he hadn't seen me naked the first time, he certainly got to see quite a bit on the second showing, before successfully closing the bathroom door with him on the other side of it.

I slapped the bathwater with my hand. "Henry!"

After a few seconds I heard his mumble. "You should lock that," he said.

"I did!"

"The lock is broken, it would seem."

"Yes, I suppose it would seem that!"

As I pulled the stopper from the drain I could hear Smidge's delighted peals of laughter through the walls.

The next time that door opened, Smidge leaned in wearing a green spaghetti-strap dress under a black cardigan. Her hair pulled high atop her head and secured with a white flowered barrette, she was beautiful—exactly as tragically beautiful as she would've wanted it to be if only everybody knew how sick she was. I am sure it bothered her that she wasn't able to milk her frailty for maximum sympathy.

"Smidge!" I said, not equipped with enough hands or limbs to cover everything I needed to hide from her view. I finished wrapping myself in a towel, wondering why I even bothered with modesty.

"That is the funniest thing I've ever heard!" she said, stopping only to make an actual hooting sound. "Henry!" Smidge shouted down the hall. "Come back, she's out! Now you can see the rest of her! Not just a titty preview!"

"Why can't you be a normal sick lady who wanders around

in a blanket asking for soup?" I hissed before I slammed the door in her face.

Her response came muffled but cocksure.

"You love me."

Forty-five minutes later I was sliding a pair of oxblood heels onto my feet, waiting alone in the kitchen. From the other room I could hear the murmur of Smidge fidgeting with Henry's clothes.

"Don't tuck that in, why would you tuck that in? It's dinner, not your mama's house after a funeral."

Henry entered the kitchen a few minutes later, head down as he finished buttoning his cuffs. His hair was still damp, swirled, and pushed into dark blond tufts that would relax once they dried into his composed, thick tousle. A heavy cloud of woodsy cologne followed him as he passed, and I found myself hit with an unexpected and sudden ache for a male counterpart.

From the living room, I could hear your mother saying good-bye to you, forcing you to do Odd Hugs and promise to be home before curfew. I heard the heavy slam of the front door as you left.

Henry limped around the kitchen on one shoe, searching for the other. I saw it peeking around the corner in the other room. He busied himself, rustling through the kitchen drawers, pulling one open before closing the last. Utensils rattled and clanked as the junk drawers sprang open like impatient jack-in-the-boxes.

"I need a shoehorn," he muttered.

I spotted one in the drawer he'd left open closest to me.

"Here," I said.

As I went to hand him the tortoiseshell tool, he simultane-ously reached back to grab it, misjudging the distance be-tween us. The next thing I knew his hand was jammed in the crook between my upper arm and my right breast.

"Jesus Christ." He spun on his one shoed heel and marched out of the room.

"It's okay!" I weakly shouted after him. I'm still surprised he didn't faint with all that blood rushing to his head.

Smidge danced in, humming. "This is all good," she said, pointing with two fingers at my black dress, my hair pulled back into a high ponytail, my heels. She flipped up my hem, flirtatiously. "Dig them stems, missy."

"Thanks. Your husband just accidentally touched my boob."

She smirked, squinting. "Maybe no accident. That man can't resist an off-the-shoulder dress. He was probably aiming for the other side where you're more naked."

"It is weird, what you are doing. You know that, right?"

"What, teasing you?"

"No, acting like you're setting me up with—" I stopped myself, lowering my voice to a furious whisper. "Like he's not your husband."

Smidge hopped herself onto the counter so that she was sitting eye level with me. Her legs in the space between us, her bare knees grazed my stomach. We were close enough so that I could see where her eyeliner was smudged. She had one false eyelash coming loose from its adhesive, curling upward.

She licked her lips, top then bottom, like she was choosing her words carefully. "I don't know why I can't get this through to you, Danielle," she said, her voice trembling around the edges of her words. "So let me try one more time. I know what I'm doing. I know why I'm doing it. And I know this is best. So if you want things to go more easily, *get on it*."

"I just think—"

"Stop. Thinking." Her lips had gone thin with frustration. "You want me to cry every day and *woe-is-me* in my bed until the tumor gets big enough to fill my throat? You want to wait until I can't jump or move or lift my arms? You want to wait until it's too late? Or do you want to do me a favor, act like someone who is supposed to love me, and just *get on it*. Suck it up and deal."

My tongue felt like it had turned into a lump of damp paper shreds. A useless, aimless pulp. I meekly nodded as my stomach shot a fierce bullet of pain into my sternum.

"Sorry," I managed to stammer.

"I've been giving you a little while to grieve and whatnot, but it's go-time now, okay? No more whining like you wet your pants."

"You sound like your dad."

"Good. That man knew how to make me do what he wanted." She rocked back and forth on the counter with hands on her hips like a cowboy. She pretended to have a wad of tobacco tucked in her cheek, transforming herself into the perfect image of Mr. Carlton from the waist up. "Now *yew* be a good *gurl* and *git on it*."

"I miss your dad."

"I'll tell him you said hi."

# FIFTEEN

We were overdressed for the wet mess of crawfish dumped onto our table, but nobody minded. Sometimes it was nice to look fancy while being busy with your hands. The four of us sat in silence as we focused on ripping the boiled red crustaceans in half, pausing to suck their briny heads before shredding their crunchy legs to the table. A final pinch to the tail revealed sweet, white meat. The process was time-consuming and labor-intensive to the newcomer, but we were like an experienced knitting circle, heads down, fingers working, pausing only for the occasional sips of beer or an appreciative grunt before taking a bite of spice-rubbed corn on the cob.

No one was quieter than Henry, who had refused to meet my eyes since our bathtub encounter. His discomfort seemed worsened by what became the topic of conversation. Me. Tucker asked questions ranging in scope from something as broad as my neighborhood back in Los Angeles, to something as minute as my plans for Monday. Often before I could respond, Smidge would interrupt to answer for me, but direct it toward Henry.

"Isn't that interesting, Henry? Danielle's neighborhood in Los Angeles just got a new bakery." Like I was their foreign exchange student, or more accurately, was on an extremely awkward and terribly inappropriate first date.

I kicked at her under the wooden table, hoping she'd get the message that she needed to lay off, but she chose to ignore me.

"Maybe you could show her how good you make biscuits, Henry. Since Danielle doesn't have Monday plans."

I kicked again, this time finding her shin.

"That's a bruise," she said quite loudly.

I stopped, but my brain continued the violence.

Once Henry excused himself to the bathroom, Tucker took the opportunity to snatch his seat, sliding up next to me, his elbow resting against mine. Even though his white shirtsleeves were rolled to his elbow, he had damp spots in the fabric from where he was careless. A smear of copper-colored sauce in the shape of a thumbprint marked his collar.

"I just wanted to make sure you knew how pretty you look tonight," Tucker said.

"You are hitting on me," I informed him.

"Barely. And that's only because I'm a little bored. Why don't you do something interesting?"

"How's this?" I asked, and then tossed the remains of a crawfish exoskeleton at his face. It hit his cheek with a satisfying pop before he batted it aside.

Tucker laughed. "Feisty. What else do you want to throw at me tonight?" He slurred slightly as he leaned into me, bumping my shoulder with his own. "Can I make a few suggestions? A request?"

"You get forward when you're drunk," I said. "I don't remember that. Is that new?"

"About as new as your divorce, darlin'." He leaned in for a wedge of potato. "I'm just playing," he said. "You can stop looking like I served cat shit to the queen."

Suddenly my shin exploded in pain. My eyes locked with Smidge's. She was shaking her head like she just caught me licking the inside of her cookie jar, her dagger eyes trying to stare-stab me back into submission.

"That's a bruise," I said as I pressed my palm against the throbbing in my leg.

Henry returned to the table with an announcement. "It seems I've found someone we know."

"Hello," said the woman attached to that ridiculous parrot necklace.

"Vikki," Smidge said dismissively, like a substitute teacher taking attendance.

"I see y'all went ahead and had Tuesday-night dinner with some new people," Vikki sniffed, the words *new people* coming out of her mouth the way some people say "mucus plug" or "fetal pig."

Smidge handed a wet-nap packet to Henry, who immediately opened it for her. "I didn't think it was a tradition," she said. "What, did we come here, like, twice?"

"Five times," Vikki snapped. "Always on Tuesdays, like tonight. Which sure seems like a tradition to me."

Smidge countered with, "And you're here tonight without us, so looks like everybody's ignoring this so-called tradition."

Vikki shook her head, looking like she couldn't decide between silence and murder.

*"Ooookay,"* Smidge sang, rubbing the napkin between her palms. "We should get dessert, right? I need cobbler." Her hands shot toward the ceiling, fingers wiggling like she was at a church revival. "Peach!" she cheered. "Henry, find out if they have peach cobbler."

Alcohol loosened Henry into even more the doting husband. I think as he lost control of his faculties, he liked being pointed in a direction, kept busy with simple tasks.

Vikki gripped the back of my chair with enough strength I could tell she'd love nothing more than to catapult me out of the building still strapped to my seat. "Smidge," she said, her voice calm and compliant, a negotiator dealing with a hostage situation. "Is there a reason you haven't been returning my calls? I mean, a reason I need to be concerned about, and not just that you've been busy with your lingering visitor?"

Smidge's face took on a look of carefully composed fake innocence. Her hazel eyes turned near black from their lack of compassion, round with feigned concern. "Have I been ignoring you, Vikki?" she chirped, her voice reaching a pitch that could summon local wildlife. "Is that what you want to know? Is that what you are asking here at Plantation of the Sea? Is this worth making a scene in front of all these people?"

Vikki had gone still, straight as a stick. Her hands clasped solemnly in front of her bulge of a stomach, as her thumbs kept busy in a quiet wrestling match with each other. "I just wanted to know if you are mad at me," she wondered, and the question quietly descended upon us in a fog of discomfort, resting heavily on the backs of our necks, for we all recognized the voice of someone banished from Smidge's inner circle. It's confusion mixed with shame, and a desire to apologize for slights unknown.

This was not when Smidge was at her finest. She tossed her used wet-nap into the pile of refuse. "I will be mad, Vikki, if you keep talking about this over my crawfish."

"You'll talk to me later, then?" Vikki moved her hand across the back of my chair, sliding along the dark oak. A damp palm print remained near my shoulder.

"We'll see!" Smidge sang, and in that second I hated her. It was an instant fury, a flash flood of anger for pretending any of this was about Vikki. I knew Smidge wasn't mad at her. With all that was going on, she just forgot she existed. But there was no way Smidge would ever cop to being neglectful. To her, it was better to have Vikki feel scared than indignant.

Vikki gave pleading looks to each of us, but Henry busied himself stacking crawfish shells, forcing some kind of order to the situation. Tucker fiddled with a toothpick, looking absolutely carefree. All I could give was a weak shoulder shrug.

"You people," Vikki marveled before she turned and left.

"She was with her husband anyway," Henry said as a consolation.

"Hey, spider lady," Tucker said, pointing his toothpick at Smidge. "Tell me, does it feel better when you trap them in your web, or is the real fun later when you suck the blood out of their struggling bodies?"

I've always admired the way some people can be threatening while remaining still. My emotions take over; I always sound exactly how I'm feeling. But Tucker practically had his feet up on the table, that's how cool he was.

Smidge stood, adding enough dramatic flair to make her chair scrape along the wooden floor. There was an offended look plastered across her face, but I could tell she was already over the whole thing. Something was wrong, and it wasn't about Vikki.

"I'm going to the bathroom." Her announcement was directed so sharply at me I halfway expected to be teleported there merely by the power of her thoughts.

As I took to my feet, Tucker gave his lap a double strike with one hand. "Go on, little doggie!" he grunted before slapping another *pat-pat* against his thigh. "Your master's calling you!"

No matter how deep into the restaurant I got as I headed toward the bathroom in search of Smidge, Tucker's laughter found me.

"Vikki's right." He chuckled. "This is a great tradition!"

## SIXTEEN

O nce inside the bathroom, I ducked my head to spot Smidge's legs peeking from underneath a stall. She was on her knees. One of her strappy yellow heels was tangled in a lengthy strip of toilet paper. Her other shoe was overturned, the stiletto angled toward the sky like a dangerous weapon. The stall door was closed.

"Smidge? Are you sick? Are you throwing up?"

"No, but I can't stop gagging."

The struggle sounding from deep inside her body was as if her organs were wrestling each other, trying to break free. Eventually she fell into softer sputters and spits. "Block the door!" she shouted, her words echoing through the hollow of the white-tiled bathroom. "I can't have someone walking in on this."

Trembling with adrenaline, I found myself trying to jam a wicker chair underneath the doorknob, a move I knew only from television shows, and had no proof actually worked. There was no lock; I didn't know what else to do. Eventually I opted to sit in the chair, hoping my weight would be enough.

"I've got the door," I said. "Are you okay?"

Beside my head was a framed old black-and-white photo. A young girl held an umbrella and a damp kitten. She had huge, sad eyes, looking like her entire world had been crushed now that her pet had gotten wet. I could feel the judgment in her eyes as she transferred her disappointment with the weather onto me.

*Are you really listening to your best friend cough up a lung in the bathroom of a seafood restaurant and all you can come up with is "Are you okay?" Next, why not ask her, "Do you think it's the cancer?"*

From inside the stall, Smidge gasped, "Oh, shit."

Dropping to my hands and knees, I crawled over to her as close as I could, while keeping one foot firmly pressed against the chair. I stayed ready to spring back to the door if I needed to. Reaching under the stall, I found her arm and squeezed. Her hand was cold and trembling.

"There's blood, Danny," she whispered, and then exhaled a shaky, shocked sob. "I don't like it when it looks real."

"Let me in. Unlock the door."

She didn't. Instead she rocked back and forth on her heels, clutching my hand to her chest as if she were praying. I could feel her breath hot on my fingertips. My arm was bent at a strange angle, but I didn't dare adjust myself. We stayed like that for a moment as I tried to come up with something to say.

Then Smidge asked, "Did you know Alexa Chambers was a whore?"

"Who?"

"I'm just reading the stall wall in front of me. That's what someone wrote. 'Alexa Chambers is a useless whore.'"

"Well, it needed to be said."

"Gimme something to write with."

I crawled over to my purse and to my surprise found a black Sharpie tucked inside a notebook. While Smidge was busy working up her rebuttal, I busied myself washing my hands.

The stall door swung open. Smidge was already collected, fluffing her hair. But she hadn't seen what I could see: a small line of blood smearing from the corner of her mouth up toward her ear. Quickly I wet a paper towel and handed it over as I pushed past her, pretending I desperately wanted to read what she'd written, giving her a moment of privacy to clean her face.

Underneath *Alexa Chambers is a useless whore* was Smidge's unmistakable handwriting, neat and curved like a schoolteacher's.

*While you are wasting your life writing on the bottom of a shit-stained wall, Alexa's out getting laid. Life is short. Flush your tampons.*

"Kinda long," I noted.

Smidge smiled, all traces of illness erased from her face. "I like a lengthy legacy," she said.

"And I don't think you're supposed to flush tampons."

"I am not leaving my DNA in a box next to a toilet, bouncing around with other tampons. That's disgusting."

A spine-bending screech filled the bathroom as the wicker chair clattered to the floor. Vikki entered, confused at the commotion she'd just caused.

"Vikki!" Smidge cheered, sounding like this was the one person she'd been hoping for. She bounded toward her with arms outstretched. "Come here, girl." Smidge latched an arm around Vikki's freckled shoulder and leaned in close enough to kiss that parrot. "Did you really think we didn't want you to come to dinner? I was just playing with you."

"What?"

"We were in here trying to figure out the best way to tell you it was a joke."

Vikki gave me a horrible look. "It was *not* funny," she said. "So, you're not mad at me?"

"Mad at you? Vikki, to be honest, it seemed more like you were mad at me! You hadn't been coming around and I know you're jealous of Danielle."

What your mother did there was one of her special skills. Vikki was immediately on the defense.

"I'm not jealous of Danielle! Why would I be?"

"Well, I figured you thought she was taking your place, which she's *not*."

I never knew what to say or do when your mother was busy manipulating women. It felt like being the world's worst wingman. I usually ended up standing there mute. Since my silence could be easily misinterpreted as disdain, I'd lost more than one friend over the years when they figured I was on Smidge's side.

―――――

We got home from Plantation of the Sea that night only to have things turn worse.

If you haven't yet remembered which night this was, let me start by telling you that you weren't there when we got back. It was the first time you'd ever broken curfew. You didn't answer your phone immediately when your mother called. Instead you texted back something brilliant like, *1 sec.*

Your stall was enough to let Smidge know her daughter wasn't lying in a ditch, the place all mothers assume missing children end up. Once you were proven alive, she was free to plot the demise of her offspring. She paced between your bedroom and the kitchen, stopping only to take another sip of wine. *"One sec!"* she yelled in astonishment. *"One sec!* Like I am writing to her from *homeroom."*

Your next text was the famous one, the line that still makes me laugh every time I think of it. It was just so desperate and bumbled.

It read: *Don't call Angie's mom.*

Which is what your mother immediately did, which is how she learned you were never at safe, nerdy friend Angela's house, but somewhere else entirely.

This is when Tucker turned and asked, "Do you want to go sit on the porch with me to wait this one out?"

"Aren't you going home?"

"Aren't you?"

I stopped, my hand on my hip. "What is with you tonight?"

"I bet you'd like to find out," he said, grabbing two beers from the fridge.

Henry appeared in the doorway, blocking the entrance to the hall. He braced the frame with his hands, eyes closed as he took a deep breath and slowly exhaled.

Smidge's voice poured over his shoulder from the other room. "This is the night I am going to stand there and watch while you kill her!" she shrieked. "If you loved me, Henry, you would do this for me! Kill her slowly. Kill her twice."

Tucker flicked his finger against the small of my back. "Last chance," he said, quickening his pace toward the porch. I followed him out the door.

Our feet were propped up on the ledge between two thick, potted ferns as we shared the small bench. I tried to smooth my skirt over as much of my legs as possible, determined to feel casual despite my outfit's restrictions.

"It's okay," Tucker said. "I'm not looking."

He slid one of the open beers into my hand. I took a moment to hold the wet bottle to my forehead, cooling my skin. "Maybe I've already had too much to drink," I said. "This night feels endless. And this day has been going on for seven years."

I closed my eyes as I rested my head against the sturdy wood of the house. The porch light's hum vibrated the beams, making my skull buzz.

This is when Tucker kissed me, hesitant and soft, but like he'd done it before a thousand times. I was so shocked, it took me a few seconds to realize I was tipping my bottle. Beer splashed onto my thighs in a bubbling froth, splattering onto the floor.

I jumped, but not before Tucker accidentally bit my upper lip.

"Wow," he said. "That did not go like I thought it would."

He dabbed at my leg with the bottom of his shirt, apologizing. But there was too much beer and not enough shirt. In a final effort to soak up the mess, he dragged his hat across my knee.

He looked different without his cap. I stared down at the mop of Tucker's blond curls. He looked all of seventeen again, on his knees and awkward around me. The superhero in him deflated.

Those walls we build and fortify so purposefully crumble beyond our control in seconds, long before we'd ever suspect they'd give out. We're all just trying to make it through the day without accidentally showing up to a dinner where we were not invited, coughing up blood in a bathroom stall, or wiping beer off a girl's leg with a battered baseball cap.

"I'm okay," I said as I gently placed my hand on his chest. I could feel his heart pounding through the fabric of his button-down. "It's okay. You can get up."

"I'm really sorry." He searched my mouth for blood.

"Is it swollen?" I asked.

"Like you got kissed by a hornet."

There were no more attempts at affection. We finished our beers quietly and then he left with a cowboy tip of his hat.

I lingered over the memory of Tucker's mouth on mine, not only because I liked it, but because it felt like I had just cheated on my best friend.

By the time you came home I was already in bed, but I could hear the fallout over the next three hours. You'd been out on a secret movie date with that boy Aubrey; you knew your parents wouldn't have let you go. Smidge finally got you to admit that you held hands at this movie, and I believe she called you something just shy of what poor Alexa Chambers was accused of on the bathroom wall at Plantation of the Sea.

You cried and wailed and begged Henry to make your mother stop. But he didn't. I think he was scared. Of both of you.

Then I heard you shout, "But it wasn't a secret! Danielle knew about Aubrey! I thought she told you!"

You threw me under the bus, you little shit.

I'm sorry you suffered that night, Jenny. But I have to say, it was really nice hearing your mom get to be so normal. You probably only heard her hysterics and outrageous threats of violence, but I could translate what was under it. She was being your mama. I hadn't heard her sound that happy in a long time.

## SEVENTEEN

It must have been a week later when my left arm started tingling. It felt like my skin had a surface burn, as if I was being attacked by fire ants. I held my arm flush against my churning stomach, mashing one ache against the other.

I was in need of some coffee. It might be that I was having a heart attack or the beginnings of pancreatic cancer, but before I found out either of those things, I needed more caffeine so I could deal with it. I could just imagine the diagnosis: sympathy cancer.

When I walked into the coffee shop I saw Smidge sitting at a table with Seth Sampson.

Seth Sampson (referred to always with both names by everyone who has ever known him, including family members) was my unofficial boyfriend for all of four and a half minutes at the beginning of my senior year. He was a football player and completely out of my league; I thought I had suddenly become the Chosen One of Neville High when he asked if he could come over to my house one night. I didn't know if he was going to ask for a date or to see my calculus homework, but I didn't care. I felt important.

Turned out Seth Sampson wanted to sit next to me on the stairs outside my front door and get to third base, skipping bases one and two.

I sat there as his fingers prodded my thighs, groping past my underwear. Fear kept me still as I worried, *What if he doesn't kiss me?*

He didn't. He eventually got bored with his exploration and left without a word.

He must have known how mortified I'd be if anyone ever found out I'd let someone walk right over and treat me like someone checking to see if dinner was done. He was right to assume I'd never tell anybody, not even Smidge. I couldn't face her. She'd be so upset that I hadn't stuck up for myself; demanded something other than misery and confusion in return for his spelunking expedition.

And now Smidge was huddled up with Seth Sampson at the coffee shop, one hand playfully flirting along his arm as he made what I assumed to be a series of idiotic jokes. The way she was cackling you'd think it was Open Mic Night and Smidge was three drinks past her two-drink minimum.

"I'm so *sure!*" she guffawed, her voice bouncing off the walls of the mostly cement room. The other patrons gruffly squared their shoulders, harrumphing around their laptops, hunched over their paperbacks, exaggerating their actions so that Smidge could catch a hint. She didn't, even when the couple finishing their breakup coffees gave her red-eyed glares.

I was one hundred percent sure Smidge had never come close to betraying Henry, and this seemed like a very weird time to start doing it. Maybe she had decided to spend more time with the people she previously wouldn't, just so she could leave more strangers with a great impression of her. Her legend could live on in even more minds. Maybe she thought you got into Heaven by the number of attendees at your funeral.

Seth Sampson raised both his hands like he was reffing his own touchdown as he shouted, "I swear to God!" as Smidge made a sound like a frightened chicken. I decided to wander over before it got any worse.

"Hey, Danielle," Seth Sampson said with a cheery smile, as if he didn't remember anything, as if we were the oldest of bestest friends who hung out in coffee shops telling jokes all the time. Just a regular Rachel and Joey.

Smidge presented Seth Sampson to me as if I was an adoring crowd. "Look who's back in town!" She placed her fingers to her cheeks, but it didn't hide her flush of emotion. "Did that sound celebratory?" she asked him.

"I like it," he said.

"Well, I didn't mean to cheer, it's not appropriate. Seth Sampson is back home to help his mother, who's not feeling well, bless her heart. Dans, isn't it nice of this boy to come home to help take care of his mama? Isn't he a nice son?"

Seth Sampson fiddled with a wooden stir stick, flipping it between his thumb and forefinger as he looked me over.

"Danielle Meyers," he said. "I hear you've done all kinds of exciting things in your life. Like move to California."

I narrowed my eyes in disdain. "Are you being sarcastic?"

Smidge waved a bony arm toward me, as if shooing a gigantic fly from her picnic table. "Forgive Danny," she said. "She sometimes speaks in Asshole."

Later that night on the porch, Smidge studied her toes while I tried to figure out the best way to start asking questions about Seth Sampson.

She had her feet perched up on the wall in front of her, wineglass dangling from her left hand. Her toenails were meticulously painted and it occurred to me that she was either doing her own toes or she was somehow finding time to sneak away for secret pedicures.

If I were dying, I'm pretty sure the first thing I'd stop doing is worry about the state of my feet. In fact, my impending death would be a fantastic excuse not to think about *any* of my twenty nails. My fingertips would become a wasteland of ripped cuticles and sharp, jagged edges.

I launched into my best impression of Smidge, raising my voice an octave, heavy on the drawl. "Oh, Seth Sampson! I just don't remember you being so *real*-funny! But you sure are a hoot and a holler, I'll tell you what. Is this coffee spiked? Because I am drunk off of how awesome you are. Can I feel your muscles?"

Smidge raised herself in her chair, already on the defensive. "Oh, you know," she tossed, as if that was enough on the subject.

"No, I don't. That's why I'm asking."

She draped one arm over her head, rotating her hand at the wrist as she stared off into space, formulating an answer. "Well, *Mother*, since you're so curious about my social life, I will tell you that I just happened to run into him."

I'd yet to hear back from the Lizard. I briefly wondered if I should give it another try, or if silence was her answer to the situation and the extent of her willingness to take part.

"You just *happened* to run into him?" I asked.

She leaned over to the side table, examining the label on the wine bottle.

"Yes, just like how you *happened* to run into us," she said.

I couldn't let it be. "You guys were sitting kind of close, is all."

Smidge let her spine unhinge at her neck; her head dropped and rolled to the side as her eyeballs bulged, like she had been struck by a temporary possession. "We were sitting at a table. For two. Like two people."

"I'm just saying—"

"Oh, okay, Danny. You caught me. I wanted to see if I could bag the head boy from high school. I wanted to know if this sickly ass still had the hotness."

"Just because you say it sarcastically doesn't mean it can't be the truth."

"I see what you're doing here," she said. "And it's not going to work. Back to the plan, missy. No more stalling. What it is time for you to do is: a Henry experiment."

"Right now?" Henry was upstairs in a battle with a certain brand-new ninth-grader over an essay she hadn't finished writing for her English class.

"When he comes back to the kitchen, I want you to chat him up."

"*Chat him up?* What does that even mean?"

Smidge tucked a hand across her waist and held her wineglass with the other, like she was wandering through an art show. "He needs to get used to you being close to him," she said. "If not, it won't happen after I'm gone because he'll think it's like a betrayal or something. We have to have it already in his head that you are a separate, sexual being."

"Please don't call me a sexual being."

"Look, I'd probably find someone to have sex with him even if I weren't dying. Then I could finally live in peace. I love him, but I don't need to have him in my face every night."

"Smidge."

"Pawing all over me."

"Smidge."

"You'll have to get used to that. He likes grabbing butts."

*"Smidge."*

She was on a roll. "Married people should only have to do it once a month. When you're with Henry, I say you don't have to do it more than four times a year. But you should probably do it more often at the beginning. You know, if he's sad."

"Please stop."

"Although, I admit I don't like thinking of you two kissing. I like how Henry kisses."

"I am so uncomfortable right now."

"Then go in there and flirt with that man. Bump into him. Touch his hand. See if he looks you in the eye and gets real close."

"Give him the old Seth Sampson treatment?"

Smidge pinched my arm. "I wasn't flirting with Seth Sampson," she insisted.

"I'll do this only if you promise you won't see him ever again."

Smidge launched into a full-scale production of moral outrage, putting her glass down onto the table before adjusting it like it was the sole audience member for this monologue she was about to deliver, ensuring it had the best view.

"I didn't even *try* to see him! I *ran into him*. I already said that!"

"Then it's easy to make this promise."

She tucked her lips into her mouth, scrunching her face in frustration. It's possible the difficulty she was having wasn't over getting to see Seth Sampson again. It was in letting me tell her what to do.

"Fine," she said. "Because I don't *ca'yir*. I promise."

"Who's making promises?" Vikki had let herself in through the screen door and was wearing some kind of yellow house-dress that had seen better days and what appeared to be several lonely nights. She had her hair pulled into pigtails, of all things, topped off with a trucker cap that read *Rest Stop*.

"Knock, knock!" she added as an afterthought.

"It's Vikki!" Smidge cheered. "Come sit. Danny's gonna go into the kitchen and get us all some more wine and you can keep me company."

Vikki practically pushed my ass off the bench. "Sounds fun! Now, what were you promising?"

"Ohhhhh," Smidge said, drawing the word out for a few seconds. "Just that I wasn't cheating earlier, when we were playing a game. Right, Dans?"

I held my hand on the doorknob. "I didn't say you were cheating. I said it looked like you were thinking about it. Like it looked fun to you."

"Thinkin' ain't cheatin'," she said, turning her back to me, fluffing out her hair. "Ain't no thought police up on this porch, right, Vikki?"

Vikki looked from Smidge to me and then back again, her overglossed mouth a twisted pout of confusion. "Well, I'm sure I don't know what y'all are talking about, but that wine sounded like a good idea."

"One second," I grumbled as I pushed my way inside.

I'd hoped fate would be on my side and I'd find an empty kitchen, but no such luck. Henry was at the sink, scouring the roasting pan from that evening's dinner.

"Let me ask you something," he said, drying his hands on a nearby tea towel, slapping it back and forth between his palms like he was making a tortilla. "When exactly are you going home?"

"I don't know," I said. "Smidge asked me to stay."

"Yeah." He turned back to the sink. "I know. It's just . . . the school year already started and . . . Am I going to have to buy you a Christmas stocking?"

I stood there, unsure of what to do next.

He opened the cabinet to his left and grabbed a bottle of whiskey. "I'm drinking this," he said. He took a step toward me and then another and suddenly he was right next to me, reaching a hand just past my cheek to open the cabinet door behind me. "Need a glass," he explained.

"Oh, good!" said Smidge as she made a beeline to where we were standing. "My two favorite people, right next to each other." She smirked before looking over her shoulder toward your bedroom. "Since Jenny's on my shit list tonight for that essay bullshit."

As she chattered on, her hands went to work. One was on Henry's arm, the other my hip, gently pulling us into what was threatening to become a group hug. I tried to wiggle away, but she gripped my side, pulling me into the position she wanted. Smidge slid herself into the space between us.

Reaching toward the speakers on the counter, she decided, "This should be louder."

Once satisfied with the volume, she snapped and bounced, eyes closed. "Nnh!" She grooved, turning the two-by-two space in front of the sink into a dance floor. "Oh, people!" she moaned. "I forgot how good this song is." She hip-bumped me into Henry before shimmying off toward the porch. "I miss my drink!" she shouted to no one in particular, then disappeared around the corner.

"Your wife is crazy," I said.

"She sometimes still feels guilty about James is all."

"What do you mean?"

Henry cleared his throat. "I don't know. Just forget that."

"Forget what, exactly?"

The sudden clamor on the porch announced Tucker's arrival. "Howdy, ladies! How is your Friday going? Good, good. Henry in here?"

Henry tried to scoot past me, but I stepped in front of him, grabbing his arm.

"What did you mean?" I asked again, a sense of dread rising in my stomach. It felt like I was peeking inside a darkened room with one hand on the light switch, not quite ready to flip. I ducked my head, trying to force him to look me in the eye. His cheeks were flushed as his lips pursed and twisted, searching for some kind of emergency exit.

"Nothing," he said. "Smidge said you might have left the bathroom door unlocked on purpose, so I figured this was about James. But she was joking; I get that now. I forgot how you didn't—"

"What is going *on*, people?" Tucker's booming voice was laced with accusations as he took in the scene he'd stumbled upon in the kitchen.

"Nothing," Henry and I said at the same time.

"Then why are y'all standing like that?"

Not Tucker's question. Yours.

I'll never forget the sound of your voice right then, Jenny, so uncomfortable and unsure. I don't know how long you'd been watching us, but any length of time was probably too much. Once your father uncharacteristically yelled at you to go to your room, everything looked even more suspicious than it had already been.

"Yes, sir," you said, your voice already cracking from tears, as you ran full speed into your bedroom, slamming your door with all your force.

Tucker gave me a sarcastic wink. "This place is a whole lot more interesting now that you're becoming a sister-wife."

# EIGHTEEN

I had been awake most of the night trying to figure out what Henry was talking about. What kind of secret about James would Smidge be holding from me?

In the morning I stepped out of the shower to find a small, square rash on my back, just to the left of my spine. It extended outward in a small line toward my armpit. I probably should have been instantly alarmed, but all I could muster was a weary sigh.

Considering all the ailments and unknowns I was enduring, a rash seemed like one I could handle. Nothing too serious could come from a visit to the dermatologist.

Dr. Fowler's eyes bulged behind round, thin glasses with a yellow tint, and she started each of her sentences in almost a whisper, a mumble that built up steam as she tumbled toward the final punctuation. She sounded like a fleet of police cars on the chase.

After giving my back a perfunctory inspection, she said, "*Thrmrrfuhl* say-that's-either-shingles-or-*HERPES*."

That has to be pretty near the top of the list of words people don't enjoy getting yelled at them.

"Herpes?" I asked incredulously, which is the only way anybody ever asks that question.

"*Impra* probably-SHINGLES."

"I thought shingles was restricted to the elderly."

Dr. Fowler left the room, presumably to mumble-yell an order to a nurse. A few minutes later I met Glenda.

She was cheerful, the opposite of Dr. Fowler, with a shiny bob that gave a perky swing as she nodded, which was something she did constantly, as if she were continually agreeing with her own happy thoughts. Her dark eyes seemed unnaturally round, as if she had just come back from having them dilated.

"Okay, Danielle," Glenda said, smiling wide enough that I was tempted to start counting her teeth. "I hear you got the shingles," she said. She shoved her fists into her lab coat pockets and shuddered, but never once lost her smile. It felt like she was hosting a children's show and I was today's special lesson. "I bet you're in a lot of pain!"

"I thought maybe I was dying," I confessed.

"I bet you did." She tsked.

Glenda swabbed the blisters on my back as she told me the test was just a formality; she was pretty sure I had shingles. She gingerly placed a hand on my shoulder. Her eyebrows were plucked to two thin strands, her forehead wide with calm.

"I'm sorry to tell you, sugar kitten," she said, "but it's about to get worse."

"My life?"

She laughed. "The pain! But, yes. Your life, too, I suppose. By the way, the medicine we give you is the same we give people for herpes. So if you use the pharmacist down on the first floor, you pay no attention to the look she might give you."

Then Glenda turned serious. "This is from stress," she said. "Something's going on with you that you can't quite handle. Your skin looks like someone's been rubbing sandpaper on a baby lizard."

That's when I realized the most important question: "Is this contagious?"

"To people who haven't had the chicken pox, it is, *immhmm*. But you'd be giving someone chicken pox, not this."

Smidge had never had the chicken pox. She bragged about this on all of her online profiles.

*"Short. Talky. Never eats meringue. Never had the chicken pox."*

As I was getting back into my clothes, the sleeve of my shirt brushed against my arm. It felt like I'd just tried to wear a coat of fire. I became one of those cartoon characters whacked by a frying pan, spine all wiggly, face stretched in pain.

Glenda gave me a comforting pout. "Shingles is an inflammation of a nerve, the whole nerve. On you: your left side, spine to fingertip." She gestured down my arm, two fingers extended like a flight attendant pointing out the exit doors. "Everything that touches you along this line for the next couple of weeks is gonna hurt like hell. Load up on painkillers, stay inside, and try to sleep this off."

It is possible that I sounded a little too relieved when I

called Smidge from my car to tell her I needed to fly back to Los Angeles, that I was contaminated and couldn't be around her.

She didn't take the news well.

"Oh, so you're abandoning me, is that it?"

"It's not abandoning. I'm sick and I can't be near you."

"I've been sick and near you before. We shared a toilet during the Food Poisoning Epidemic of 1995."

"This is different. If you caught the chicken pox, it could— I'm not sure, but I know it would probably make things worse."

"Uh-huh."

"Maybe get Vikki to help you," I offered. "She'll like that, and you can boss her around and she won't ask as many questions as I do."

"Ugh," Smidge grunted. I could hear her washing dishes, the rush of water splashing against the sink, the *clink* of plates piling.

"Besides, I need to check in at home. Business is piling up and I have a few clients I need to tend to."

"Oh, for your dumb job where you teach people how to open their bills and buy carrots in a bag? You're right. That sounds *real* important."

"I'm sick, Smidge," I whined.

"Are you sick?" she mocked. "Do you have an owie on your arm?"

She interrupted herself with a coughing fit. I could picture her struggling against the sink to choke down the spasm inside her lungs, angry that she'd had to take a break to catch her breath.

"I'm sorry," I said.

"You should be." She waited for me to respond, to take it all back, to drive over wearing a hazmat suit, I guess. It was that time in our fight where I was supposed to bend to her wishes. But I couldn't.

My e-mails were piling up, clients were starting to get frustrated, my future income was threatening to dwindle away. My website was down for three days before I realized it. No telling how much potential work I lost during that time.

Plus I was just too sick. I didn't think I could handle anything other than getting into a bed and swallowing a painkiller.

I heard the squeak of her faucet as she closed the tap.

"I'll come back," I said. "You know I will."

"Frankly, I don't care if you do," she snapped. "You obviously don't give a shit about me, or you'd think of something, you quitter."

And then she hung up on me.

If only Mr. Carlton were still alive, I could call him for advice. He was the one who really knew how to deal with Smidge, who always stuck up for me. "Now you be nice to Danielle," he'd tell his daughter. "She's gonna be the only friend you have left one day."

At this point Smidge didn't look too terribly sick. It's not like people were stopping her at the grocery store to ask if she was okay. My point is, Smidge wasn't dying that day, and she wouldn't die the next. She hadn't died in the months I'd been on pause, living under her every whim. I dropped everything because it seemed like after she said she was sick, there was no tomorrow and even less of a guarantee for a day after that. With a terminal diagnosis, "the end" seems at once an immediate terror pressing down and this fuzzy finish line way out in the impossible distance. When each day passes without death, you start to believe it will never come.

I needed to be by myself for just a second. If I was really possibly going to give up my life and everything in it to morph into someone else's, at least I could mourn the last of my independence, the shreds of what was Danielle Meyers. I couldn't ask Smidge for that, but I could take it.

Smidge could probably use some time away from me, too. She should be alone with her family; stop thinking of it as a project that needed finishing. Henry was clearly getting suspicious and frustrated. You were acting up so often at this point you were basically holding a sign that read *I need you to talk to me, Mama.*

If I removed myself, not by choice but by doctor's orders, perhaps the family could return to a unit of three, and I could go back to a life that seemed quite quaint in comparison.

Unfortunately, I wasn't getting out of Ogden that easily. That podunk, stupid-ass town only had two flights out per day, and I'd already missed my second chance at freedom. That left me with a night where I was effectively, electively homeless.

The cost of a flight to Los Angeles was more than most people in Ogden pay for a mortgage. No wonder people end up staying forever. *I could visit my cousin in Manhattan, or I could feed my family for the next two months. Guess I'll never leave. I've seen New York on the TV, anyway.*

The Cottage, Ogden's only decent hotel since the Chesterfield closed long ago, was booked solid. The only other option, the 75 Motel and Diner, was a known bedbug factory. Not to mention I believe you aren't allowed a room unless you plan to turn tricks in it.

I just wanted to be somewhere quiet where there was a bed and maybe someone to run a bath for me. I needed someone who wasn't Smidge. Someone who didn't mind the attention being placed—even temporarily—on me.

I called Tucker with a single question.

"Have you had the chicken pox?"

# NINETEEN

---

Tucker answered his front door wearing a surgical mask.

"That's very funny," I said.

"Smidge gave me this actually. It's from that time you guys were traveling in dangerous areas. Jenny got a dollhouse. Henry got a knife. Smidge got me a three-cent SARS mask."

Tucker welcomed me in with a hospitable pat to my arm, which caused me to double over in pain.

"Ohhh," I moaned, gripping my biceps as my vision whitened hot into stars. "This thing is terrible."

"My grandfather had it once, up near his eyes," Tucker said. "It's the only time I ever saw that man cry."

"Please don't touch me. I'm in so much pain."

"I think you wrote me a poem that went something like that our senior year."

"You wish."

"No, not then. You weren't the prettiest thing back then, California. No offense."

"You're lucky I'm so tired."

"Your sickbed, ma'am," Tucker said. "Please take to it."

The couch was folded out into a bed, complete with clean sheets and lots of pillows. On the side table rested a bottle of Advil and an unopened plastic jug of water. A stack of fashion magazines sat beside a mason jar filled with yellow daisies.

"This is the nicest bed I've ever seen in my entire life," I said, desperately wanting to flop into the safety of warm blankets and soft pillows. But *flopping* was definitely on my list of forbidden verbs. I opted for a more gingerly slide.

Tucker ducked into the other room as I inched myself toward a reclined state. He came back holding a laundry basket, which he unpacked at the foot of the bed.

"Okay," he said, quickly giving his ball cap an official adjustment before he presented a pair of fuzzy slippers and a robe. "I don't know your size, but I saw these at Walmart and it seemed like the kind of ugly thing you'd like to wear when you don't feel good. I do mean *you*, specifically. You strike me as a girl who goes pretty ugly when you're unwell."

"You're right."

Next came a heating pad. "I don't know if this will help, but Pee-Paw clutched this to his chest and cried a lot, so maybe if it gets that bad, there's this."

I closed my eyes and tried to stop myself because I could feel the laughter bubbling up inside. *"Huhhrrrrrrr,"* I said.

"What is that, what you are doing?"

*"Hhrrrrrrr,"* I said again, determined to keep my shoulders from shaking. *"Hrrrrreeee."*

Tucker gave a slow, disappointed shake of his head. "You're trying not to laugh."

With the little that was left of my breath I managed to whisper, "You said '*Peeeeee-Pawwwwww.*'"

"Nice. Real nice."

"Please say it again."

"You know, I hope you *do* laugh, and I hope it makes your skin burn, you ungrateful woman."

He twirled on his heels in mock offense, stomping to the kitchen. "Just for that, I'm going to go make your soup too hot," he announced.

*He was making me soup.*

I was the closest to happy the shingles would let me be.

Two hours and two bowls of soup later, the painkillers were starting to work.

Tucker sat across from me in a chair, watching with an amused expression.

"When is your flight?" he asked.

"Tomorrow." I smashed my face into the pillow.

"I don't think so," he said. "Look at you."

"Look at *you*," I said. "*This* is what you're supposed to do for someone when they're ill. You did everything right. I'm such a bad person."

"Change your flight," Tucker said. "Stay here and get better. Then you can go home. Don't take this the wrong way, but you look like shit."

I felt myself dozing off. Still, I managed to say, "Thank you."

It was dark. When I woke up, Tucker was still watching me from his place on his recliner. An open book rested in his lap.

"What's going on?" I asked, disoriented.

"You were talking," he said. "Just now. You asked me if she's going to be mad at you."

I tried to sit up, but it hurt too much. I needed another pain pill. "I said that?"

"I'm guessing you meant Smidge. But you also said something about a lizard, so it was probably just dream babble. You've got a little drool on your chin. I wasn't going to say anything, but I just did because I don't want to stare at it."

I wiped my face and checked the time. "It's late. Really late."

"Yeah, I'm going to bed. I just wanted to make sure you were okay." He stood, stretching out his back. "Plus, I don't sleep too much. You take another pain pill now. I'll wake you up for breakfast."

I raised my hand to touch him. He was too far away, so I stroked the air between us like he was a beautiful mirage.

"You are . . . so amazing," I said. "Why, sweet angel, have you landed in my life?"

"That's more like it. Danielle Meyers, *this* is how you're supposed to talk to me."

———

For the next three days I faded in and out of consciousness as Tucker made sure I occasionally had a shower, changed pajamas, or ate some of his amazing roast chicken.

Sometimes that's all that matters about a man, Jenny. That he knows how to cook a meal. Give me someone who knows what vegetables to toss into a roasting pan and into which part of the stove it all goes once he's done.

The last night before my morning flight to Los Angeles, a night when I was feeling three hundred percent better— enough to wear actual pants—Tucker created a "dinner table" out of his bed, with equal amounts of pillows and trays, so that I could recline while eating. There was even a place to rest my wineglass.

There was a basket of bread, a butter dish, a liter of bottled water, and a small bucket of ice. He'd placed two Vicodin on a saucer for my "dessert."

"I probably could have eaten this one at your actual table," I told him. "I'm feeling much better."

"I like that we've eaten half of our meals lying down."

"I'm doing my best to try to eat this like a lady, but this chicken is made for eating with my hands."

"Do it," he said, reaching over to grab a drumstick. "When chicken's this tasty, I say ditch the forks."

"I'd toss the bones when I'm done, but I don't want to ruin your carpet."

"Reason enough why I need to get another dog."

"No, the reason you have to get a dog is because you have dog toys in your Jeep like you still have a dog."

"How do you know that?"

"I saw them when you picked me up at the airport." I looked around his bedroom, which I'd spent quite a bit of time in, considering I had kept my clothes on the entire time. "I can't believe you live in this big place all by yourself."

Tucker snapped his napkin. "I wasn't supposed to. That dog left with a lady, remember?"

"I do, but when was that?"

"About six years ago."

"Six *years*? You act like it was six days! You've still got her stuff in this side table!"

"You went through my side table?"

"That is not the point."

"It might be."

I dropped back against the pillows. "You don't have any-thing hanging on your walls. And look at that." I pointed at his closet. "It's half empty, like you are waiting for someone to move in. Like you can't take up all the space or it's bad luck."

He rubbed the back of his neck. "Okay, okay."

"No, seriously, Tucker. That is nuts."

"She might come back."

"Isn't she still in Germany?"

"Kentucky."

"Well, she's practically a neighbor."

Tucker stacked his plates, cleaning up the space in front of him even though he was nowhere near finished eating. "I guess you're just fine being divorced and it never bothers you."

"I didn't say that. But I don't live like we might get back together."

"You don't even know her."

"Well, she left you, so I know she's an idiot."

Tucker slid a tray off the bed and carried it to the kitchen. I knew his feelings were hurt, but it didn't feel like I'd said the wrong thing. It was like trying to talk someone into riding a roller coaster. It was only scary when you hadn't done it yet. Unless he was afraid of heights. Then it would probably never be fun.

"I'm sorry, Tucker!" I called out. "Come back. I'm sorry."

"You sound like her," Tucker said as he returned.

"Your ex?"

"No. Smidge. Don't do that. Don't talk to me like I'm stupid. Like you have all my shit figured out. You don't know everything."

I found myself rubbing my chest in shock. "I'm sorry."

"Everything reminds me of her, and I hate it. That's why I asked you to stay. You make it different."

"And I'm already in your bed."

He patted my knee. "That's not what I meant."

"I know. I'm just ruining the moment with jokes."

"I appreciate that. I really do."

"Maybe it's because I'm afraid you're about to try to kiss me again and last time there was personal injury. To my face."

He nodded. "Don't worry. Trying to kiss a girl after talking about your ex is tacky. But how about this?"

He leaned over and pressed the smallest kiss to my forehead, like he was wishing me good night.

I considered it for a second. "No, not very satisfying," I said.

I kissed him because when a man makes roast chicken as good as Tucker's, he deserves to be kissed. I pulled him to the bed because he'd relinquished that bed to me for the better part of a week without a single complaint. I pulled his clothes off because he'd given me medicine, on time and accurately, since I'd walked through his door. I pulled *my* clothes off because I could, because it no longer hurt to have skin, because Tucker had taken care of me like I was important. We pushed and kicked the plates, glasses, and trays to the floor because when two people tumble into bed after waiting the majority of their lives to find out what that might be like, no piece of glassware or cutlery in their proximity is safe.

We fell into that bed, into each other. There's no other way to describe something that was at once unpredictable and inevitable. Our mouths and bodies locked on each other and stayed that way for the rest of the night.

I will not ruin your ideas of Uncle Tucker with any other details. I'm sure that's more than you wanted to know. I only told you because sometimes I feel like you never really knew me. You had a lot of ideas of what I was all about, particularly once you got older, and I'm hoping this right here shows you that I wasn't trying to hurt anyone. Especially you.

# TWENTY

In the morning I woke to find Tucker on his back, staring down at his chest while rooting around his belly button.

"The magic is over, I see," I said with a yawn.

He turned and grinned. "There's bread crumbs in there," he marveled. The curls on one side of his head were mashed flat. A long line from his pillow cut his right cheek in half. "Your lips are still wine-stained," he said, reaching over for another kiss.

When I opened my eyes, I saw the clock over his shoulder and jumped out of bed.

"I have to pack! I'm so late! Is that really the time?"

Pointing at the doorway, Tucker said, "You're fine."

There were my suitcases, packed and ready. My purse rested on a nearby table. My cell phone was plugged and charging.

"You packed all my stuff?"

"Not everything. I left your toothbrush and good-smelling face soap next to the sink. I don't want to tell you that you're in desperate need of those things right now, but I guess I just did."

"You packed all my clothes," I said, flattered.

"It wasn't that hard, really," he said. "You weren't wearing anything. I did put out some jeans and a shirt for you. Not that I'm dressing you. I just put out that thing you like to wear a lot. I told you I don't sleep very much."

Thirty minutes later I was scrubbed and dressed, debating how best to say good-bye. In the shower I'd gone over a million different ways to tell him what I needed to say. I found him back asleep.

I was tempted to leave before I said something stupid, but his eyes popped open.

"Hey, pretty," he said.

"Don't get up," I whispered.

"When are you coming back?" he asked, his voice low and hungry enough that I wanted to fold myself back into the warmth of his blankets, curve around the heat of his body.

"I don't know," I admitted. "But can you do me a favor?"

"Sure, that'd be new for me."

"Could you not tell Smidge about this?"

His face froze as he made sure he'd heard me correctly. He sat up, still in awe. "Amazing. I've never actually felt myself stop caring about someone so specifically, so acutely before."

"It's not what you think."

"What I think is you can go ahead and get on that plane."

"Tucker."

"Hurry! We wouldn't want Smidge to be unhappy. She might tease you about me, and wouldn't that just be too much for you to handle?"

"That's not it. It's hard to explain."

"I'm sure it isn't. You just don't want to."

"I'm sorry," I said, as I reached for my bags.

"No, don't apologize for being you," he said. "This is my fault. I'm sorry I forgot you weren't your own person." He rubbed his arms, like the room had a sudden chill. "Just how indentured of a servant are you? Or is it really all about you not having a backbone?"

"Don't be an asshole, Tucker."

"There we go. That's how I like an exit."

I unplugged my cell phone and threw the charger into my purse.

"She's a cancer," he said.

It stopped me cold. "She what?" I'd misheard, but he didn't notice my fear.

"You know what cancer does?" he asked. "How it mutates? How it jacks all the cells up, tells them to keep growing, keep making more cancer cells, and that's how you get a tumor?"

"I know how cancer works."

"Well, that's how your little friend there works, too. She infects people with the wrong ideas. She makes them sick, and then she spreads her evil until the bad stuff grows, until they wither up and die. With you it's even worse. You let her get inside your bloodstream, move up to your head, and mutate your life."

"Good-bye, Tucker."

"You can fix that," he said as he followed me into the living room, the sheet wrapped around his waist, gathered in his fist. "She doesn't affect me because I'm not scared of her. She knows if she ever tried some shit with me, she'd get knocked down so fast her bony butt would snap in half."

"Big talk." I opened the front door and stumbled over my luggage onto his front porch. "Like you'd ever hurt a woman."

"Ask yourself something, Danielle," Tucker said, standing in his doorway half naked and resigned. "You got a dog with rabies, does it really matter what gender it is before you shoot it?"

## TWENTY-ONE

I shouldn't have been too surprised to find your mother sitting on top of a suitcase at the Odgen airport, sipping an iced coffee, flip-flops tossed aside on the carpet. Her toes were spread, nails unpainted; a pair of sunglasses shaped like two red hearts rested on top of her head.

"Surprise!" she cheered. "Isn't it nice to have someone meet you at the airport?"

I didn't want to talk to her. My head was still swimming from what had just happened with Tucker, something I couldn't, and certainly didn't want to, discuss with Smidge. Then there was everything Henry was alluding to about James that I was actively trying to ignore. I had to get on that plane. I may not have had much of a life to go back to, but it was something, and it was mine. Besides, she hadn't checked on me once since she'd hung up on me days ago, and now she wanted me to pretend that it was nothing.

"I have to check in," I said, looking over her head toward the arrivals gate, wondering if anybody would help me toss this little woman onto the curb. Only a single willowy blonde with penciled eyebrows and sad shoulders stood manning the computer. She wasn't going to be muscle enough. I'd need a couple of guys from baggage claim.

"Guess what?" Smidge waved her yellow, floppy hat like it was a victory flag. "I'm coming with you!"

"To where?"

"To California, dummy! I want In-N-Out and some palm trees. I told you I'd pay you back that vacation. Here it is! Let's go. I'm freezing."

"You can't come with me."

She reached into her giant purse and revealed what appeared to be a boarding pass. "Uh, I think that I already am. So, stick that in your mouth and suck it."

Stunned, I asked, "How did you know my flight?"

"I called and asked!" She pointed at the skinny woman at the arrivals counter. "Bella was in my knitting group that five months we all thought knitting was fun. We used to be the best of besties before she started dating that guy who looked like Tom Petty."

"It can't be legal that she told you my flight," I said to nobody in particular as I hustled to the counter.

I gave Bella the glare of a lifetime as she began the approximately thirty-seven thousand keyboard strokes and clicks necessary for anyone to receive a boarding pass.

"Come on, Dans," Smidge said, knocking into my side. "Don't be sore with me. You know we need to have one last trip, and this can be it."

I turned to her so quickly the little hairs around her head

floated in the breeze. "You don't pull that card on me right now, Smidge."

"Oh, I'm pulling it," she said, standing on her tiptoes for extra importance. "I'm pulling that card right now in front of you." She held her boarding pass inches from my nose. "Here's the card. It's pulled. Look *at* it. Besides, you owe me for not taking all my calls."

"What are you talking about?"

Her chin dropped until it just about folded into her neck. "Uh, what are *you* talking about? I called you and Tucker every day, but he said you weren't taking my calls. I can't believe you stayed at that man's house. You probably have scabies now."

"How did you know I was at Tucker's?"

"Henry went checking on you for me."

"He must have deleted your calls from my phone."

"Well, I hope your privacy is all that man invaded."

What if something had happened to her?

"Here you go, Miss Meyers," chirped Bella the Snitch. "Enjoy your upgrade!"

"Upgrade?"

Smidge grabbed my hand. I felt her cold, sweaty palm in mine and realized there was a different look in her eyes. For the first time in our lives, she looked genuinely frightened, as if she was unsure she was going to be able to gain my forgiveness this time.

"Do you know how many miles I had saved up?" she asked. "I cashed them all in for a free flight for me, and first class for both of us. Well, first class once we get to Houston.

You know this shit-kicker town has to puddle-jump us out of here first."

That was an official Smidge apology. Not with epiphanies or remorse, not a heart-to-heart that ended with a hug and some tears. Smidge gave oversize gifts and unnecessary acts of kindness that stated silently, yet at a million decibels: *"Okay, get over it now. Here's your present."* With Smidge it's the grand gesture followed by a huge sweeping under the rug of everything that should have been said.

"I haven't seen your place in ages," she said. "Does it still smell like mice?"

My apartment *never* smelled like mice, but it was most likely filled with dead plants.

"What about Henry? And Jenny?" I asked, my voice already sounding defeated. "Don't you need to stay with them? I mean, shouldn't you?"

I felt as helpless as my suitcase motoring away on the conveyor belt, overturned and stamped with only a slight promise it would reach its final destination.

Smidge paddled my butt with both hands. "Let's get on board, missy!"

Once we were on the second plane, the one with the pre-flight mimosas in first class, after they'd whisked away our empty champagne glasses and asked us to turn off all electronic devices, Smidge decided to get down to business.

"Oh, I opened a safe-deposit box for us," she casually said as she adjusted her overhead air-conditioning button. "For you," she added. "For things you aren't going to be able to hold onto while you wait around for me to die, because that's going to be obvious. I mean, we don't really know when I'm going to go, so we shouldn't pretend it's tomorrow. Right—that's what you figured out? And why you were being such a butt-face?"

I sighed, letting the alcohol relax me away from her verbal bait. "I suppose."

"And you're right. I ain't dying tomorrow." She dug into the front pocket of her jeans, an effort that seemed to take a lot out of her. Her chest heaved; her rib bones raised the surface of her skin, which had goose-bumped in the chilly cabin temperature. "But just in case I do," she said, "here is the extra key. Right now all I have in it are the duplicates to my car information, registration and insurance stuff. Henry never pays attention to the cars, so you have to do that. Make sure they're clean. If it were up to Henry we'd only drive dusty kidnapping vans and mud-splattered Jeeps like that Tucker."

I was happy to latch onto a new subject, no matter how dangerous it was personally. "Do you know Tucker still has dog toys in that thing?" I asked.

"And do you know he still puts a stocking up for that woman every Christmas?" she countered.

"You're lying."

"He does. Somehow he got it into his head that she'd come home for the holidays."

I tried to picture Tucker staring at an empty stocking, having made too much roast chicken for one person.

"That's rough," I said.

"It's stupid and pathetic, is what it is. He is the worst."

"Smidge. That's not nice." I was weak in my defense; half-way worried that she'd notice I was taking up for him, the other half wondering if I should. This new, additional secret was weighing more heavily on me than I'd like. If Tucker felt that strongly about how I seemed to let Smidge control things in my life, there's no way he'd be okay with the truth of what we were discussing while sitting on a tarmac in Houston, Texas.

Smidge gave a tsk. "That man lets himself be miserable and he won't listen to anybody who tells him how it is. He acts all tough when I'm around, like he's a hillbilly robot. I know his sissy truth. He cries more than my teenage daughter."

"I had no idea you thought that way about him," I said.

"Well, it's not nice to call a man weak, but that's what he is. Henry won't let me talk about it anymore around him. Gets him riled up not knowing how to stick up for him when he agrees with me. Hey, did you two have funny business while you were staying over there? You better say no."

"Smidge. I was sick."

"So nothing happened?"

"No."

"Good."

The seats started rumbling as we gained speed down the runway. I looked past Smidge's shoulder to the small window, watching the airport blur by. I felt better knowing we were finally headed toward my home, away from Tucker, away from Smidge's house. All of Ogden was behind me, and for once it felt like I was fleeing the bulk of my problems.

"That's another reason I want you with Henry," she said.

"If he doesn't have anybody, it'll be all 'Sad Henry the Widower' hanging out with 'Lonesome Bitter Tucker' all the time. The two of them will turn into junkyard dogs. Having contests to see which one of them could grow the nastier beard the fastest. My daughter lives there; she shouldn't be subjected to male sadness. What kind of husband would she pick if that's the kind of daddy she lived around?"

Smidge unhooked her seat belt, lurched forward, and snatched her purse from the nook in front of her. "In fact," she said, "I'm adding that to the list. Do Something About Tucker."

Technically, I suppose I'd done that. It dawned on me that I could potentially destroy her entire plan right now by telling her what had happened. Would she still want me to be with Henry after that? Would she even talk to me?

Smidge checked to make sure the flight attendant wasn't looking. A devious, gleeful smile spread across her face.

"I'm not wearing my seat belt," she confessed, chuckling. "It's the little things, Danny." She shoved her purse back. "Looking over my life I would say I haven't intentionally broken enough rules."

"I imagine this happens every day now," I said. "You think of another thing you regret about how you lived your life."

"No, not really. I don't believe in regrets. What happened, happened. Nothing you can do about it. People waste too much time trying to reassess blame, put everybody's feelings into proper perspective. I say just shut up and move on. What good is all that lingering?"

The plane lurched, and people gasped. As we bobbed and jolted for a few moments, I could feel some people on the plane definitely having moments of regret. Smidge wasn't clutching her seat. She was distractedly hugging her right side as she scribbled into her notebook.

When the plane settled and the overhead light made its comforting *ding*, Smidge leaned back, stretching her shoulders, rotating one after the other.

"You wanna play a game of cancers?" she asked.

"A game of what?"

"You've got questions, and I've got answers. With a *C*." She drew an arc in the air with her fingertip. *"Canswers."*

"That's clever."

"Not really. I saw it on a brochure and it made me angry. I don't like it when they try to make this thing cutesy."

"Me neither. But lung cancer doesn't seem to get cutsey. I mean, what color would that ribbon be? Brown? Gray?"

"I can tell you want to know what it's like."

"Does that sound morbid? I just want to understand."

She turned toward me but didn't look me in the eye. I could see her debating the right words. Maybe trying to decide what I could handle.

"Give me your hand."

I held out my right hand, but she swatted it away as she took my left. She placed it against her right side, just under her arm.

There was a bulge pushing through an unnatural space between Smidge's ribs, like a golf ball had gotten lodged into her side. The lump seemed both solid and fragile, human and unhuman.

"That's a tumor, sissy," Smidge said.

Dazed at the realization I was holding cancer in my

hand, I lost my breath completely before pulling back like I'd been singed.

"Every question you've got for me ends with that answer," she said, tucking her hands under her legs with a chuckle. "Sorry, I mean it ends with that *canswer.*"

We were quiet after that. She had stunned me out of feeling anything other than helpless grief.

Smidge slept for almost the remainder of the flight; a deep sleep that kept her out during beverage service, a meal, another snack, and a pretty rough patch of turbulence over west Texas. I did my best to keep her covered with a blanket, but it repeatedly slid to the floor. I tried to answer e-mails or write myself a to-do list, but I found I just kept staring at my sleeping friend, wishing I knew what to do, wondering if she felt that mass in her lung with every breath.

Would she fight for me the way I wanted to fight for her? I know she'd be forcing me to get treatment, marching me straight into chemotherapy, holding me down while they injected the chemicals. She wouldn't let me bow out. She wouldn't give me the chance to die.

*"Fix this!"* she'd yell at every oncologist, at anyone within earshot. "Fix my friend, she can't be sick, I need her!"

When the flight attendant began to serve small bowls of ice cream, I made sure Smidge was awake. She'd be furious if I let her miss that.

"Vanilla is just better than all the other ice creams," she said around a mouthful of iced sweetness.

I poked at my strawberry scoop with regret. "I think you're right."

"I *am* right. Death brings you clarity," she said. "Why does strawberry act like it's so special? Just because it's pink? No. Vanilla is perfect. Clean and white and pure and all you need. And don't ruin it by dropping nuts on it."

Our peals of immature laughter woke everybody else in first class.

# TWENTY-TWO

"Los Angeles is brighter than other cities," Smidge said, shielding her eyes as she watched me struggle with our luggage up the flight of concrete stairs to my apartment.

"Everybody always says that when they first get here," I told her. "I think it's the pollution."

Smidge joined me on the second floor, just as out of breath as I was. "I like how you make up science but present it like you read that somewhere."

I opened the door.

"Oh, this place," she said as she walked in. "What did you do to it? It used to be *so nice*."

"Might I remind you I've been unexpectedly out of town."

She wandered, hands pressed to her hips, like she couldn't figure out which piece of furniture to toss first. Was it the coffee table, where the half-filled coffee mug I was drinking from the morning I left still rested, looking rather moldy? Perhaps it was the disheveled couch, which had been doubling as the house sitter's mail receptacle. I felt bad for being embarrassed by my lumpy green corduroy sofa, especially since it had been there for me through many lonely nights.

If I'd known Smidge was coming, I'd have at least cleared the clutter off my dining room table, which was also my desk, which was really more of a recycling bin. It looked trashed. Papers, magazines, and half-read paperbacks scattered across the tabletop, spilling over until they were stacked on the chairs. No fewer than eight pairs of shoes were in sight, pushed aside like a dance contest had been in full riot before everybody disappeared. A lonely fork rested on the table next to a dead plant. A sock had fainted next to the sink. I couldn't imagine what it would look like inside my refrigerator. My place resembled a crime scene, frozen, waiting. Like if you pushed on into my bedroom you'd find my stone-cold corpse. It did make me wonder why more people hadn't been asking where I'd been. I made a mental note to make more local friends.

Smidge slept most of that first day away, which gave me a chance to focus on the things that had fallen behind. It was unsettling to be suddenly back at my desk, a mug of coffee next to my laptop in the place where I liked to keep it. My toes were dug into my familiar carpeting, the grooves in my chair welcomed my body, and before long I found myself back to my familiar procrastination clicks and searches, checking on websites and social networks I hadn't thought much about since I'd left my apartment. I was finally where I'd been wishing to be, but it all felt different than I'd remembered.

There was a surreal disconnect. I was above my life, looking into it, flipping through bills I needed to pay, reading e-mails I hadn't answered from friends who would understand my absence later, but at the time would worry that we were in some kind of fight they didn't remember. There were parties I'd missed, baby showers, a wedding invitation. Life had been moving forward while I was gone, this life I'd been living for a while without noticing how much of it I did by rote. Time used to be an inconvenience, something I needed to maneuver, schedule, carve out. Time got in my way. I had to wait to see someone, sit still long enough for a client to get back to me, stall as I waited for a paycheck, a package, an answer. Time never used to seem finite. It was still my enemy, but now because I couldn't let things wait.

Rainey had definitely noticed I'd dropped off on my website, and sent a rather terse e-mail that I was making her look bad, that I was risking losing sponsors if I didn't start updating more, if I didn't take on new clients. She'd heard I'd passed on the San Francisco gig, and the consultant she went with instead was now in talks to have her own hour on a cable network.

I tried not to let it stress me out, especially considering I'd never wanted my own cable network show, but I still felt like opportunities were passing me by, that I was making myself irrelevant, obsolete.

I was struggling to determine what was important. Was it the life I had in Los Angeles, or the one that was pulling at me back in Ogden, the one that might be waiting for me in not too many days?

When Tucker called I let it go to voice mail.

*"By now you probably know she called when you were here, and that I deleted any proof of that. For what it's worth, I was trying to protect you. Let you be sick in peace. You were a mess,*

*Danielle, and she would've only made you feel guilty and—you know, forget it. I'm sorry I messed with your personal property, but I'm not sorry about what I did. The way you tore out of my place the other morning because of her only shows I did the right thing. I know she's there with you, probably saying worse stuff about me, so I won't wait for you to call back."*

On the drive to a coffee shop the next day, Smidge listed the things she wanted to do during her week in Los Angeles, including eating cheeseburgers and putting her feet in the ocean. Suddenly she squirmed away from me, rolling down her window in horror. "You stink!" she shouted.

Michelle, the acquaintance who'd survived cancer, the one with the polite daughter, had Facebook-messaged me with a few suggestions on how to make Smidge feel better without having to involve doctors.

*I know it seems hokey,* she'd written. *But aromatherapy really helped on days when I hurt. Good smells, like lemon and eucalyptus, make the brain feel better. They have healing properties. Maybe we just like lemons, and eucalyptus smells like a spa, I don't know. Regardless, it did help. And acupuncture was nothing short of an atheist's miracle for me. Please don't make me explain unblocking energy flow.*

"You don't like it?" I asked Smidge. "It's lemon and eucalyptus oil." I showed her the small tinctures of essential oils and hydrosols I'd brought along in my purse. "They're for you. They're supposed to help make you feel better."

"No, thank you," she said, waving at her nose. "You smell like an old lady's crotch."

"Well, take the lavender water, at the very least. It's supposed to be soothing."

"Meaning it'll shut me up?"

"No, Smidge. Only a bullet could do that."

She kissed the back of my hand for that one. But getting her to try acupuncture was a complete disaster.

"I've scheduled a sort-of massage for you."

She spotted my verbal gymnastics immediately. "Define 'sort of.'"

"It's a California thing, Smidge. Just give it a try. Lots of people out here like it."

She gave a quick clap. "Is it tiny ladies walking on my back? Because you know how much I love that. Can you get me one of those massages again?"

"Wouldn't that hurt your tumor?"

She looked disappointed. "Maybe. You take the fun out of everything."

I couldn't pretend everything was normal and fun; that we were just hanging out in my city like a couple of pals. It seemed like too big of a lie.

"It's acupuncture. People say that can help."

"Nice try," she said, lowering her sunglasses. "I told you I was done with needles. Even the weird ones. No more poking!"

But I had to do something. Smidge was starting to require much more sleep each day. I was so used to her constant whirlwind that to see her, head cocked back, mouth open, almost drooling on one of my throw pillows, felt like my Smidge had been secretly switched at the airport. They gave me one that was low on batteries.

At moments when she did seem more like herself, she'd be chattering full force, sticking her fingers in every pair of cement hands in front of Mann's Chinese Theatre, when she'd suddenly deflate, a wave of exhaustion leaving her crumbled. "But I wanted my picture taken with the fake Johnny Depp pirate," she said wearily, pouting as I helped her back to my car, referring to the handful of celebrity impersonators who gathered in front of the cemented tributes. Jack Sparrow had flirted with Smidge as she'd passed him earlier, something about her "booty."

"We'll come back tomorrow," I promised.

But the next day she'd moved on to a new desire, one she told me over her morning five-shot espresso. "I want you to score me some pot."

Your mother and I weren't really all that into drugs. I know that sounds like something parents say when they're trying to cover up huge swaths of stoner years, but this is the truth. We'd both tried pot in college, and your mom did acid once at a Lollapalooza concert. Although I'm pretty sure she was sold a fake and was acting to save face, as everybody else I knew who bought tabs off that guy said they were bogus. (Why is it we only use words like *bogus* when talking about people who sold drugs back in college?)

Because we were in California, one could acquire it legally, but the problem was, *I* couldn't. I didn't have a prescription. Luckily, almost every other person I knew did.

I picked my friend Mia because while she got high all the time, I can't recall ever seeing her stoned. I chose a pot person like I was choosing a wine connoisseur—someone who knew what she was talking about, but was discreet.

Mia was also one of the few people I knew who wouldn't want us to smoke it with her after she bought it. I learned that inconvenient rule the last time I thought about buying marijuana. Smidge would never agree to such a stoner tax; she would balk at the idea of hanging out in a stranger's living room for hours. Not that I have any desire to get high and then wait out having to go home. I'd never stop being paranoid.

The one time I did get high before going to a movie, I was convinced everybody in the theater—and even the people *in the film itself*—knew I was high. I was sure the police were on their way to arrest me. I fled to a Pinkberry, ordered "all the toppings without the fake yogurt crap," and ate candy, fruit, and nuts until I no longer felt like I was being persecuted by the fuzz. After that experience, I try to put myself under house arrest if I'm going to smoke.

Mia's wrists were loaded with bangles. Leather bracelets twisted halfway up her arms. She jingled and clanked as she drove her Prius down Sunset Boulevard. She wore purple sunglasses that hid half of her face. Her dark, glossy hair was tied in a knot above her right shoulder. One spaghetti strap of her tank dangled in a lazy, sexy way, highlighting the white line that cut across her deep, soft tan. Her lips were pink and glossy, the only hint of a cosmetic. She was all summer on top but winter below; a battered pair of Uggs adorned her feet. This was standard outfit for a girl in Los Angeles running errands in late autumn weather. You can determine the season only by thickness of her scarf. Mia's was thin, made of T-shirt material.

She pulled into a strip-mall parking lot. Surrounding us were a 7-Eleven, a nail salon, a dry cleaner, a Thai delivery place, and a nondescript storefront I knew was the dispensary because of the seemingly ubiquitous sign of a green cross on a white background.

"Okay, you two," she said after she'd parked. "I need to know what you want."

"Duh!" shouted Smidge, clapping her hands together like someone had just brought out a birthday cake for a two-year-old. "We want pot. The weed. Drugs, please."

Mia nodded, unfazed. "I meant how much."

"Oh, I should give you money," I stammered, digging into my purse. This whole thing, as legal as it was, still felt shady. I guess because what *we* were doing wasn't legal. We were in a parking lot handing over cash so that someone would buy us drugs. I was already getting paranoid, antsy to get this over with.

"Do you want me to buy stuff for you guys to eat, to smoke, to drink?" Mia asked.

"Yep," said Smidge. "All of it."

"We don't need to smoke anything," I said, handing over eighty dollars. "Is this enough?"

She smirked. "God, I hope so."

"And buy some for yourself, too."

"Thanks, Danielle. I was going to do that, anyway. Now I don't have to steal it from you."

"Hey, what do *you* have?" Smidge tapped Mia on the bare shoulder with a sudden interest.

"What do you mean?"

"What do you have that makes you need pot?"

"Uh, a job I don't like? Debt?" Mia looked at me, confused.

"Smidge, it's not polite to ask people their medical history."

"Oh," Mia said, nodding. "I have *anxiety*. That's how I got the card. So much anxiety."

Smidge looked at her hands. It wasn't often you would catch her in a moment of naïveté. When it happened it felt like a glitch in her whole system. "I'm like country came to town," she mumbled.

Mia ducked out of the car, telling us to wait. She disappeared into the dark building, sliding between heavy curtains that hung just inside the door.

Smidge spritzed lavender water on her wrists and inhaled. "You were right. This stuff smells good and makes me feel better." She opened her door to let the sun shine on her face. "All this stuff makes me feel better. Why doesn't everyone live in California?"

"Maybe you should shut that," I said, concerned.

"Why?"

"A police car has pulled into the parking lot."

Smidge leaned forward, her face going pale. "Oh, my God. It just hit me, what we're doing. And now the cops are here. Danielle! What are we doing? We're criminals!"

I thought she was teasing at first, but she seemed actually scared. "I don't know," I said. "Calm down. It'll be fine."

"But what if the cops ask Mia who she's buying the drugs for? What if she tells them the truth? Do we go to jail for that?"

"I don't know."

"Maybe we should get out of this car!"

I looked around. "And go where? That Thai food joint?"

"Don't say *joint*! Oh, my God! I can't wait here! I ain't no sitting duck!"

Smidge shot out of the backseat like a bullet. She wiggle-stepped over to the 7-Eleven, half hurrying, half trying to look nonchalant. She even mimed tipping a hat toward the officer, who was taking a break, leaning against his car.

I couldn't just leave Mia's car. If she came back and both of us were gone, she might drive away. I certainly would've, if the people I had just bought drugs for skipped out when a cop parked next to my Prius.

Ten minutes later Mia still hadn't appeared and the police officer hadn't budged. Smidge came wandering back, sucking an enormous Slurpee. She knocked on my window. Smidge lowered her voice, trying to sound official. "Ma'am, can I ask you why you're sitting in this parking lot?"

"Get in the car and shut up."

As Smidge slid back into her seat, Mia opened her door and dropped into the car before lowering a paper bag into my lap. It was heavier than I expected and I heard glass bottles clank against each other.

"It's okay that there's a cop right there?" I asked.

Mia laughed. "Is that why you two look like you just pissed your pants?"

Smidge looked over her shoulder out the back window. "Drive!" she shouted. "What are you waiting for? Let's go, let's go, let's go!"

Mia slowly backed up. "You are a trip," she said. "I think this is going to be actually medicinal for you."

"In many ways," I said, leaning back into my seat, relieved to be done with our dangerous errand.

But once we were sitting on the floor of my living room, red-faced and breathless from laughter, eating cheeseburgers while ordering a large pizza, I was grateful we'd made the journey.

"I have never been this happy in my entire life!" Smidge shouted over the phone to the pizza deliveryman. "You are bringing a pizza and therefore I may just kiss you. Consider yourself warned, pizza man!"

As she searched my pantry for Doritos, she wondered, "Why haven't we been stoners our entire lives? This is my one regret. I should've felt like this more often in life. I haven't been in this much *not* pain in a very long time. Everything just feels so good, so good, *soooo gooooood*!"

"When did they say the pizza would get here?" I asked. "I'm still hungry."

"They said it will be here any minute," Smidge replied, standing on her bare tiptoes to nudge a box of Raisin Bran from the high shelf. Reading the side of the box, she asked, "How much fiber is a bad idea for one night?"

My head felt fuzzy, but in a good way, like it was formulating something important. "That's not true, is it? That the pizza will be here any minute."

Smidge was counting on her fingers. "What are you talking about?"

"Well, it can't be here *now*, so there's one minute that can't count as 'any,' because it's not here. Also, it can't have been here the last minute."

"Oh, you're saying if 'any' refers to the *concept* of 'any'—"

"Which means all things, right?"

Smidge was getting it. Her eyes lit up as she rubbed her nose excitedly. "Right. You're right! The pizza won't be here 'any' minute. Because the pizza will not arrive during the French Revolution."

I raised one finger. "Our pizza will not be here when the Beatles sing on *The Ed Sullivan Show*."

"Our pizza will not arrive that time Marty McFly went back to 1955."

"Smidgey, that's fictional."

"Even better! All fictional minutes should count in the concept of 'any'!"

"Genius."

"I know. We totally wasted our lives not being genius pot-heads. Dans, I love you the mostest. Thanks for letting me be a druggie."

That night she taught me how to snap a bottlecap across the room. She French-braided my hair. We had a slumber party that ended with us falling asleep in front of the television about six minutes into *The Legend of Billie Jean*.

I love this memory of your mom because it wasn't often she'd allow herself to be truly free. That night she couldn't have cared less what anybody thought about her, including when she actually tongue-kissed that pizza deliveryman. Your mother would kill me if she knew I told you this story, but there it is. I think of it every time I want to imagine her giddy and satiated, and truly at her silliest. When she just loved me and loved being together. No agenda. No judgment. It had only the parts of her that made up the best of who she was.

I often think of that night for another reason. It was the last time I ever let myself believe she would find a way to live forever.

## TWENTY-THREE

We'd reached one of the six days of the year when it rains in Los Angeles. There was a late-October storm that would be gone within an hour or two, but would tangle traffic for the rest of the day. This was, of course, exactly when Smidge and I were headed to the beach. Consequently, we'd been stuck in traffic on the highway for more than an hour before she broke what I sensed was a thoughtful silence.

"Do you remember that idiot cat you had with the missing eye?" she asked. "In that apartment before I met Henry, the place we left because of the termites and Bucktooth Betty with the tap shoes?"

"Sprockets," I said.

Sprockets wasn't a very smart kitty. He had depth perception problems because of his eye, and he seemed to be in a constant battle with what his whiskers were telling him about his world compared to what he could see out of half of his head. Consequently, Sprockets often would get lost in a corner, standing still, staring at the wall until someone came over to turn him around. Sprockets almost drowned in the toilet one night. He burned his tail on a candle. Sprockets was a bit of a sad case.

"You hated that cat," I said.

"I did not. Please don't confuse apathy with hatred. But you loved Sprockets. I guess because he *was* so pathetic."

I got a little misty at the memory of his lopsided, orange face, how his weird eye socket made it seem he was an abandoned stuffed toy. "He was a little pathetic," I admitted. "He was sweet, though. He liked to sleep on my feet."

Smidge took a sip from her coffee. It was after three and she was still drinking hot coffee. I don't know how she could do it; I would have been up all night. "What happened to Sprockets?" she asked me.

I had to put him down. She knew this. "What is your point?"

"You found him under the building. You knew he'd been hit by a car and had dragged himself under there. What did you do?"

"I accused Bucktooth Betty of running him over because she always drove so fast in the parking lot."

"And then you wrapped him in your flannel and you took him to the vet, where you had him put down."

I swallowed the lump rising in my throat as I tried to focus on the personalized license plate of the car in front of me.

Up until the moment Sprockets' body went limp, I'd never seen anything die. It wasn't peaceful to me. It was awful. It felt like someone had robbed my cat of its very catness, as I stood by, helpless to stop it.

The license plate read: SUPRSTR8. I couldn't tell if it stood for *Super Star 8* or *Super Straight*.

"I'm no different than Sprockets," Smidge said.

Maybe *Soup or Street*?

"My grampa went down the long way," she continued. "He wasn't that old, but he was really sick. He spent years withering away, and I had to watch it. The Lizard would take me over there and I'd have to sit with him in his hospital while he stayed hooked up to machines. He went away piece by piece. Sometimes he'd lose a memory; sometimes he lost control of his bowels. Sometimes the Lizard had to feed him."

"When was this?"

"I was eight. That man had fought wars and won medals and now we had to take a break during Christmas so my grandmother and my father could tag-team changing his diaper. He didn't die until I was almost Jenny's age. One day he told me about the cyanide capsule they made him carry on his uniform during the war, in case he was ever captured. Told me he'd been dreaming about cyanide pills for months. You know what he said to me then? Well, he thought I was Ginger Rogers so he said, 'Never let them do this to you, Ginger. Find the way out.'"

I gave her a couple of seconds before I made my point. "Smidge, that was an old man, and he lived a full life. I bet your grandfather wouldn't want you to do what you're doing. He'd say maybe stop focusing on whether or not *I'm* wearing the right nail polish, and look into seeing if taking some fish oil and niacin pills might keep you around for another year or two."

A space opened up to the right. I pulled in and drove alongside the Lexus that was previously in front of me so I could put a face to the personalized license plate. I glanced at the driver, who was an older, Hispanic female. She was shaking her head while talking on her Bluetooth headset, fingers outstretched on her steering wheel.

I'm gonna go with *Superstar 8*.

"I *hatechoo*," Smidge said.

"Why? Because I don't support you on your little death wish?"

"Because you think things can be simple and then you judge me for not doing what you want me to do. You think I'm weak when I don't do what you think I should do."

"I cannot believe you just said that." I felt my neck wrench as I turned to face her. "How is that any different than the way you think of me?"

"It is completely different."

"In what way, Smidge?"

"I can't believe you live twelve miles from the beach and it takes an hour to get there. This city is fucking stupid."

It took another fifteen minutes to get to the water, which was the same length as the heavy sigh that came out of me.

Smidge jammed both of her feet into the sand and took as deep an inhale as she could muster. "This is good," she said. "Can you bottle up *this* smell? This feels like it could help."

I was still too upset to pretend everything was fine. I kept my fists in my pockets as I stared out at the horizon, shaking my head.

"Okay, that's it," Smidge said as she pushed me backward onto my butt, plopping directly into the damp sand. I was unprepared for her strength.

She straddled my stomach, sitting over me like an older brother about to spit in my face.

I didn't struggle. "Get off me."

Sand stuck to her cheek. She ran the back of her hand across her forehead as she sneered.

"This is officially the last time I talk to you about this," she said. "*This is it.* I cannot get better. It sucks and it ain't fair, and it's embarrassing enough without you trying to make it sound like I am doing some kind of high-horse bullshit, which I assure you, I am not."

She lifted her head to gasp a few breaths, trying to calm down. The tide was coming up around our feet, chilling the backs of my legs. My toes were numb from exposure.

Smidge continued. "You're all I've got. I hate that I need you, but I do. When you were gone over at Tucker's, I was lost. I tried to do it alone, and I couldn't. I was miserable and terrified, and I couldn't bring myself to tell Henry. Don't make me break my husband's heart. You need to start acting like my best friend. Not a husband, mother, teacher, or doctor. Do you understand?"

I lifted my left hand to her torso, and gently pressed my palm against her rib cage, cradling where I knew she was the most broken.

"Damn, Smidge," I said, tears streaking across my face until they dripped warm into my ears. "Why didn't you just say that in the first place?"

## TWENTY-FOUR

———————————

I felt different after that. I don't know how else to explain it, other than I had a purpose that was *with* Smidge, not because of her. I let our remaining time in Los Angeles play out as our last vacation together. We decided to cross off a few of Smidge's wishes that had nothing to do with the business of her family.

Starting with skydiving.

She made me promise not to tell anybody, which is why this is probably the first you've heard of it. She somehow got it into her head that it was one thing she always wanted to do but had been too scared to try.

"What's the worst that could happen, I die?" she asked. I was very concerned about her lungs at high altitudes, but her doctor told her by phone that the most dangerous thing was that she could panic. "I'll be fine," she insisted.

But I made the mistake of staying up the night before on the internet, reading about the risks. "Thirty-five people a year die doing this!" I told her as we headed toward what I hoped wasn't going to be my final destination.

"Only thirty-five?" Smidge marveled. "I would've thought it'd be higher."

I chickened out. It wasn't my dream, and it wasn't like we were going to hold hands as we went down. She'd be strapped to an expert, lost in her own tandem jump. I waited on the ground with a camera for what felt like forever.

Smidge wasn't consistent in her fearlessness. The woman jumping out of that plane would leap just as high if she suddenly found herself standing next to a clown. Your mother never took you trick-or-treating because she was frightened by small children wearing masks. Henry did all the door-to-door stuff, shuffling you around on the early shift so he had time to get back home to deliver candy to the neighborhood ghosts and goblins knocking at the door. Smidge would hide in her bedroom, drinking, doing a horrible job of pretending she wasn't terrified a child would break through the entryway and come running down the hallway, hell-bent on stealing her soul.

A girl with blond dreads, somehow looking shapely in a blue jumpsuit, pointed toward the sky. "There's your friend," she said.

At first it was just an orange dot. But that dot grew in size, twirling and swooping as it got closer to the ground. Eventually I could make out a parachute followed by the humans dangling underneath. The rest of it happened quite quickly. Smidge and her instructor swept one way, turned another, and then came to the ground with a thud.

"I did it!" she shouted at me, arms raised, struggling to move inside all that protective gear.

"Are you okay? Did it hurt?"

"A little, but I don't care! This is so much better than acu-puncture!"

Dinner that night was straight out of Smidge's medical-marijuana-fueled fantasy: mac-'n'-cheese-'n'-In-N-Out—a double-meat cheeseburger stuffed with macaroni and cheese, slathered in heart attack. My friend might have been wasting away, but as we entertained her whims, I could feel myself growing larger.

"I just fell out of the sky!" Smidge said, cramming a hand-ful of french fries into her mouth. "I couldn't think of any-thing but that. No cancer up there. Just me falling to the ground, deciding to come back to the planet."

She had repeated that story to me at least five times. With every retelling she'd remember another detail—how she wasn't scared until the instructor asked if she was ready; how her brain initially disconnected from the experience as it looked like the earth was curved below her; how peaceful it was once the parachute took over, gently gliding them back to the ground. "I didn't even think to be scared," she always concluded. "Next time I bet I'll be. This time I just did a lot of looking."

She must have seen my face as I silently debated the proba-bility of there being a next time. "I'm telling you, I feel great," she said. "I feel so healthy. Maybe this is the secret," she said. "Extremes will help keep me alive. Adrenaline and shock."

"And heavy foods?"

"Yes. The heavier, the better! My body won't have time to replicate mutated cells. It'll be too busy keeping up with me. I love that I'm finally hungry again."

I lifted my glass. "Cheers to that."

She was halfway through getting a tattoo when I finally asked if there was a chance this was a version of a midlife crisis.

She stared down at the raised, red skin tight against her right hipbone. The thin, dark line would eventually form the name *Jenny* in cursive, discreetly hidden just below her waistband.

"Technically we can now confirm I had my midlife crisis at eighteen." She winced, exhaling through a pucker.

She was trapped underneath the steady hand of a tattoo artist named Tiger, a white man with dark eyes and a thick, black bar driven through his septum. I decided to use her imprisonment to attempt to get some truth out of her.

"Henry said something the last night I was at your house," I started, pausing to scratch my arm. "He said you still sometimes feel bad about James."

"Bad? About your divorce?"

"Maybe. But I don't know, he used the word 'guilty.' And then he wouldn't tell me what he meant. You know what he meant, don't you?"

She went still. "I suppose you're a big girl now," she said.

The back of my neck became sticky and hot as the blood left my toes. Smidge had something to confess. I could tell because she wasn't relishing this moment. Her face was a complete blank.

"You're already divorced, so it shouldn't matter," she said. "But your husband once made a pass at me. There. The end. Weight lifted."

Time slowed to a crawl. "What kind of pass?"

I hated how she would make me fish for painful information, yanking the truth out of her crumb by crumb until we
dug into what really mattered. I'd sometimes have to embark
on an hour-long excavation in order to finally start hacking at
the most important bits.

She pretended to be concerned with her tattoo. "Do you
need a drink of water, Tiger? You've been working for so
long."

"He's fine," I said. "Answer the question."

"He made the kind of pass that men shouldn't make at
their fiancée's best friend."

"*Fiancée?* When did this happen?"

"That's such a specific question."

"That's the point."

"I punched him in the balls. Don't you want to hear that
part?"

Tiger pulled back in his chair. "Do you ladies need a moment?"

"No," Smidge said. "I might need a witness."

I didn't appreciate her trying to lighten the mood. "What
happened?"

"You were fixing to get married and I didn't want to ruin
anything."

"Ruin what? How 'fixing' were we?"

She didn't answer.

"A month?" No answer. "A week?" Still no answer. "A day?"

"Yes. A day. *The* day. I mean, technically."

"*The* day? My wedding day? It happened on my wedding
day and you didn't tell me?"

Was it okay to punch a woman with cancer? There had to be times when everybody would get behind it. What if she were kicking kittens, or sitting on a baby?

I left Smidge trapped in that chair so I could pace the parking lot.

No wonder she was so supportive of the divorce. She practically moved all my furniture into that empty apartment all by herself. The weight certainly had been lifted, not just now when she told me, but back when the final papers were signed, when she and James no longer held a secret bond.

That must be why she thought I could just *be* with Henry once she wouldn't be there anymore. If she could have such intimate knowledge with *my* husband, if she could be a part of that marriage without me even having a clue, why wouldn't she think of a husband and wife as an arrangement, an agreement, and not much more?

"Hey!" It was Tiger, half leaning out the glass door of the tattoo shop, his face pale and strained. "Hey, your friend needs help! I called 911!"

———————

The ambulance came quickly, and as they worked on your mother, Tiger told me what had happened.

After I stormed out Smidge tried to make a few jokes with Tiger, but instead began to cry. I told Tiger he must be mistaken. Smidge never cries.

"That's the thing," he said. "I know she was crying because she tried to blame it on the tattoo, that I was hurting her, but I wasn't inking her at the time. I had just finished. Then she started crying harder, started choking or coughing. That's when I first got worried."

Tiger told me Smidge then stood suddenly, possibly to come find me. She lost her footing, wavered slightly, and passed out, slamming her head on a table as she fell. The paramedics revived her, applied ice, and administered fluids, but her blood oxygen level was low enough they felt she needed to be admitted for monitoring.

I waited for hours at the hospital before she had a room I could visit. When I finally saw her, spread thin under the sheets like a mottled paper doll, quietly gasping under an oxygen mask, I briefly lost my own breath. After all that life Smidge had been living the week she'd been in California, she looked frozen in a moment quite close to death.

There was a dark lump on her forehead, just below her hairline. Smidge lifted her puffy eyelids to look at me. She couldn't speak because of that mask, and was too weak to move. She did nothing more than hold my gaze for a few moments before closing her eyes again. But I'd heard what she was telling me as clearly as if she'd just yelled it straight into my ear.

*Shit, Danny. It's starting.*

I reached the foot of her bed and told her what I'd been thinking since we arrived at the hospital.

"I think you came to Los Angeles to die." I said it loudly, so there could be no doubt it reached her ears over the beeping and wheezing of the machines, through the thick haze of selfish thoughts and self-protective acts she'd been using as insulation. "It was a hunch I had at first, but I'm sure that's what was going on. You thought you could come here and wear yourself out and then die on my couch so I'd have to go home and deal with your family."

Smidge's eyes met mine with a weary, guilty stare.

"Well, that's not what's going to happen, you coward," I said. "And I can't believe you thought I'd get tricked into that."

I stood over her and readied myself, hoping I could handle what I was about to say.

"I'm in charge now," I said. "I run your life. And first things first: we have to get you home, you stubborn bitch."

From under that oxygen mask, even through the fog of condensation, I swear I saw your mother's crooked smile.

# TWENTY-FIVE

I must've woken Smidge close to fifteen times to make her walk around the airplane during those flights home. The doctor told me of her elevated risk of blood clots, and I wasn't taking any chances. I could just hear the gossip in Ogden if something happened.

*Smidge was fine until she went to California. Then Danny brought her body back dead with a tattoo.*

Smidge engaged in a gentle form of calisthenics at the front of the plane, chatting up the flight attendants until she came back with a plate of warm chocolate chip cookies.

"They're real nice ladies," Smidge said. "They're also bringing over some champagne. I think they're being all Make-A-Wish."

"They kinda are." I stared at the foundation-caked lump on her forehead and wondered for how much longer we were going to keep her secret.

Smidge told me about the weeks leading up to finding out about the cancer's return. She'd been under a lot of stress, and almost ended up in the hospital with pneumonia, which settled into a cough she couldn't shake. At the time she'd been hoping to run a marathon with a couple of her friends from down the street, but when she could no longer keep up with them after mile eight, she knew something was more serious. She went to her doctor, who confirmed her deepest fear. Her cancer was no longer in remission, and it had metastasized. Maybe a year, maybe less.

"I didn't tell anyone for a while. When I went to see you that last time I already knew. I didn't want to pile on to your divorce sadness, but I was also in a panic, Danny. I thought maybe if I never mentioned it to anybody, it would go away. I went crazy not telling Henry, since I saw him every day and he knows when something's bothering me, but the hardest was keeping it from you. It felt like I'd started cheating on you, having an affair with my disease."

I thought about telling her right then about Tucker, how I'd been doing the same kind of hiding. But I didn't want to risk a new fight. I wrapped an arm around her and pulled her toward me. I kissed the top of her head, resting my face in her hair. "Hey, I'm sorry we never got on that cruise ship."

She admitted, "I already did it with Jenny."

I pulled back in surprise. "You did? When?"

"Right after the diagnosis. It was a tiny trip, just for a few days, right when she got out of school for the summer. I told her not to tell you."

"She didn't."

She laughed. "I told her you'd be mad."

"I wouldn't! But I would've known something was up."

"Exactly."

"How was it?"

"How do you think? Trapped on a boat with a bunch of strangers and only one real place to eat. It was awful. And, Jenny can't drink, so she was pretty useless." Then she added, "I don't really mean that. I'm the worst mother."

"What do we do now?" I asked. "I mean, I know I'm in charge, but say that I wasn't. What's next?"

She studied her fingertips like she was debating getting a manicure. "Well," she said. "*Palliative care.* That's what we're doing now. It means make sure I'm constantly happy until I'm dead."

"Then you've been in palliative care pretty much since you were nine."

"My birthday is coming up. Can I have a party?"

"Are you asking me for permission to do something?"

The overhead light dinged. The flight attendant informed us that we were prepping for our initial descent. Smidge nodded.

"Okay. Then I grant you permission to have a birthday party."

She smiled, and that's when I had that familiar rising in my stomach, the one that meant I'd been tricked again. "And guess what will happen when the party is over?" she asked casually, staring down at her seat-back button.

"Tell me," I said, my tongue heavy with dread.

She sat up, fidgeted with her T-shirt, fluffed out her hair. She popped her knuckles at the middle joints, one at a time. "You ever searched 'dying of lung cancer' on YouTube?"

"No."

"Nothing but a bunch of withering, gasping zombies praying for death. There's no way I'm putting Henry and Jenny through that. I can't let that girl remember her mother that way. I'm going to die with a little dignity. Just as soon as everything's in order, I'm going out like a rock star. And you're going to help me."

"You're asking me to commit murder."

She tossed that aside with a grunt. "Don't be so dramatic. I'll find a way to make sure you don't get in trouble. But I like how you're immediately making this all about you."

"It's not about getting in trouble. Morally—"

"*Soooooo,*" she sang as she lifted the shade on her window to watch the landing. "I don't think you get to have an opinion about this."

"Of course I do," I said to her back.

"You don't." She didn't look at me when she said her next sentence, and that's how I knew it was the most honest thing she'd ever say to me. "You skipped out on me last time, Danielle. You weren't there. I've said nothing for years. I know you feel guilty, so here's your punishment. This time it's on you. You said you're in control of my life now? Then you have to be the one to end it."

I lurched forward to grab the paper bag from the seat back in front of me, flipping it open just in time before I threw up all over myself.

Smidge went back to studying her nails. "So dramatic."

---

## TWENTY-SIX

It seemed like everybody in Ogden had a secret they were keeping both with me and from one another. I felt like the center of a sticky web. Surely it was only a matter of time before something got caught in it, but I had no idea how I was going to react when that happened.

I felt like all of you were in denial. I kept assuming someone would ask, someone would say something, *someone* had to make the truth come out. But when nobody wants to know anything the truth stays hidden much longer than it deserves. I was desperate for one of you to turn to me and ask, "What exactly is going on?"

I knew Tucker had said something to Henry, because both of them were carefully avoiding me. Tucker wasn't calling, and Henry would find an excuse to leave the room the second I entered it. I didn't know what to say to either of them, but I felt like it was time to start preparing people.

There was a new sound in Smidge's cough, a lurch right in the middle of her hacking that was followed by a quick sniff, a gasp. Her doctor gave her an oxygen tank, but she would sneak away to use it, driving to the parking lot behind the library. She chose a place where Ogden's homeless gathered, as it was the only spot she knew she wouldn't run into anybody. But someone had to have seen her, if not in her backseat, pulling breaths from a plastic tube in her nose, then when she was hauling an oxygen tank out of the Ogden Medical Center. I bet she told people she was volunteering at a senior citizen home.

"I'm trying to get some morphine off the internet," she told me. "And I wrote up a DNR." Her voice was icy with decision. "Not long now."

Something had shifted in Smidge since we got back. A hardening. She had a look I recognized from when she drank too much. She could get mouthy; a careless fearlessness would overtake her, ensuring she would piss off at least one person in the room. I knew she had the potential to be even more unpredictable.

"Henry isn't happy to see you," Smidge admitted.

"I bet not. He doesn't know why I'm here. You need to tell him. You need to tell him first and then everyone else. It's time, Smidge."

She folded her arms as she stared at the floor. "You're right," she said. "I will do it right after the party. Let me get one last memory of everyone happy before they all start looking at me differently, okay?"

I decided to give her that one last request. A *last* last request. At the time, it didn't seem to be an outrageous one. I also knew Smidge would find some comfort in the process of planning. Party prep always made her happy. She got adrenaline jolts from crossing things off a list. Any list. And this party had *lists.* The invitations, the decorations, the food.

Since she didn't have the stamina to run these errands, she'd send me out to do the work. If I wasn't heading toward Lavender's Flowers and Stems ordering a massive delivery, I was at Brandy's Baked Goodness making a deposit on a cake. Often I was on the phone with Smidge listening to her mentally process which runner would look best on the entryway table.

I faded out during a particular one-sided phone conversation as I watched dark clouds swirling overhead. The skies turned an ominous green color, making me wonder if I was about to become the center of a natural disaster. I knew if I returned to Smidge empty-handed, having to inform her that a tornado stole the helium tanks, she'd spin me right back out with her own funnel of energy.

A thunderclap so loud it sounded like someone had shot up my car interrupted whatever it was Smidge was saying.

"I am going to die!" I shouted into the phone.

"Not before you go get cupcake papers!" Smidge shouted back. "I need them pronto!"

The world overhead broke open as the storm hit. Sheets of rain pelted my car. It sounded like I was inside a popcorn maker. Visibility shot, I dropped the phone into my lap and slowly made my way to the side of the road.

I checked my e-mail, and was shocked by the number of requests and questions. Rainey must have put out some kind of call for new clients.

A mother who "desperately needed" me to help her solve a problem with her daughter biting other kids on the playground asked if I would e-mail her toddler a video request to behave. "She responds well to things she sees on the computer," she had written.

Before I had a moment to second-guess myself, I wrote back, "I'm sorry. My best friend has terminal cancer and I am unable to attend to your request."

*Send.* I just did it, before I could stop myself.

Trembling, I pulled up another e-mail. This client was furious that I hadn't called her florist to stop her weekly delivery. "You can tell me that I can't afford it, but you can't find the time to make it stop? You want me to humiliate my-self by admitting to this flower-pusher that I can't have nice things?"

I wrote back, "I'm sorry. My best friend has terminal can-cer and I am unable to attend to your request."

*Send.*

I went down the list, sending the same response to client after client, feeling nothing but the empty ache of freedom that comes with the truth. From food issues to construction woes, from the parents who felt pressure to have cloth diapers to the parents who felt pressure to tell their neighbors to have cloth diapers, I e-mailed each and every one, "I'm sorry. My best friend has terminal cancer and I am unable to attend to your request."

This decision was final. I couldn't do those things anymore. I didn't want to. I didn't care about them because my best friend had terminal cancer and I was unable to attend to their requests.

I'd never made a peanut butter sandwich without the crusts for a small child. I'd never carried a feverish baby to the hospital in the middle of the night, terrified that something was wrong. But I went on television with these opinions on homemaking and childraising like it was easy. I made money off people who were feeling lost and helpless, and I never thought before about why people were willing to do that.

When you feel that helpless, that useless, you desperately want to find a right answer. I'd told married couples how to work out their sex lives when I knew next to nothing about the sexual history of either person. I had no training in therapy whatsoever, and yet at one point I felt qualified to create calendars for people with date nights and "sexy time." I recommended lingerie and games. How bold I was, thinking I knew anything about the lives of strangers, as if coupons and chore wheels were all anybody needed to save their relationships. I sold a fantasy and even worse, I made it seem like any life could be had, if you just chose it.

Maybe it's true I never asked for the job, that originally I was just trying to help a friend, but as my client list grew and people had more and more outrageous requests, I tried to fake it until I made it. I should've stopped when I knew I was bluffing. People just kept thanking me, and then referred me to their friends. Why could I do what Smidge did, but only if I was talking to people who weren't really in my life? And why didn't I ever see I was being exactly like her?

The culture I'd created for myself as someone who knew how to make hard things look easy was just that: an illusion.

I couldn't fake it anymore. Real life was much harder than achieving perfection.

I pressed the button for my website app on my phone and began drawing up a new entry. It was an open letter to my clients, past and present. I let them know that I had a newfound respect for what they'd done to get this far with each other, how they stay together even though life gets scary and sad.

That while I appreciated our time together, and it'd been an honor coming into their homes, getting to know them, they had the power to fix themselves. They always did. They just forgot to trust it.

I finished with, "I'm not trying to get preachy here. I want you to know that you can do this. Do not spend your life worrying what others think of you. They aren't in your house. Only you are. Fill it with love, and don't worry how many crumbs are on the floor. That just proves you lived there."

When I hit Send I realized I'd effectively destroyed my own business. And not to get too mystical about it, but at the same moment, the rain abruptly stopped. It got silent in my car, quiet enough that I looked around, spooked. Had I just gone deaf? Had my life been put on pause?

Down South, Mother Nature was just like any other Southern lady. All hellfire and crazy for five minutes, making you worry everything you love is about to catch on fire from a lightning bolt. But then, just as suddenly: sunshine and breezes. Everything's a little cleaner and the sky looks like it has no recollection of what it just did.

I'd pulled my car to the side of the street, but only now was I given the chance to gather my whereabouts. Turns out I wasn't too far from the party supply store; it was just up ahead a couple of blocks. I leaned forward to peer at the sky. That's when I saw another looming pool of darkness headed my way at a steady clip. When I looked back at the road, there was Tucker, running down the street in his escape clothes.

I got out of my car and headed toward him.

# TWENTY-SEVEN

It isn't easy to run alongside a man who's pretending he's not trying to outrun you. I wanted it to come off like it was no big deal to trot alongside of him, but I was in a pair of Chuck Taylors, feeling the gritty, slippery concrete through the thin rubber bottoms.

Tucker seemed torn between showing off and keeping pace to hear what I had to say. He opted to stare straight ahead, soaking wet, rainwater dropping from his curls like he'd just stepped out of a shower.

"I wanted to apologize," I said, already feeling the burning in my lungs. Fifty yards in and it was the most exercise I'd done in months.

Tucker didn't respond. He just kept jogging, his tongue jutting a lump from the inside of his left cheek.

"You're not going to talk to me?" I asked.

I stopped running and had to drop my hands to my knees. "I cannot believe you're letting a girl chase you down the street."

Tucker swung back around to me, stretching his arms behind him. "You aren't the first."

We took a moment to catch our breath.

"Thanks for stopping," I said.

"Hey, what's your business is your business. I no longer care."

"Please don't be like that."

Tucker walked in a circle, hands on his hips, his breath quieting as he shook his head in amazement. "I have a feeling you are about to ask if we can just be friends," he said.

"I don't even mean it that way."

He flipped his head back toward the darkened sky as the wind picked up around us. "Why do women always need to decide on everything?" he asked. "Why must it be discussed until it is boring? Can't some things just suck or be broken and then we leave them alone?"

"Are you talking about us?" I asked, confused.

"*Us?* What *us*? You haven't even called me."

"I wanted to."

"She wanted to," Tucker said to a passing mother seeking shelter. She was frantically pushing a stroller toward the nearest building, unaware Tucker was talking to her. "I like how you *wanted* to. That's touching, really."

My skin was sweaty from the jog and damp from the humidity. I always forgot how the heat could stick around until November sometimes. Just under my right knee, a mosquito bite was reddening on my shin. "I did want to, Tucker. I thought about it."

"I feel stupid for thinking things were better when I was with you," he said.

He started walking away, but I followed. "It's not stupid," I said. "I feel better when I'm with you, too."

"That's because you're away from Smidge. Henry's miserable, do you know that?" A breeze flipped his hat, exposing swirls of damp hair clinging to his forehead, his neck. Before it hit the ground, Tucker bounced the hat off his knee and caught it. "You two aren't fooling anybody, and I just hope you know what you're doing. Because it sure does seem like . . ."

"Like what?"

He exhaled here, incredulous. "I don't know. Forget it."

Heavy drops of rain started to fall, pelting the back of my head, gaining intensity by the second.

"What do you think it is, Tucker?" I asked, hoping he'd say it. Just say it, and we could move on, we could get to the part we all needed to get to.

Suddenly the sky lit white, flashing like the gods were taking our picture. A thunderclap immediately followed. But we didn't move. We didn't stop standing at that curb, not fifty feet from a convenience store where we could have safely waited it out.

"Do you like me?" he asked, a surprising change of subject. "Seventh-grade-question time. Do you like me?"

I nodded. "I do."

"Good, because I like you, too." Tucker put his arm around my head and clamped his hand over my mouth. "No more talking. Drive me back to my house, let's get in the shower, and then you are going to get in my bed."

I moved his hand. "But I have to pick up cupcake papers."

"Woman, don't make me do this!" He picked me up and carried me to my car, splashing through every puddle.

This time I didn't resist.

# TWENTY-EIGHT

---

I thought I'd be so strong, all business, when I got back to Ogden, but your mother and I were both dragging out the part before things had to get real, pretending we didn't have something looming. I was sleeping with Tucker again, and from the smell outside the house as I walked up, Smidge was busy making cookies.

She didn't ask where I'd been all day, even though it was after dark when I walked in wearing slightly damp, wrinkled clothes, holding a definite lack of cupcake papers. It didn't take long to see why I was the least of her concerns.

She was firmly in the middle of an enormous fight with you.

You were both in the kitchen, standing on either side of the island, arms up to elbows in brightly colored mixing bowls. You were crying and Smidge was as close to it as she got, her face orangey-red.

"Why are we crying and making cookies?" I asked, trying to sound casual.

Smidge shouted, "Because it's important to make memories!"

"Just let me leave!" you screamed.

"No!" Smidge shouted back. "Not until we've made six dozen cookies for my birthday party!"

Face streaked in tears, cheeks flushed pink, a glob of something that looked like butter stuck to your cheek, you turned to me and screeched, "Why is she being so mean to me?"

"Danny," Smidge said, "tell this fool child that she needs to learn her mother's cookie recipe and to stop being an asshole."

This was not a good situation I'd walked into.

"Mom said I could go over to Mandy's party and now she's making me stay in just to make stupid cookies with her! On a Friday night! She's so unfair!"

"Maybe I just grounded you again, how about that? Maybe I'm not done being mad at you for parading around with boys, lying behind my back, and going out asking to get pregnant."

"That was forever ago! You go wherever you want. All the way to Los Angeles. You're selfish, skinny, and gross, and I hate you!"

My heart was whacking against my chest. I had no idea what to say or do here, but I knew this was an important moment for Smidge, and one you'd remember forever. I had to do something.

"Okay," I said, hands outstretched like I was entering a lion's den. "There's a compromise here."

"Agreed," said Smidge. "Remind this hateful, evil little girl that I'm her mother, so she should *compromise* to what I say."

I peered inside your mixing bowl. "Chocolate chip," I said. Sweetly, like I was talking to a kitten. "Those look good."

"They look stupid," you said. "I hate cookies."

"Okay, that seems like a lie," I said.

"Danny, tell my child to behave," Smidge said.

"You could be a little nicer to your mother," I admitted.

You looked at me like I'd just slapped you across your face. "She called me an asshole!" you said, eyes wide and mouth flapping like a giant trout who just realized he's not in the water.

Smidge was licking cookie dough off a spoon, one bare foot crooked up against the inside of her thigh. "Did you get cupcake papers?"

I gave her a warning look that made her straighten up.

"Jenny, look. You only have to do this until the cookies are done," I said. "Then you can go to Mandy's party. Okay? I just declared that, and your mother's going to agree to those terms."

"But I'm supposed to be there already," you said, chin quivering as your tears resurfaced. "I don't want to be late. This isn't fair."

"Life ain't fair," Smidge said, leaning over the counter, taunting you like she was by your locker at school. "You'd better learn that right now."

"Make her stop," you begged me, tugging at my arm, wailing as if you were going to be forced into the oven with the cookies.

"Okay, everybody," I said. "Let's just calm down, take a second, and focus on finishing mixing."

You whacked and stabbed at that bowl like you were holding a machete. Meanwhile, Smidge pretended to be very interested in a single chip that had fallen onto the counter. She carefully placed it back inside her own bowl.

"That's good, everybody," I said, sounding like I was teaching a cooking class in an asylum. "See, we can do this."

You wiped your face, angry at your own tears. Smidge gave a small cough and a sigh. It fell quiet again, but the tension was still there. It took a second to talk over this absurdly overheated situation.

"You know, some people believe that the cookies won't taste good if you don't have fun while you make them. The cookies can sense if you were angry when you were combining the ingredients. So let's all think happy things right now, okay? Jenny, what are you thinking of? What's your happy thought?"

I remember you were mashing a wooden spoon against the side of the bright green bowl you held against your chest. You were looking down at the dough as you mumbled, "That one day my mom will be dead."

You said it like a curse, like a wish, and like you knew exactly what you were doing. It sounded so awful, Jenny. I couldn't believe you were capable of that. You were never young again.

I immediately said to your mother, "You know she didn't mean that," but the damage was already done.

Smidge faced the refrigerator, hiding her expression. She struggled with her breath like she'd been kicked in the stomach; a grunting gasp accompanied her swallowing as she stretched her neck toward the ceiling.

"Jenny, tell her you don't mean that," I said.

You threw yourself against the counter. "Whatever. She doesn't care."

Smidge snatched the spoon out of your mixing bowl and used it to smack you over the head. She didn't hit you hard, but it made such a terrible pop it startled us all.

You stood there waiting for her to say something, anything, but she didn't. She couldn't do it, Jenny, without telling you everything. Her pride and her fear got in her way.

You just held the top of your head, staring at your mom, waiting for her to fix what had happened. Instead, she sent you away.

"Just go," she said. "I'm sick of looking at you. You'll regret this so soon, you won't believe it."

Before I could say anything, you were already gone, running down the sidewalk toward that party, which must not have been too much fun after that.

Smidge calmly spooned balls of cookie dough onto waxed paper atop metal cookie sheets.

"How 'bout that for a memory?" she asked.

"Smidge, she's just a child."

"You don't know my daughter better than I do, so quit it."

"I had it all wrong. It's not your cancer that's selfish. It's you."

---

I left the house, driving slowly to see if I could find you on the street, but you were gone. I didn't know where that party was or I would've found you. I wanted to take you to Waffle House to tell you everything, but instead I ended up at The Pantry.

I figured I could just sit there and drink until I was ready to deal with Smidge again.

Sitting at the bar was Vikki, legs spread as she bent over to pick at a scab on her knee.

"I am warning you that I am drunk," she said as I approached.

"That's okay with me," I said. "I plan on joining you."

"Bad day?" she asked.

I plopped down onto the other stool. "I just watched Smidge smack her daughter on the head with a cooking utensil."

"Where's Jenny now?"

"At a friend's. I went looking for her, but she's not answering her cell phone. She's probably mad at me, too. She didn't call you?"

"No, she didn't call me," Vikki said, not bothering to hide her resentment. "Jenny doesn't call me if you're in town. In fact, that whole family forgets I even exist when your perfect ass is floating around Ogden."

She looked so weary, that same face Henry was wearing, this look of bewilderment, like the life she knew had been erased while she was sleeping. "Even Tucker," she continued, "who I almost wrote off as secretly gay, gets all moony when you're here. Is it your perfume? Do you spray some kind of potion at them? I just don't get it. What is just so great about you?"

"It's not that," I said. "I know this all must seem really confusing."

"Well, thanks for your pity."

"It's not about me."

"Nothing I ever do is good enough for that woman," Vikki said with a shake of her head. "I have changed my hair for her, did you know that?"

"I've done that."

"I stopped wearing plaid."

"I had to throw away my jeggings."

"Well, that was just good sense."

We both smiled. Vikki gave a quick gesture to the bartender and within seconds we had two cold beers in front of us.

"Thanks," I said. "You know she says these things out of love. Twisted love, but still. She thinks it's a special bond, like she's telling you something nobody else has the guts to tell you, which is why she's being a great friend."

"I used to think that," Vikki said, pausing to take a sip. "But then I realized she's the only one coming up with a list of my flaws. I bought a special whitening toothpaste from Italy after she told me the color of my teeth made me look 'slightly ignorant.'"

"That's rough."

"When I heard she was having a birthday party, I tried to help, but it was all 'Danny's got this' and 'Danny wants to do that' and 'Danny says she'd rather she did it herself.'"

"She told me you were doing things. I thought you went to the party store. You didn't get the streamers?"

"I brought some streamers over because I had them and I assumed she'd want them. But no, she wouldn't let me do anything. I kept asking if I could go with you on errands, and she said you didn't want me to."

"That didn't happen. I understand why you'd be mad about that."

Vikki rolled her eyes. "Oh, hell, Danielle, I don't give a shit about planning that party. You really do think I'm an idiot."

She dropped her elbows to the bar with a heavy thud. "I'm pissed because her cancer is obviously back and she won't admit it."

There it was. Finally. Someone had said something. It's all I'd been wishing for, but I never thought it would come from Vikki.

"You're right," I said, quietly.

"I know I'm right. She's acting like the world's smallest dick so I'll go away. She knows I'll tell Henry. She knows I know, that little shit."

"How did you know?"

Vikki rubbed her fingertips across her forehead. "Because I'm a goddamn nurse, Danielle. Didn't you know that?"

I shook my head, openmouthed.

"Well, ain't that something?" she said. She lifted her beer bottle. "Nice to meet you. Sorry I curse so much when I'm drunk. It's unladylike."

I sat there piecing together Smidge's abrupt dismissal of Vikki, how she always found a way to separate us within minutes. Of course she would want to pull away from the one person who would recognize her symptoms.

As I tried to remember what made me dislike Vikki in the first place, why I had such a visceral reaction to her, I thought about the stories Smidge told me of Vikki's clinginess, her tendency to show up unannounced, her nosy nature. I remember Smidge informing me that Vikki's husband was "stuffy." I thought about the car trip to the giant chair, when Smidge shared the tidbit about Vikki's "raisiny ovaries."

I shouldn't have known these things about Vikki.

Then I remembered that right when she first started coming around, Smidge told me that Vikki thought I was "opinionated." That I talked too much for someone who was visiting. I remember that, because it seemed odd: I couldn't comprehend why I should be quieter just because I was company. I tossed it aside as asinine, but it changed the way I thought about Vikki. I never actually asked her what she meant, or if it was even true. Then I wondered what exactly Smidge had told Vikki about me. I couldn't imagine all the things Smidge had shared that made her feel entitled to put me in my place.

This could be considered the work of a very successful sociopath.

"Vikki," I said, "I think I owe you an apology. And there's a good possibility you've been told some things about me that aren't true."

"Oh, you think? Like how you never asked Smidge to tell me you didn't want me hanging around?"

"Yeah, I never said that."

"She told me you thought I was white trash."

"That's terrible. I never said it."

"Maybe you thought it. I can tell you don't like me."

"I was probably being selfish at first when I wanted time with Smidge alone, because . . . Oh, I can say it now. Because of the cancer."

Vikki nodded. "I get that."

"But now she wants me to do this thing I can't do. I don't want her to suffer, but I'm just so mad at her, part of me doesn't care if she suffers. And that makes me feel terrible."

Vikki gave a rough pat to my shoulder. "Don't take this the wrong way," she said. "But I think you need my help."

"Thank you," I said, and as the words came out of me, something slid away. The giant weight placed on my shoulders shifted, eased into a new position.

"No offense, but I can't believe she didn't choose me," she said. "I'm great with sick people."

"I don't think she wants to be thought of as sick."

Vikki brought both her hands behind her neck. "I'll tell you one thing I'm happy about," she said. "That I don't have to wear this ugly-ass parrot necklace anymore. Can you believe Smidge told me you hated it? It's the only reason I wore it." She flipped the parrot by the chain. It landed in the oversize tip jar. "What a weird lie to tell someone," she said.

I kept my mouth shut.

––––––––

I felt like I'd had too much to drink with Vikki, so I walked back to Smidge's, my head stuffed with questions so twisted, I was grateful for the night air. Henry was waiting in the living room, standing in the center of the room, when I got home.

I could hear Smidge throwing up in the bathroom.

"She's not feeling well," Henry said.

"I know." I was too unsteady on my feet; it felt like the floorboards were shifting in their grooves.

"The party is tomorrow," he said. "You leave after that."

I didn't bother to try to explain or convince him of anything different. Tomorrow was bringing a whole new reality crashing down on Henry's shoulders.

"And I think you should stay at Tucker's tonight. We don't need you here anymore."

Henry went off to take care of Smidge, as I stepped outside for some air. That's when I found you hiding behind the cars. I saw you smoking that cigarette and I just panicked.

I shouldn't have hit you. I hope you can understand it was a complete and total reflex. I was trying to smack the cigarette, but I was too upset, too scared, and your face got in the way. All I could imagine was your mother catching you out there, and what might have happened if she had seen you smoking in the dark. Not in the state she was in, not with how tired and angry she was. Not with the way you two had just been fighting. Her heart wouldn't have been able to take it, her baby girl pulling smoke into her lungs.

I knew you were just trying it out. I could tell in the way the cigarette was precariously perched between the very edges of two fingers, like you were holding a dead rat by the tail. It wasn't in the hope that one of us would see you. This was your quiet rebellion, all alone and just for you. I'm sorry I ruined it. You were thirteen and curious, and you happened to turn that confusing age at a time that was extremely inconvenient for the life going on inside your house.

Do you remember what you said to me after I knocked that cigarette out of your mouth and onto the ground?

"Bitch, that was my last one."

# TWENTY-NINE

---

"You've had quite a night," Tucker said. He was at his dining table focused on replacing the mechanism that flipped the digits inside an old plastic alarm clock. "Beating up a kid, getting kicked out of your house. Drunk-dialing your secret boyfriend in the middle of the night for a rescue."

"My car's the only one in the lot at The Pantry," I said, taking a seat next to him. "Thanks for picking me up."

"I didn't want you sleeping on the streets. I try not to date homeless girls. Anymore."

"I thought I could be in control of this situation," I said. "Now it's all just a mess. It fell apart all around me."

Tucker twirled his screwdriver between his fingers. "I swear, Danielle." He wiped his face and shifted in his chair. "I know you like to act like the world is happening to you. You've worked hard to make it seem like you just fell into a job, your divorce sort of 'happened,' you're only here because Smidge asked you to stick around. But that's not how life works. You're making choices. Active choices."

"Like how I'm choosing to be here with you right now?"

"You're only here because Henry kicked you out. Don't try to sugarcoat that one, sweetheart. I'm glad my friend finally did something, though. Henry drives me nuts even more than you do."

He plugged the clock into the wall. A bright green light flooded the face as the machine hummed to life. The numbers seemed to throb as they waited to do their job.

"Sixty seconds," Tucker whispered.

"You don't know everything," I said. "I'm not trying to be some kind of victim."

Tucker smirked. He stuck the edge of his screwdriver underneath his thumbnail, sliding it across to clean it. "Every time you take a step in the right direction, Smidge gets in there and destroys all your hard work. Doesn't that get tiring?"

The far right tile on the clock face flipped. The sound was loud enough to make me jump in my seat.

"It's not like that."

"It is. You just don't like to see it."

"She's my best friend."

"Please don't take what I'm about to say the wrong way. *In title only.*"

"You know, right now you seem just as stubborn and cocksure as she is. Must drive you nuts, how alike you actually are."

He stood, and stretched his arms toward the ceiling before holding his hand out to me. "You coming to bed?"

Before I could decide, my cell phone rang. Tucker smiled. "Right on time."

"She's gone, she's gone," was all Smidge could get out when I answered.

"Jenny?"

"She's not in her room, her backpack is gone. She's not here, she's not answering her phone. Henry's out looking. I need you, Danny. Come help me look."

"I'll be right there."

Tucker was already holding my purse. "A predictable ending to this evening," he said. "It's three in the morning; why wouldn't you be headed over to Smidge's house after an emergency phone call?"

"Jenny's missing."

"If it wasn't that, it was going to be something. That girl has two parents. *Two.* It is their job to find Jenny, wherever she is. And you know she's fine. We all know she's fine! This town is the size of my Jeep. But this woman calls your cell phone in the middle of the night and suddenly you have to—"

"Tucker, shut up! I have to go do this, okay? It's my fault she's gone. You don't know shit about what's going on, so just shut up."

He stood over me as I shoved my feet into my shoes. I knew I was about to lose this chance I had with Tucker, but I had to let go of this relationship. It was too difficult because we weren't the only ones in it. We were outnumbered.

"This is how it's always going to be with me and Smidge, and I can't be with someone who doesn't think very highly of me because of it."

"It's not about what I think of you, Danny."

"Then how you think about women, I don't know. But I have to do it this way. Not because she told me to, but because it's right." I reached for the doorknob as I said, "Goodbye, Tucker. Again."

As I turned to leave he was suddenly behind me, his arms around mine, his hands clutching my wrist, keeping me from turning the knob. His mouth found my neck, his body pressed into mine. I could feel the heat of him, the urgency for me to stop.

"Don't go," he said into my skin. "Please. I want you. Listen to me, I won't talk like this again. This is our last moment, if you go."

"She's dying, Tucker."

I said it as I yanked the door open. I said it to stun him, to give me just enough time to be strong enough to escape his arms.

## THIRTY

---

By the time I'd sprinted to The Pantry from Tucker's I was fine to drive, but even if that hadn't worked, I'd have been completely sober three seconds after seeing the state Smidge was in.

She was pale, gaunt, and gasping like she'd just run ten miles. I fished out the oxygen tank from where we'd hidden it in my trunk and forced her to use it. I told her she wasn't coming with me, that someone needed to stay at the house in case you came home on your own.

Smidge adjusted the plastic tubing against her septum before checking her phone again. "She won't answer my texts. She hates me." She sniffed and huffed around the oxygen, struggling to calm down.

"She doesn't hate you. We'll find her. We'll find her or she'll come home."

Smidge pressed her forehead to her hand. "She has to spend the rest of her life telling people her mom died of lung cancer. They'll all think I'm a bad mother, a dirty smoker who didn't take care of herself, who didn't want to stick around to see her daughter grow up."

"But that's not what happened," I reminded her.

"How does that matter? Like anybody's going to do some research. They'll hear 'lung cancer' and think *horrible mother*."

"They won't."

"They will. I can't handle them thinking that about sweet Jenny. That her mother didn't love her. Just like how they thought about me."

"People won't think that."

"I'm a monster, Danny. I hit my kid in the head with a spoon."

"You were mad. You didn't mean it."

"She doesn't know that."

"She does. She will."

"When, exactly? How long after I'm dead?"

I covered her hand with mine.

Smidge closed her eyes. "Do you remember when she was younger, she used to go to that summer camp? She'd have this list of things she had to take with her. I'd be so busy going to the store, getting her the right sunscreen, the right bathing suit, the right poncho. I'd talk to her about mosquito repellent, what girls she shouldn't hang out with, and not to go skinny-dipping. I just hounded her with things she could and couldn't do until she was sick of me, until she couldn't wait to get rid of me. So she never once missed me the entire two weeks she'd be gone."

This is where your mother cried, Jenny. It only took her entire life, but here is where real tears fell from her eyes.

"Well, this time it's not two weeks. It's forever. I keep thinking of other things I need to tell her and I'm just so mad that she doesn't want to listen, and I'm even madder that I can't remember everything I need to say."

I picked up my phone and texted you. *Tell me where you are right now.*

I don't know why you chose to respond. I don't know if you were scared or ready to talk. I just know you wrote back.

*Scoreboard.*

Smidge stopped crying pretty quickly after that. She hustled herself out of the car, easing herself around the oxygen tank she dropped to the lawn.

"Go get my baby," she said. "Tell her that I love her and make her believe it."

# THIRTY-ONE

I'm still shocked you made me break into a high school to come find you. You were smart to know the last place anybody would come looking for you was above a football field. By the time I reached you I could tell you were ready to come down from your perch on that metal scaffolding under the giant Neville Tigers sign, but you stubbornly waited for me to climb up there to join you.

I was breathless by the time I finally made it to your side. I swung my legs over the railing and dangled my feet alongside yours.

"So, how was your day?" I asked.

There were pen marks on your jeans, a red heart drawn in marker. You'd pulled on combat boots from somewhere and had tucked your cuffs into them. A kelly green hoodie was pulled tight over your head, the string cutting across your forehead. You kept your hands shoved tight into your pockets as you leaned against one of the metal railings that ran in front of us. You left me to do all the talking.

"It's scary up here," I noted.

You shrugged.

"Aren't you worried you'd fall? I almost fell coming up here in the dark. It's not lit very well."

"Don't care," you said. "So I fall. So I die."

"Probably you'd just snap a couple of leg bones, which would feel worse than dying."

You hunched yourself over even more. "Everybody dies," you said.

"That is true."

"Like my mom. She's gonna die."

I could hear a dog barking down the street and my heart beating in my ears. Like a sad little monkey, you curled around your knees, rocking yourself. "I hate you for taking her last days from me."

"I didn't—"

"She's sick," you said. "She's so skinny, she's coughing all the time. I don't know why y'all are lying to me."

"Lying about what?"

You sprang up onto your feet like someone had shot you with adrenaline. It took me much longer to find my own way upright, our age difference suddenly becoming more apparent.

"I was on her laptop," you said, grabbing the top of your hood, yanking it backward. It parked itself on your shoulder like a deflated balloon. "I saw her cache. I saw what she's been researching. DNRs? Morphine? I looked up Seconal. I'm not a little baby."

I tried to step closer to you, but you pulled back.

"Tomorrow's her death party, isn't it? You think I'm too stupid to know what's going on? My mother's dying."

It only took a couple of steps for you to be balanced over a tight space that made me extremely nervous. I wasn't afraid you were going to jump, but there was a very real possibility you could fall, as upset as you were and hovering over the edge of that scaffolding.

"Jenny, come down."

"Just tell me it's true and I'll come down."

"Come down and we can talk."

"Tell me it's true!"

"You should talk to your mom."

You sent one leg over the railing. "Tell me or I'll jump."

"Don't."

You leaned into it. Your foot twitched. "I should die before she does. That'll show her. Why can't she just talk to me? Why does she always have to talk so mean? I wished she was dead, and she just took it. Why'd she do that? Why didn't she tell me what was going on? Why didn't *you*?"

While you weren't looking, I took a step closer to you. And then I took another. "I'm sorry," I said.

"I'm telling my dad."

"You can't, Jenny. It's not yours to say. That's your mother's right."

"You got to see the world with her and I didn't. One stupid cruise, and you know, she was crying, like, the whole time. She told me not to tell you. Why's she always telling us not to talk to each other? Why do we do it?"

"She scares us."

"I'm tired of her telling me what to do and not what is actually happening. I hate her. It's not fair."

Another step. "No, it's not. And you don't hate her."

"It's bullshit," you said. "I don't care anymore."

You turned too quickly, lost your balance on the beam, and lurched forward, trying to compensate. It caused you to flip forward, going over the rail. You cried out as I grabbed you by the waist and pulled you back into me just in time.

We tumbled onto the metal grate beneath us. The wind was knocked out of me, and you'd smacked your head against one of the beams. Both of us stayed flat on our backs, silently rubbing our injuries.

It wasn't until right then that I remembered you had much more living to do without Smidge than any of the rest of us.

And I realized none of this was happening because of Smidge. It was because of *you*. For you.

You were right. It was so not fair.

I found your hand not too far from mine, open and cold, waiting. I held it as I told you then, "Jenny, I'll make sure you get everything you were supposed to get with her."

"You can't promise that," you said.

"I can. I'm doing it, right now."

After all these years of silence, Jenny, if I could ask you only one question and have you answer it truthfully, I would want to know if you thought I kept my word.

# THIRTY-TWO

The party started well. I'll give it that. I was shocked at the number of people who turned up. I hadn't recalled the guest list being so large. Smidge must have made some extra invites. They were mostly ladies from various groups Smidge had jumped into and out of over the years. I was slightly uncomfortable when I realized I mostly knew these women from the gossip Smidge had told me about them; I was recognizing people not by their names, but by their awkward plastic surgeries, lesbian partners, or impermeable cliques.

Then there was one mystery woman, standing off to the side near the fireplace, overlooking the scene while sipping a Chardonnay. I eventually called Vikki over to have her identify the rail-thin redhead in a long green dress and wearing an impressive diamond the size of a hard candy.

Vikki shot a look of jealousy-filled disdain. "That's Tori Payne. Her husband owns a bank or something. And she runs that fancy-pants cemetery for the VID."

*"VID?"*

"Very Important Dead."

Tori Payne happened to be the director and chief executive of Serenity Hilltop, the cemetery Smidge was planning on crashing. Smidge was hosting her graveyard audition.

As she flocked from attendee to attendee, around thirty-five in all but growing in number by the minute, Smidge was beaming like this was her cotillion. She wore a long-sleeved navy dress with a bright red brooch. A thick Bakelite bangle in the same color red hung from her wrist. The temperature had dipped slightly, but not quite enough to explain the dark stockings she was wearing. Cherry-red patent-leather stilettos completed her outfit. She looked like a flight attendant from the sixties, perky in her French-braided hair and red lipstick, makeup covering any trace of how pale and paper-thin her skin had become lately. If she was in any pain as she played the merry hostess, flitting around her home holding a martini, she was hiding it well.

I located my glass of wine before diving back into the throng of women. I was hoping to find Smidge without being sidetracked by awkward small talk.

"The birthday girl is fixing to speak!"

Smidge was teetering along the ledge of her brick fireplace, drink raised like a torch. Someone lowered the volume on the music.

She cleared her throat, exaggerating for effect, like she was about to launch into a big speech. It got the crowd chuckling, which covered as she gave her real cough, the one I'd come to recognize. She placed a hand against the painted brick behind her to steady herself before she continued.

"I wanted to thank all y'all for coming today," she said. "It's real nice of all of you, and I know it's been some time since some of us have seen each other. Look how pregnant Amy is, for instance."

The stunning Asian in a black, fitted dress sporting a modest, five-month pregnancy bulge smiled as she gave a regal wave to the room. "Yes," she bellowed. "I am huge."

There was more polite laughter accompanied by a few murmurs about her in vitro fertilization. The woman behind me barely tried to speak at a polite volume as she noted to her friend, "I asked Smidge, but she didn't know who Amy chose as the father."

I shifted uncomfortably on my heels and searched the room for Tucker. I didn't know whether or not to expect him, but I could imagine him showing up, claiming to be there for Henry.

Smidge continued. "Before I open these presents, I've got my husband out in the kitchen cutting y'all some cake. I want us all to have something sweet in our hands."

She took the last sip from her drink and put it aside.

"Where's Danielle?" she asked, looking over the crowd. It took me a second to recognize my own name, I was so unused to her calling me by anything so formal. I found myself standing there with my hand in the air.

"Well, come on up here!" Smidge smirked.

As I walked through the crowd, Smidge explained, "I want everybody to appreciate this cake, because my friend Danielle here went through a lot of trouble to get it. Poor woman was out in that storm making sure there was enough buttercream and fondant for all of us."

Unsure of what else to do, the women gave a brief, gentle round of applause. Again I found myself raising my hand in acceptance.

Smidge put an arm around me, gripping me by the elbow. "Danny here," she said, and then she suddenly stopped, dropping her face toward the floor. Mouth twisted to the side, chest heaving, I realized Smidge was holding back tears. She lifted her head, her chin raised higher than normal, and gave a quick gasp. "Danny here is my best friend," she said.

It felt like someone had tied ten-pound weights to both corners of my mouth. Smidge kept her voice steady.

"She's also my partner in travel, my partner in life. We've seen way too much together. And yet, we still haven't seen enough."

The grip Smidge had on my elbow tightened as she took a breath.

That's when I saw Tucker wandering in from the kitchen, a beer dangling from his hand.

"Danny's been through a lot lately," Smidge said. "And wouldn't you know it: I went ahead and put her through even more. But I wanted to thank her, in front of all of you, because I know I don't tell her that I love her enough. And I love her the mostest."

"Aw!" That came from Tori Payne at the front of the crowd.

Smidge hugged me then, just as I saw you in the back of the room, holding your father's hand, tears streaming down your face. Henry also looked troubled as he watched this scene on his fireplace, this outpouring of womanhood splayed out all over his living room. The question burning in his eyes read loud and clear: *What does everyone know that I don't?*

Looking over that crowd of tense, saddened faces, I realized exactly what was going on.

They all knew.

*Everybody knew.*

Their eyes were wide as they attempted to hide their own fears, their own worries of death coming for them at any moment. If it could happen to Smidge, it could just as easily swipe them from their husbands and children, knocking them right out of their designer heels.

At one time or another Smidge had terrorized their church groups, their book clubs, their parent-teacher conferences. Nobody in Odgen got away without coming face-to-face with Smidge Cooperton at some point. And yet, here they all were, paying silent, secret, last respects.

They all loved her just as I did: wholeheartedly, in a most terrified way, unable to stay away from her, and worried they'd never really be close enough.

I was floored with gratitude.

I called for a toast to the birthday girl.

"Danny, I can't believe how many people are here," she said to me as her crowd sipped and shared teary glances. "It's enormous! It's all of Ogden!"

"It does look like that, doesn't it?"

"Danny, I am *loved*. Beloved. I am not a mean spider. You see that?"

Women began seeking out their husbands in the crowd, clutching them a little tighter. Men were carrying their children, cheeks were being kissed. Over by Henry, people were shaking his hand. A receiving line was threatening to break out.

That's when Smidge cocked her head. "Wait. You don't think . . . they don't know, do they?"

I shook my head. "No way. This is because they love you."

She smiled as she relaxed into a pleased nod. "Yeah, I think you're right."

When Smidge started giving away her things it was like a joke at first, a bit of charity. That girl who used to coach soccer at your high school had knit Smidge a sweater. Overwhelmed with the amount of work that went into a gift like that for a person she hadn't seen in more than a year, Smidge pulled the yellow bracelet from her wrist and handed it over to her, insisting, "It will look so much better on you."

The girl was so confused she accepted it, perhaps unsure of the etiquette.

Smidge smacked her palms together. "Wait! Amy with the baby! I just remembered something important."

Using my arm as an anchor, Smidge dropped herself to level ground and headed in a speedy shuffle straight to her bookshelves. After a quick scan, she gave a squeal of success before pulling a heavy white book from one of the lower shelves.

"I still have your Nigella," she said. "I must have borrowed that six years ago! And wait, whose *Middlesex* is this? I know it's someone's here."

"Mine." It was one of the moms Smidge used to sit with during your ballet recitals. The heavyset brunette giggled like she'd won a contest as Smidge placed the hardcover into her waiting hands.

"I'm sorry I had this so long," Smidge said. "I never did get around to reading it."

"You can keep it awhile longer," the woman said. "It's really very good."

"No," Smidge said, a peaceful look overcoming her, like she'd just been sainted. "I'm afraid I won't find the time."

Smidge found excuses to unload her Harry Potter books, a first edition Agatha Christie, and three copies of *The Great Gatsby*. "I guess I liked this one," she said. "So nice I bought it thrice!"

Smidge told each guest to pick a book, any book. "I don't want you going home empty-handed," she said. "Party gifts for all!"

This was something bigger than a free paperback. This was an olive branch Smidge was extending to each of them, for whatever slight that had caused them to drop away over the years. Taking a book with a smile was an easy way to declare all water officially under the bridge. It was a peace offering and a farewell. The women looked relieved.

Henry stepped in. "Some of those books are mine," he reminded his wife, trying to elicit a chuckle, while letting people know they could stop pilfering his book collection at any time.

"Point taken," Smidge said, before jutting one finger into the air. "Here is what is all mine: Ladies, I have dresses."

"Smidge," I said, knowing she was going to ignore my gentle reminder that she was about to go too far. Two-thirds of those women would never fit into any of her small clothes, risking the chance that each of them could be insulted anew.

Smidge turned to Tori. "I have the perfect dress for you," she said. "Danny, you remember that dress I wore to the gala last year? The green one? Wouldn't Tori look amazing in it?"

"I don't know which dress that is," I admitted.

"Well, I'll go get it and show you. Tori should have it."

*"No! You said it was mine!"*

Your voice cut through everything. All of the women fell silent, aside from the one or two who gave an audible gasp.

You approached us, stomping heavily. "You said it, Mama," you repeated.

"Did I? I don't remember saying that," Smidge said, wavering just a bit on her feet.

"It's okay," Tori said, smiling wide enough I could see metalwork on one of her molars. "Your daughter can have the dress. I'm sure it's too small anyway, Smidge, you're such a slight gal."

"Jennifer, will you please meet me in the bedroom?"

Your mother's formal invitation was enough for me to know that I needed to follow as you once again stomped through a cloud of competing feminine perfumes.

I found the two of you standing in your mother's closet, ripping dresses from the hangers, tossing them over your shoulders as you searched for that one Holy Grail of a dress.

It was like a final clearance sale. You were in a race, both of you dead set on winning, and it was eerily quiet.

"Please stop," I remember saying.

"It's *my* dress," you muttered. "She said I could have it."

Smidge said, "You can't have everything you want, Jenny. Learn a life lesson."

"Maybe it's time for you to learn something, Mama." You grabbed my hand and clutched it, keeping me from going anywhere. "Tell her, A.D. Tell Mama what to do."

This was it. There was to be no more stalling, no more excuses. I couldn't believe you were making this happen after all this time, after all the reasons not to, you just cut it all away and demanded that it end right then and there.

"You have to tell them good-bye now," I found myself saying, the words barely audible, my voice breathy with emotion. "You have to tell them, Smidge, while they're still out there."

Smidge was shaking her head. "No. No, I don't want to," she said, sounding so small herself, even smaller than she'd already become.

"Look at those women out there taking your books and thanking you for them. Why do you think they're doing that? They *know*. You can pretend to be mean and selfish and spiteful all you want, but we all know what you're doing. You're trying to slink away. Well, you owe it to us to die like a decent person. Quit being scared and fix it. We all have to be here once you're gone, so let us say our good-byes."

"Wait, we need Daddy," you said, wiping your eyes. "Mama, we have to get Daddy and then we can tell everybody else."

"Tell everybody what?"

That was your father, of course, standing in the doorway, walking straight into the end of his life as he knew it.

## THIRTY-THREE

This story gets harder, Jenny, because you know as well as I do that it is winding down. I'm going to do my best to shelter you from any of her suffering.

It happened so quickly. She was fine, so fired up with direction and to-do lists, until one day, when she just wasn't. Her voice had gone raspy, every breath rattled. Her shine was gone, and I knew it embarrassed her to look that way, unable to style herself the way she liked. I tried, but it was such an effort just to get her to the bathroom, doing anything that required washing her hair grew difficult. She stayed in bed, attached to a small oxygen machine.

One day she made me do fifty jumping jacks, right at the foot of her bed. Then she ordered thirty squats. "Look at that," she said, sinking back into her pillows as I bent and stretched, grunting and gasping. "Look how healthy you are. That's amazing."

"Don't tease me. I'm so out of shape."

"You're doing it. That's impressive. I can't do that. Look, something you're finally better at than me. Do it again."

"Can I catch my breath first?"

She smiled. "Yeah, you go ahead. Show off."

One morning we were going through photographs. Smidge always made prints from our digitals, and I'd never been so grateful that she'd been so meticulous in documenting our trips.

"This whole plan," she said, as she closed the book from our trip to Thailand. "I can't believe how you just dropped everything for me. That was nice of you."

"It was. Especially since you've been so mean about it."

"Well, listen. I free you. You're fired. Whatever it is you need to hear."

I smelled the beginnings of one last trick. "Right."

"I'm serious. After I'm gone, you do whatever you think is best."

"Passive-aggressive freedom."

She patted the back of my hand. "Take these albums, by the way. They're yours now. I'm so happy you get to have them."

"I can't believe you just said I'm not taking over your life. After all this. Why are you saying that?"

"Because I know what's going to happen," she whispered, and then she fell asleep. She kept doing that, by the way, giving out little psychic warnings and then passing out, like all this paranormal activity was just too much for her.

———

Smidge had plenty of morphine, but she didn't want to take it. Besides making her feel "swimmy," it would make her fall asleep. She didn't like sleeping away her days. She wanted to be alert enough to boss us around. Henry and I each had a notebook that we'd keep on ourselves at all times. We never knew exactly when Smidge would remember another task one of us needed to take care of after she was gone. One day she spent an hour telling me exactly how to tend to her irises. Maybe you felt like everybody treated you like a dummy, but your mother spent twenty minutes carefully explaining what "deadheading" was to me, like I was going to Edward Scissorhands her garden the second she was gone.

She must have given Henry directions for every remaining minute of his life, including the kind of woman she wanted him to marry, if it wasn't going to be me. I know she was pushing for me, openly. But Henry dismissed it. "She belongs to Tucker," he said to her then.

"I don't," I argued.

"She doesn't," Smidge agreed. "You'll see."

Then she had her Seconal fantasies. She'd read about Oregon's Death with Dignity Act, and she would talk about it with me like she was fantasizing how to renovate her kitchen. She fawned over pills like she used to gush about paint swatches.

"Isn't it amazing, what they're doing?" she asked me. "Letting people do what they want, letting people go who are ready. It's so beautiful."

I know it was the painkillers, but when Smidge would turn mystical, so angelic and peaceful, it unnerved me. That wasn't the woman we knew. She was changing. She was weakening.

---

One morning you looked out the window and asked, "Why is there a lady sitting on our front yard?"

Your mother eased her way over to you and glanced through the curtain. "That's just your grandmother," she said. "Don't go out there; she's evil. Henry, lock the door."

I jumped to my feet. "She's here? Your mom is here?"

Henry peered out the window. "So that's the Lizard. She's much prettier than I thought she'd be. Why is she sitting out there? You think she's scared to come in?"

"Oh, she tried earlier," Smidge said. "She came knocking on the door like that was okay. I told her she can crawl back under whatever rock she slithered up from."

"You have to let her in," I said.

Smidge gave me a weary glance. "I don't *have* to do anything."

"She's here for you. I haven't e-mailed her in months. Someone must have told her what's going on."

"You e-mailed her? You e-mailed my mother?"

"I thought I'd be more frightened to admit that to you, but you aren't very good at hitting, pinching, or throwing anymore, so yes, I e-mailed your mother. I thought it would help."

"You thought wrong," Smidge said, shuffling to her bedroom. "Send her away."

You frowned and stamped your foot. "Uh, excuse me, Mama!" you shouted, sounding so much like your mother in four words it froze the room. "Think how sad you'd be if I wouldn't let you talk to me right now. She just wants to say good-bye like the rest of us. Now you let her in."

Your mother finally took some orders. They just had to come from the next in line for her throne. Jenny, I must say, you took to bossing well.

———————

Sometimes she would yelp so loudly we worried what would happen if you heard her. She didn't like you coming into her room when she was in pain, and it must have seemed to you like a lot of grown-ups keeping you out of the way. Please believe it was for the best you never saw her like that. I could barely take it. Henry was a wreck. Instead of "Grampy Camp," it was "Gramma Camp," this time around, with your newfound partner in shopping and gossip. Your grandmother made sure you got out of the house and kept up with the business of being a teenager. Smidge was so worried about you during that time. We all were. But the Lizard, who preferred to be called Lydia, was there for you. She loved you from the second she saw you, and you were attached to her as well. We all ended up very grateful she came as soon as someone who'd been at that party gave her a call. She was surprisingly quiet and patient. Sometimes I feel like we all imagined her, so desperate for a guardian angel to help us navigate this unfamiliar and devastating terrain.

Lying in bed with Smidge one night, listening to the rise and fall of her chest, I watched her breathe, something that was now an active part of her. Keeping her breath going was the most important thing she was doing, what her body fought to do constantly.

"I don't like this," she said. It was quiet, plaintive.

"I don't like this either," I said, brushing her hair back from her forehead. "Why is marsala such a jerk?"

"I was supposed to go out like a rock star."

"I don't know," I said. "You're pretty gross and skinny. A lot of rock stars go out this way."

She smiled, allowing herself a small cough. "But they get to have the good drugs."

"Look on the bright side. With this tumor where it is, it's kind of like you've got three boobs. That's special."

"I hatechoo."

"Hatechoo more."

She nuzzled her head into my shoulder. "James only made a pass at me that day because he was scared. It wasn't a real thing. He panicked and shoved his hand on my breast. I was more disappointed than anything else."

"You don't have to tell me this."

"I do. I didn't tell you to be in charge of you, but because it would have ruined your day. It was *your* special day, and you were the bride. After I hit him, we never once came close to talking about it again. It was like it never happened, because it barely did. He loved you. He didn't want me. I think he was just like, 'Oh, I'll never touch another boob again. Okay, there. I just did it. *Now*, I'll never touch another boob.'"

"That makes sense. It sounds like him."

"Do you miss him?" Smidge's voice was getting quieter as she drifted off to sleep again.

"Sometimes," I admitted.

"Me too," she said. "He was good at messing with you."

———

I searched everywhere, but I couldn't figure out how to get my hands on Seconal. It just seemed impossible. People could get crack, score meth, steal babies, and rob banks, but I couldn't find a bottle of barbiturates? It felt like I'd wasted my life being a law-abiding person. It made me want to learn how to hotwire a car, make a shiv—knowing how to live a life of crime suddenly seemed more useful.

I was angry I couldn't find a way to give my friend that bowl of applesauce lovingly spiked with the contents of one hundred opened capsules. One tiny meal could end her suffering within minutes after she had wanted to. I could give this compassionate ending to her dog, but not to my best friend. Amazing that there were still new ways to feel so helpless.

One night I was so distraught I walked through the rain, wandering until I reached Tucker's house. I knocked on his door and I stood there until he opened it. "Tucker, I don't have anybody else. My whole world is dying back in that house."

"Come here," he said, pulling me into his arms. "It's okay, come here. Come sit." He brought me into the house.

After I calmed down, he said he had a confession to make.

"I have to tell you something," he said. "There's someone new in my life. Someone I'm very attached to."

"Oh," I said, surprised that my heart gave a sharp pang of regret, surprised that I could feel anything through all that hurt I'd been swimming in. "Is she nice?"

"She's nice," Tucker said, grinning, letting a slight laugh escape his lips. "She's really pretty, and sweet, and as soon as I can, I plan on making her stop pissing on my rug."

He pursed his lips and made two kissing sounds, sending the floppiest, big-eared, huge-pawed hound dog pouncing into the living room. She was nothing more than a wiggling butt attached to a pair of huge, watery brown eyes that saw only Tucker.

"She's so cute," I said, finding myself crying again, because when you're in that kind of mourning you're easily touched by the beginning of life. There it was, years of love ahead of them, a promise of a future.

"I also moved into my entire closet," he said to me. "I thought you'd like that. But I'm selling the place."

"You are?"

"I was thinking about how I'm always going to the airport to pick people up or take them there. I never actually get on a plane. Smidge is dying with twice the life experience I ever got. I can't sit around here anymore."

He pulled a blanket up over my knees, noticing I'd been shivering.

"I'm sorry for how I talked to you," he said. "I was being such a hypocrite. At least your lady-boss had your back. Mine left me years ago. And now it's time for *me* to leave."

"Where are you going to go?"

"My ex lives in Kentucky, so I figure I'll start with whatever is the very opposite side of the planet from there. Which is kind of in the middle of the Indian Ocean. But Australia's close enough. Maybe you'll come visit," he added.

"Maybe," I said. "I wish I could make you stay here."

"You don't mean that. And you don't have to stay here either," he said. "They won't make you stay."

"Nobody's making me do anything."

"You're a good girl," he said, leaning forward to give me the lightest of kisses.

I slid my hand down his arm until I found his hand. "Hey, do you know where I can score some Seconal?"

## THIRTY-FOUR

Vikki led the hospice. Turns out she was an expert at palliative care. She taught Henry how to bathe his wife, when to give her which medicine, how to prop her up at night so she could sleep without feeling like she was collapsing into her tumors. She refused to move into a portable hospital bed, insisting on staying in her room, on her mattress. There were many medicines, some of which Smidge didn't want to take. Her doctor came by, bringing even more. He charmed her until she agreed to take most of them.

I'd always heard people referring to their loved ones in end-stage care as having "good days and bad days." I quickly learned what that meant.

The good days were when people came to visit. Nobody ever came empty-handed. To this day, I can neither smell lilies nor eat macaroni and cheese without thinking of your mother's final days.

The Christmas season entered quietly, and we were all intent on ignoring it, except that Smidge wouldn't have it. "Are you kidding? I've been waiting for Christmas. Bring on the presents."

Seth Sampson brought your mother an enormous stuffed giraffe. It was apparently an inside joke between them, because Smidge let out a scream of laughter so loud and sudden that everyone came running to check if she was okay.

Thankfully, she didn't have too many bad days. Maybe because she had too many people ready to assist the second she felt any discomfort. We weren't going to let cancer be in charge. Henry and I took shifts. When one of us was with her, the other tried to be with you. Your grandmother did everything else. She was an excellent cook.

One day I found Henry in his shed, staring at his tool box. "Nothing here will fix it," he said. He was pale as a moth wing, quietly shaking.

I went searching for you, and made you do that dance number you were learning for jazz. It was soon apparent that you hadn't learned it all the way, but you kept your eyes on your father as you moved your feet. "See, and then I do this!" It wasn't until you were on your fifth encore he realized you had long ago run out of steps and were stalling.

You kept that house alive during that time, Jenny. I don't know if anyone told you that. It would have been so easy to wallow, to fall into that pit of anguish, but you were someone to protect, someone who nurtured us when we hit our low points, and you seemed so grateful to have us all together.

Which is why I was so shocked when you decided to have a "Come to Jesus" moment with me. You cornered me in the kitchen, trapping me between the island and the refrigerator.

"She's waiting for you," you said. "It's not about Christmas. It's you."

"Jenny, don't make it sound like it's up to me."

You sneered like I had stepped in something and dragged it through the carpet. "Don't be a chicken. She's going to wait as long as she thinks you need her."

There was no way it was my fault that Smidge was still holding on. Vikki kept insisting it was just a matter of time—no matter how many good days would convince us that she might live another month, another year, maybe turn around and cure herself once again—a bad day would always follow, one where she would falter, grow weaker, sleep most of the day away, and cough through the night.

"If I can say good-bye to my mother," you said, "then you can say it to yours, too."

You were right. All those years I let Smidge boss me around, be the overprotective pit bull by my side, was because I needed her to be the one coming out swinging when life dealt me its biggest blows. That's why I couldn't handle her cancer the first time around. It was too scary to have my surrogate mother leaving me, to be abandoned yet again. It wasn't fair that no matter how obedient I was, no matter how much I did everything right, she could still go away at any time.

Having a mother is only a guarantee until the day you are born.

Tucker got the Seconal. He pressed a paper bag into my hand, and like a good Southern man, he wouldn't tell me how he got it, or where it came from. His only concern was that I understood that he'd done it. The directions were on a piece of paper inside.

When I told Smidge that Tucker had scored her the "*sui-cider*," as she liked to call it, I saw the relief soothe every part of her body.

"That man's a good man," she said.

"He is."

"I shouldn't have said such hateful things about him."

"Well, you're hateful."

"Hmph. You're the one who dumped him."

"Lady, don't make me smother you with this pillow before you get to taste your *sui-cider*."

She mumbled a laugh, reached up, and wiped her mouth. Her breath was slow, rattling.

"Henry is a good man, too," she said.

"He is."

"Then why won't you be with him?"

I stroked her arm, careful to be gentle. "Because he's *your* man."

She looked off toward the window. Creaks and moans escaped her body as she seemed to be searching for something. "What if he doesn't find someone? Or what if he does and she's an asshole?"

I knew this was what you meant, Jenny. This was the moment you were asking me to have with your mother. She was waiting to hear everything was going to be okay. She needed proof before she could leave.

So I did what you told me to do. I said, "You have to let us go, Smidge. You have to let us bumble around and make mistakes and miss you." Then I cried. "I am really going to miss you."

"Good," she said. "There'd better be a planet-size hole in this world after I'm gone. That's why I stayed alive long enough to ruin Christmas forever." All that time I'd wanted her to fight, to stay around longer, but up until that moment I hadn't noticed she was doing exactly that.

She was fuzzy, blurred out through my tears as I said, "I hate that you're leaving. I hate that it's so soon."

"Then you're really going to hate that it is now."

*"Now?"*

"You go call in my family. I am going to say some good-byes while you fix Mama one last drink. I'd like some apple-juice with a hell of a mixer."

"But."

"And I'm going to drink it alone. I don't want anybody getting in trouble. After you hand me that glass, you leave and don't let anybody come back here until I'm dead."

There's never the right last moment. Even if you get to say good-bye, even if you get to say "I love you," even if you jump off a plane and get a tattoo and hug everyone you've ever met right before you drift off with a smile, it is never the right last moment. There is always more to say, somewhere to go, something to remember. Another discussion, another fight. Another day. There is always supposed to be another day.

She had her last moment with Henry, and she had her last moment with you. I don't know what she said to either of you when she took you alone in her bedroom. It's none of my business, and it's not my memory to share.

My last moment with Smidge is enormous in my heart. It has expanded to fill all of the space inside of me where she is missing. I know it was her time, I know it was what she wanted, even though it sometimes seemed like it was taking forever for her to get to the end. It really seemed somehow she'd find a way to stay alive, because she always got what she wanted. Once her last day came, I couldn't believe how fast she was gone. Just like that. Thirty-six years of that tornado of a woman on this planet and then she was gone. Forever.

It's never the right last moment.

## THIRTY-FIVE

As well as you took it at the time, as much as you surrounded yourself with the friends and family who supported
you during Smidge's final days and up until the memorial on
Serenity Hilltop, the day had to come when the mourners
weren't as plentiful, when you took off your black clothes and
realized your mother was never coming back. I resolved to
do whatever it took to make sure you never resented or hated
Smidge for leaving you so soon.

Dissolving your life into someone else's can't be a process.
It has to just happen. That way, everyone just deals with it
and makes it work.

I sold most of my things in Los Angeles and moved only
the essentials into the Ogden house. I was careful with
Smidge's money, and I made sure Henry did what she wanted.
You might remember he opened Henry's House not too long
after that. I helped with inventory and acquisitions, filling
in where Tucker would've been. Supporting Henry where
Smidge would've stood.

But always at a bit of a distance.

I stayed in the guest room for the next five years. I think you two let me stay mostly out of our mutual sadness, our loneliness. Not having someone to boss us around was difficult to get used to for a while. With Henry and me both able to focus on you, it kept us from feeling so lost.

I like to think we made the most of it. There were good times in there. We took trips, lighting memorial candles in cathedrals for your mother on more than four different continents. You let me be the shoulder to cry on for your first heartbreak. I taught you how to drive a stick shift. Every year on your mother's birthday we made cookies from her recipe, and left some out for her like she was Santa. We even went to church that one time. Your genius brain got you into college all by yourself, but I like to take at least a little credit that you applied to more than just that one where your boyfriend was going.

And then suddenly you were all grown up and beautiful, with as many of your belongings as possible stuffed into the back of the Pickle as you headed off to Austin for college. You waved good-bye toward your father and me where we were standing on the porch. As we waved back, Henry brought an arm around me, and I realized what was happening.

It was your mother's dream, her vision, just as she'd described it so long ago. She was right, once again. That stubborn woman always got what she wanted, even from her bossy porch swing in Heaven.

That's when it ended for me, Jenny. My promise was over. The job fulfilled. You were raised and you were thriving. I had done everything your mother wanted, everything your father needed.

I know it's hard for you to understand, but as much as Henry and I cared for each other, we never fell in love. We were never going to. We weren't attracted to each other, and he deserves a woman he wants to cook for and care for, as much as he did for your mother. Henry's love makes the sun wake up and circle the woman he desires, and that's part of what makes him such a wonderful man. I couldn't sit in some other woman's place, a woman he had yet to meet. His love, as you know, is a special thing.

That's why I immediately went to find Tucker, who at that point was living in London. If I fell in lust for that man when he was in a ball cap, I fell in love with him the second I saw him in a peacoat. He met me at the airport, once again, but this time when he held me, I asked him not to let go.

Sometimes our hearts make decisions long before our heads get into the game.

I know you felt like I left your daddy, that I abandoned your family, but you have to know that I couldn't have. I was your family, and I still am your family.

You got so angry with me. I know you had to. I had a feeling it was coming. Both Smidge and I lost our mothers young, too, remember. We all felt abandoned and needed someone to take the blame.

In a last act of love toward your mother, I stood in the way of your hate, and let you blame me for everything instead. I let you hate me as if my name was lung cancer.

I don't know if Henry ever tried to get you back to my side. We both knew you had waited a very long time to start to grieve, and I can assume he didn't want anything to get in your way, either.

We will do anything to get away from our own pain. We will change our lives, rip people out, swallow a bottle of life-ending pills. When we hurt more than we can bear, when our lives get that dark, it's shocking what we will do to protect ourselves.

I never blamed you for hating me. And I never stopped loving you for all these years. I hope you found peace. I know peace is basically the opposite of your mother, but at least it would be something.

## THIRTY-SIX

_____

We've come to the part where I need to get to the point of all this. If you have, indeed, read this whole thing. If you kept yourself from lighting that match.

Henry called me today, for the first time in years, to let me know what's happening. To tell me about your good news. All your good news.

Jennifer Cooperton, a young, beautiful twenty-five-year-old woman, well on her way to becoming a successful oncologist, is getting married tomorrow. I have a lot of thoughts about that.

I hope this man you have found is kind, sweet, funny, and patient. I hope he wants to have babies with you. I hope he understands the importance of your tears, and will never make you feel small. I really hope he's Southern. I hope he's ready to grow old with you, find antique credenzas for you, and I hope he knows to leave the house when your best friend shows up with a bottle of wine.

As for that best friend, I have thoughts on her, too. If I could do only one last thing on this planet before I am sent to that place where your mother now reigns supreme, I wish you your own Smidge, your own tyrant in a tiny dress. I wish you that kind of love, because it's harder to find than what you've got right now with that man about to become your husband.

I'll be thinking of you tomorrow. Please promise me one thing. If you have found your own Smidge, and if she's by your side when you stand up there in front of all those people, make sure she knows Henry is the *only* one who is giving you away. Not her. Find a way to tell her she had you before you were in love and she'll always have you, no matter what people try to put between you.

Keep that girl in your heart and protect her. Because once she's gone, you will be thrown to the ground in awe of how that pain never lets up.

I'm getting better at knowing when the hurt is coming. Sometimes two notes of a song or a glimpse of a stranger's face will knock the wind right out of me, sending me back to a time when she was alive and only as far away as my cell phone, my computer, your kitchen.

Sometimes the memories of Smidge hit so strongly I will lose the ability to stand. I reach for the lowest point in the room, stretch myself out on the ground, and weep. It's like a ghost flew in and sucked out my breath. I know that's when Smidge has found me and is demanding I acknowledge her, that the pain I might have tricked myself into thinking has dissipated or dissolved is very much *here* and *now* and it is time to deal with it again.

This is when she's haunting me, just like she promised she would. Not when I don't follow her wishes; but when I forget for a moment that she's not here.

During those moments, memories of your mother flood my head in ways I cannot control, nor comprehend. A hodge-podge of our life together, superimposed sometimes. I see us on our way to our high school graduation, when we got pulled over for speeding because we were late finding her cap and gown that had somehow fallen behind the couch. She talked the police officer out of giving us a ticket by kissing his cheek and telling him that a smooch from a graduate was good luck. He then hit his lights and escorted us the rest of the way, at speeds way over anything I'd ever dared to drive.

Then the memories stack upon themselves, faster and faster. Smidge pretending she's British and works in PR so she can get backstage at a concert of a band I can't remember any-more. The time she was almost deported trying to smuggle Kahlúa back into the States using a fake ID. The time she got a flystrip stuck to her face and screamed until I pulled it off her. The day of my wedding, when she gave me my some-thing borrowed, and told me she was my something blue. "Because you aren't just mine anymore," she said, as she held back a secret that could have destroyed me in order to keep my life perfect that day.

The freckles on her shoulder formed an extended middle finger. The pinkie toe of her right foot looked exactly like a comma. She once won a call-in radio contest by reciting all of REM's "It's the End of the World as We Know It (And I Feel Fine)" from memory. She knew all the states' capitals, flowers, and birds. She hated pistachios. She thought Chardonnay was for quitters. She never met a joke she couldn't tell, a punch line she couldn't hit. In Barcelona, she stopped a pickpocket who was trying to rob a lady on a subway by hitting him on the back of the head with her own purse and then told him to go home to his mother and apologize. In Puerto Rico, she unsuccessfully tried to steal a blue cobblestone from the street in broad daylight. She celebrated my birthday by wrapping one candy bar for each year of my life. In a couple of years I will be fifty. I know she would have stuffed me with such evil glee.

I do not know how I will make it through another birthday without her. This still all makes no sense. It will never feel real. It will never be okay.

I wrote this not only to tell you the entire truth, not just to let you know how much you will always mean to me, but to tell you something important. I wanted you to know that no matter what she said, no matter what you heard, no matter where she went or whom she met, no matter what you might have thought she said and no matter what she did actually say, she absolutely loved you the mostest, and her greatest achievement in life was you.

All my love and a million Odd Hugs,
A.D.

# ACKNOWLEDGMENTS

Everything happens because of Alexis Hurley, who continues to be the calm center of all my literary storms and the champion of my what-happens-next. This story went through many capable hands from outline to manuscript to novel, and I'm thankful for Karen Kosztolnyik (a name I will always type s-l-o-w-l-y), Jennifer Heddle (who left me for Darth Vader), Emilia Pisani, Kate Dresser, and Heather Hunt for their thoughts and guidance. Thank you to Lisa Litwack and Regina Starace for the cover art. Special thanks to Anne Cherry for copyediting with an impressive balance of skill and humor that allowed for jokes in the margin (including pointing out when I was unable to count to seven).

While every cancer story is different, I wanted Smidge's to ring true, warts and all. Thank you to Stephanie Markham, cancer survivor and the friendliest of warriors, who should teach classes on how to be good. Warm, big, happy thanks to Jennifer Saltmarsh Manullang, who got me started by swapping sad stories before helpfully guiding me through her website—where she hilariously and honestly chronicles kicking cancer's butt (http://jmanullang.blogspot.com).

The rest of my research I did anonymously, so I wanted to thank a few people for their passion and tireless energy in the fight against cancer, and their superhero boldness to share their lives with the public. Mary Beth Williams writes of her battle with melanoma with admirable wit, grace, and bravery (http://www.maryelizabethwilliams.net/). Jennifer Windrum is fighting to gain advances in lung cancer research while letting us in on her mother's struggle at "Where's the Funding for Lung Cancer?" (http://www.wtflungcancer.com).

In researching assisted suicide and the Death with Dignity movement, I spent countless hours (and cried thousands of tears) watching personal accounts shared via YouTube, and pretty much blew out a tear duct over the moving documentary *How to Die in Oregon* (http://www.howtodieinoregon.com/). I am forever humbled by the courage people can muster when faced with their most final of decisions.

Thank you to Allison "Husalin'" Lowe-Huff and Jason "Cane Pole" Upton for their patience, insight, and encouragement (and for being so lovingly Southern).

Finally, thank you to all my Southern and/or bossy friends and family who have found a way to comment one way or another on the state of my hair, shoes, nails, love life, career, family, and then back to my hair again. You know who you are. Without your voices in my head, I'd have nothing. Well, maybe a little more self-esteem. But other than that, nothing.

PS: Bailiff Ray of the LA County Superior Court, Stanley Mosk Courthouse (Dept 34)—here's your shout-out. I told you they weren't going to let me serve on that jury.

# you take it from here

## PAMELA RIBON

## INTRODUCTION

How far would you go to be there for a friend in need? In Pamela Ribon's *You Take It from Here,* thirty-five-year-old, newly divorced Danielle Meyers is forced to answer this question when her best friend, Smidge Cooperton, makes a very complicated dying request that Danielle isn't sure she can take on.

On one of Danielle and Smidge's yearly trips together, Smidge reveals that her cancer has returned. Still feeling remorse and guilt for the way she acted the first time Smidge was diagnosed, Danielle promises to be supportive in every way possible. But Smidge's request—for Danielle to take over her home when she dies, caring for her husband and raising her teenage daughter, Jenny, until she leaves for college—is more than Danielle ever expected. Written as a letter from Danielle to Jenny many years after Smidge's final breaths, *You Take It from Here* gives voice to the journey traveled by those who loved Smidge most. It is a story of friendship, sacrifice, and ultimately, of love.

## QUESTIONS AND TOPICS FOR DISCUSSION

1. Though Smidge and Danielle appear to be complete opposites at first glance—Danielle, the more introverted, practical, and patient one, and Smidge, the loud-mouthed leader who always attracts the spotlight—which traits do they have in common? Do you think it's their similarities or their differences that keep their friendship strong? Does their relationship remind you of any such ones in your life?

2. "It's a lot like having a lion for a best friend—everything is really fun and exciting until the lion is unhappy" (p. 57). Do you think Smidge would have agreed with Danielle's comparison? If not, which animal do you think Smidge would think she is most like? Which animals do you think Smidge and Danielle represent?

3. "When I die, I want you to take over my life" (p. 60). What was your reaction when you first learned of Smidge's proposition to Danielle? Do you think it is fair to make this kind of request to a friend?

4. Throughout the novel, Danielle mentions the regret she feels for not having been there for Smidge during her first battle with cancer. In what ways do you think Danielle's guilt affects the way she reacts and responds to Smidge the second time around?

5. At the start of the novel, Danielle refers to Tucker Collier as a superhero. In what ways throughout the novel does he come to Danielle's rescue?

6. In what specific ways does Jenny grow up from the beginning of the novel to the end? As she makes the transition from girl to woman, in what ways do Smidge and Danielle view and treat her differently?

7. Danielle goes into detail about both her and Smidge's family lives when they were younger. How do you think their respective experiences growing up shaped the women they became?

8. How would you describe Smidge and Henry Cooperton's marriage? What role does each of them play in the relationship? Danielle says she's never seen "two people ever fall more instantly in love" before (p. 92). What do you think it is about Smidge and Henry that instantly drew them together?

9. The moment when Vikki tells Danielle that she knows about Smidge's cancer is a moment of comfort for Danielle: "The giant weight placed on my shoulders shifted, eased into a new position" (p. 268). Why is Danielle so relieved? Were you surprised to find out why Smidge had been keeping Vikki at a distance?

10. "[E]verybody sees this disease through their own mortality, looking back over their shoulders, wondering, Would I be ready for this? Cancer is selfish" (p. 59). Do you agree with Danielle's assessment of the disease? Why or why not? Have you or anyone in your life been affected by this disease? Take a moment to discuss, or to reflect on, how your life has been impacted by cancer. Do you see any reflections of your own stories in Smidge and Danielle's?

11. Danielle sees Smidge cry for the very first time after her fight with Jenny in the kitchen. Danielle says, "This is where your mother cried, Jenny. It only took her entire life, but here is where real tears fell from her eyes" (p. 275). What emotions do you think Smidge is feeling in that moment? What do you think it is that finally causes the tears to fall?

12. Although Smidge tries to keep her cancer a secret from all of her friends and family, it becomes apparent to Danielle at

Smidge's birthday party that everybody already knows—except for Henry. How do you think Smidge was able to keep her illness from Henry for so long, while the rest of the town already had it figured out?

13. Although she debates doing so, Danielle ultimately provides Smidge with the Seconal that ends her life. Do you think Danielle did the right thing? After reading the story, do you think Jenny would agree?

14. "After all these years of silence, Jenny, if I could ask you only one question and have you answer it truthfully, I would want to know if you thought I kept my word" (p. 280). Do you think Danielle fulfilled her promise to be there for Jenny in all of the ways Smidge wasn't able to? After reading the story, do you think Jenny will feel that the promise was kept?

## A CONVERSATION WITH PAMELA RIBON

### What first inspired you to write *You Take It from Here*?

I have a few bossy lady friends, and more than my fair share of them are Southern. The idea for this novel came to me after I took a fourteen-hundred-mile emergency red-eye flight three hours after one called me in a hysterical panic, telling me that her daughter was in the hospital and near death. I'd just torn a ligament in my knee the day prior (please see my previous novel, *Going in Circles*, to find out how), but hobbled in a knee brace through LAX, uncomfortably smashed myself into a middle seat, was couriered via wheelchair to catch my four a.m. layover, and frantically fought my way to her side . . . only to be told, "She's getting released today. Um, someone might have called you after having too much wine." We had a good visit, and I eventually got to take a few painkillers for my knee, but I flew home, thinking, "I just dropped everything and went. I didn't even question it. How far would I go for this woman? And, more importantly: how much can a best friend feel entitled to ask?" Add this to my unresolved feelings about my father's death from lung cancer many years ago and the story started taking shape.

**This novel is written as a letter from Danielle to Jenny, retelling the journey she and her mother took from start to finish. Why did you decide to structure *You Take It from Here* as a letter? What about this format felt right to you?**

After I'd written more than half of it I realized it needed to be a letter. If I wanted to get to the ending I wanted, to have the feeling on the page that I felt in my gut, I was going to have to change my approach to the story. That realization came with such a sense of loss, knowing that I was going to have to go back to the very beginning and change almost every sentence to make it right.

These kinds of confessions—about the love you have for a friend—are best done to the only other people who know how crazy they can make you feel: their children.

**Did you know all along how the story was going to end? Or did the "right" ending reveal itself along the way?**

I knew Smidge's ending, and at first I wanted it to be a bit of a question what Danielle ultimately decided to do, but the wise women who counsel me with my writing suggested I needed to tell more. This is how it became a letter to Jenny, the only one who had the right to judge whether or not Danielle had kept her word.

**One of your main characters is named Smidge. Why couldn't she be a Jessica, Denise, Lucy, or any other common name? Why did her character call for such a unique name?**

Because there could be only one of her. For the sake of everybody and everything.

**Have you ever been given a nickname that stuck with you?**

The very first nickname I ever got was "Pamie," right when I was born. I think my mom was actually trying to name me "Pamie," but the nurse thought, "That tired woman who just went through thirty-six hours of labor meant 'Pamela.'" Other nicknames have come and gone, though "Wonder Killer" has stuck, mostly due to self-promotion.

**Do you see more of yourself in Danielle or Smidge?**

I know I'm very much Danielle, but I have fantasies of being bold enough to be Smidge, even for only one day. Just to get some things done that I would normally consider beyond my control.

**You've written for television, for blogs, and for the stage. How is the experience of writing a novel different?**

When writing a novel, the period of time where one is isolated with one's own paranoid, anxious, soul-crippling thoughts of imminent failure is much longer. You spend months convinced you have made a series of irrevocable mistakes and soon everything you care about will be gone because you have no business stringing words together. If I only wrote novels, I would no doubt develop agoraphobia. With a blog, I know right away if what I wrote worked for the reader. With a novel, I'm the only one who's going to write it, from start to finish; that's my job. But with television, the work gets spread around. (So does the blame.) I like the collaborative nature of television as well as the deadlines. You're putting on a show every week, not waiting a year or more to see the final product.

**Were there ways in which writing *You Take It from Here* differed from writing your previous books? Which book was the hardest to write? Which was your favorite to write?**

When I'm writing a novel there inevitably comes a point where I say out loud, "Why did I do this to myself?" Whether I'm writing about divorce, death, separation, depression, loss . . . usually around the third pass of the manuscript I curse myself for having to sit with these feelings and memories once again. I don't have a favorite novel of mine, and I don't go back to read them. They feel like old diaries, in a way, because I remember where I was when I wrote them and how my life was going at the time.

**In reviews of your books, readers often point out how skilled you are at creating novels that are both poignant and funny; novels that make readers laugh just as much as they make readers cry. Is it difficult striking this balance?**

I don't know if I'm consciously trying to strike that balance as much as I know I prefer reading a story that takes me through more than one emotion. I write toward that destination.

**What are you currently working on?**

I've been having a very good time writing an original movie for The Disney Channel, and partnering on a graphic novel for Oni Press with the extraordinarily talented Emi Lenox.

## ENHANCE YOUR BOOK CLUB

1. To keep their friendship strong, Smidge and Danielle take yearly trips together. Ask each member of your reading group to make a list of the top five places they would choose to travel to in the world. Then, compare lists: Are there any matches?

2. The relationship between mothers and daughters is a theme that is explored throughout the novel. With your discussion group, write the novel's mother/daughter relationships on a series of index cards—Smidge and Jenny, Danielle and her mother, Smidge and Lydia/"the Lizard," and so on. Then have each group member pick an index card and talk about that

pair's particular relationship. How did each woman fulfill her role as either mother or daughter? Ultimately, was that character successful in her role? Finally, discuss: Which characteristics, if any, do you find that all of the mother-daughter relationships in the novel share?

3. Lung cancer is the number one cancer killer in the United States, killing more people each year than breast, prostate, colon, liver, kidney, and melanoma cancers combined. To learn more about cancer, visit the American Cancer Society's website at www.cancer.org. To help in the fight against lung cancer, visit the American Lung Association at www.lungusa.org.

4. For more information on the Death with Dignity movement, please visit the Death with Dignity National Center at www.deathwithdignity.org.

5. For more information about Pamela Ribon and her books, visit her personal website and blog, www.pamie.com, or like her fan page on Facebook at www.facebook.com/PamelaRibon, or follow her on Twitter @pamelaribon.